Free Agent

USA *TODAY* BESTSELLING AUTHOR
CATHERINE GAYLE

Free Agent
Copyright © 2018 by Catherine Gayle
Cover Design by Kim Killion, The Killion Group
ISBN 9781942177364

For more information:
catherine@catherinegayle.com

Author's Note

A lot of people have a lot of opinions about weight-loss surgery.

Some say it's cheating. Some say it's a mistake and a surefire way to ruin a life. Some say it should only be used as a last resort. Some say it should only be offered to the most extreme cases. Some say it shouldn't be covered by health insurance as it's an elective procedure.

If you believe any of these things or anything else remotely similar, please refrain from sharing those opinions with me. I thoroughly researched the subject matter and am fully aware of all potential pros and cons related to this and other procedures of the sort. Anyone considering undergoing gastric bypass or any other weight-loss procedure should discuss the same with their health care provider to ensure proper education.

Chapter One

Blake

Let it be known that my assholish tendencies have never been in doubt, and I have always been aware that I am a fucking douchecanoe. Absolutely, without a doubt, I *know* I've got issues. I even realize the shit that comes out of my mouth is bad.

Problem is, most of the time, I recognize the issues with what I'm saying after the fact—once it's too late, and the words are already out there and I can't take them back. That's especially troublesome when I don't even mean the shit I say, which happens more often than some people might believe.

I just don't have a filter—don't take the time to think about the ramifications of what I'm doing and saying until it's too late. Occasionally, if I'm lucky, I'm able to recognize there's a problem even as the idiocy is falling from my trap.

The warning bells never seem to go off in advance, though. Or at least not when it matters—not with enough time for me to put a cork in it and keep my lips zipped. But if I catch my mistake before I've turned the situation into a mammoth problem, I can usually do damage control.

Every now and then, I'm able to sense the douchebaggery before I let it fly, and I can stop it in its tracks. I doubt anyone believes that ever happens, though, because of how often I do and say stupid shit that I immediately regret.

Maybe my grandma believes it, but she knows the reason behind it all. And besides, she's my grandma— the only person in my life who's ever given a shit about me.

Everyone else, though? It's extremely doubtful that they believe I'm not the jackwad I come across as being. Even the guys I consider to be my friends probably believe the worst of me nine times out of ten.

Still, whether people believe it or not, I try to keep as much of my worst behavior contained as possible. Maybe I fail more often than I succeed, but I am at least *trying*. And I'm getting better. I'm succeeding more often than I'm failing in these kinds of endeavors.

Or at least I think I am.

Most of the time…

But then there were days like today, which made me question everything I thought I believed about myself. Maybe everyone else was right and I was wrong. Maybe I *was* just an ass, underneath it all.

It was sure starting to look that way.

This was the shit racing through my head on my way between having a game-day meal with my Portland Storm teammates at Amani's Family-Style Italian

Restaurant and facing my impending doom in the general manager's office.

Because—as already mentioned—I'm an asshole, and I have a problem keeping my lips zipped. Or in this case, my problem had been with knowing when *not* to put one of the dumb-ass thoughts racing through my head out there for the whole world to see on social media.

My idiotic tweet had been deleted less than three minutes after I'd posted it, but in those two-plus minutes of its existence, it'd been re-tweeted and screen-capped and spread all over the world. By now, less than two hours later, no fewer than three of the biggest hockey blogs following the NHL had posted about my thoughtless stupidity, and it was sure to be news on every major sports news site before the day was out.

Hence the reason I was sitting just outside the team's general manager's office, waiting to have my ass handed to me on a platter.

Rachel Campbell, the GM's assistant and wife of my teammate, Brenden "Soupy" Campbell, kept giving me I-can't-believe-you-were-such-an-idiot looks over the top of her computer screen in between answering phone calls and doing Lord only knew what on her computer. She was a master at those looks. Probably gave them to her four kids all the time, not to mention to her husband. Soupy might not be as much of an ass as I was, but surely he had more than his fair share of idiotic moments.

At the moment, he was sitting beside me, along with a couple of our other teammates, Cam Johnson, and our team captain, Jamie Babcock. Ostensibly, all three of them were here to keep me from bolting or something. Well, Jonny had practically hauled me here on his own, so he didn't exactly need the help of the other two. But still, I wasn't going anywhere. I'd done the crime, and now I had to do the time. Maybe I was an asshole and a fucking idiot, but at least I always owned up to it. I wasn't too chickenshit to face the music.

"What the hell were you thinking?" Jonny asked me quietly. He was staring down at his hands, cracking his knuckles. Not in a menacing way, though. It was more that he had to crack them to keep them from freezing up on him or something. Jonny was getting up there to still be playing pro hockey.

Not that I'd ever say something like that to his face, if I could manage to keep it all inside. I didn't have a death wish.

Instead, I said, "I was thinking someone asked me a fucking question on Twitter, so I answered it." Simple enough, right? Truth was, I *hadn't* been thinking. Which they probably all knew already, anyway. If I would have taken just a moment or two longer to think things through, I would've realized it wasn't a question I should answer.

Jonny snorted, and Babs shook his head. Soupy just scowled at me like I was the biggest idiot he'd ever had the displeasure of meeting. Too bad for him—hell, for all of my teammates, really—they were stuck with me, at least for the foreseeable future. Unless this meeting was all about how fast the team was planning to ship me off to Timbuktu or Abu Dhabi so I could spend the rest of my playing days all by my lonesome.

But then Rachel's phone rang again, saving me from the need to come up with some better response than what I'd given them. She pressed a button and said,

"Yeah, Jim?" into her headset. Then a moment later: "I'll send him straight in." After pressing the same button again, she gave me a pitying look and said, "Jim's ready for you."

"Should we go?" Soupy asked his wife.

She shook her head. "He wants all of y'all, actually." These days, most of Rachel's Texan accent remained hidden—but a *y'all* or an *over yonder* came out every now and then, reminding us all of where she'd come from.

I tried not to scowl as my teammates ushered me into the general manager's office. Surliness wouldn't help my cause.

Mr. Sutter sat behind his desk, and the entire coaching staff was positioned throughout the room. The assistant GM was here, as well as a few people from the communications department and almost half a dozen other people whose jobs I didn't even remember—only that they worked for the team in some capacity or another. Paying attention to details, at least when they didn't pertain to me? Yeah, not my forte.

"Have a seat," Mr. Sutter said, folding his bifocals and setting them on the desk in front of him.

I plopped down in the chair he'd indicated, but when I glanced up, he'd spun his computer monitor around so everyone in the room could see it. A screen-cap of my idiotic tweet filled the screen, blown up to larger-than-life size so everyone in the room could witness just exactly how much of a moron I'd been.

Must be a retard to think it's okay to hit chicks.

My laughing, fuck-you-all-very-much face was sitting right next to the words, complete with me flipping off the photographer. Probably another strike against me, but they'd never tried to police the photo I used on my social media profiles before.

Didn't matter that I'd just been responding (like the moron I was) to some fan who'd asked what I thought about some douchecanoe in the league who'd been suspended for beating up his girlfriend. Didn't matter that I'd been condemning behavior that every fucking person in this world with any goddamned sense ought to condemn.

The only thing that mattered was that I'd used the very same word that I'd always loathed anytime someone had used it against me. *Retard*.

If the evidence wasn't staring me in the face, I might not believe I'd done it. Somewhere in my mind, I might have been able to convince myself it was a hoax. Staring at that word on Mr. Sutter's screen made me feel physically ill. I wanted to puke, but giving in to that sort of weakness would only prove I *was* a chickenshit. So I swallowed down the bile and forced myself to look at that fucking tweet without showing everyone in the room how it made me feel.

"We have a bit of a situation," Mr. Sutter said, his words coming out calm and smooth, somehow, even though I knew he had to be almost as pissed at me as I was at myself.

"That's putting it mildly," Mattias Bergstrom bit off. Bergy was our head coach. I'd never seen the guy look so pissed off before, and that was saying something, because pissed off was his usual state of affairs when it came to dealing with me.

"I didn't mean—"

"I don't care what you did or didn't mean," he growled, cutting me off. "You know what I care about? I care that Sophie's going to hear about this, and I'm going to have to deal with convincing her that one of my players doesn't think she's *a fucking retard*."

That stung worse than anything else to this point. Sophie, his stepdaughter, was one of the sweetest kids I'd ever met. And she had Down syndrome.

I fucking adored that little girl, and I would never intentionally say something that would hurt her.

But I had.

Goddamn fucking pisswanker, *why* could I not rein myself in before I did stupid fucking shit like this? I needed a keeper. I needed someone to commandeer my phone and computer. Someone needed to take over every aspect of my life to keep me in check, but fuck if I'd ever let that happen. I was too much of a control freak, always needing to be in charge of every aspect of my life so something wouldn't send me into a tizzy.

Grandma was going to rake me over the coals as soon as she heard about this. I could hear her voice now, even though she was thousands of miles away. *You're better than this, Blake. You're only hurting yourself.*

But this time, I wasn't only hurting myself. What I'd said had the potential to hurt all sorts of people…including a lot of people I cared about. Like Sophie.

I sank lower in my chair, wishing it would swallow me up. No such luck. The weight of a dozen stares wasn't enough to push me under.

"It goes a lot further than our own families, though," Jim said, sobering me to an even greater degree. "This is going to be a PR nightmare."

"You going to trade me?" I asked around a thick tongue that felt too large and too dry to belong in my mouth. That was what my previous team had done, and I hadn't even fucked up this badly when I was with them. It was just a bunch of my usual shit, not anything so blatantly callous and unthinking.

"Trade you?" Mr. Sutter's eyebrows went up almost comically high into his hairline, and then he gave me a kind smile that I definitely didn't deserve. "Why would I trade you?"

"And who'd want you in return?" Soupy added.

"Plenty of teams would—including us," Mr. Sutter said. "We still love what you bring to the table on the ice, Blake."

I shrugged. "But then I could be someone else's problem."

He stifled a soft laugh and shook his head. "We knew what we were getting when we brought you here, son—both on *and* off the ice. We did our research. We were prepared then, and we're even more prepared now that we know you as a person and not just as an athlete. But we do have to act fast, see if we can turn the tide of public opinion, maybe find a way to spin this in a more positive light."

Unbidden, my gaze traveled over to Bergy. He looked like he was having extreme difficulty biting his tongue.

Maybe Mr. Sutter wouldn't hold this against me for too long, but Bergy? I'd be living in his doghouse for the rest of my days playing in Portland. There wasn't a snowball's chance in hell that he'd ever forget my unfortunate choice of words or let *me* forget them, either.

"So how do we do that?" David Weber, one of the assistant coaches, asked.

"First," Mr. Sutter said, scanning the room to include everyone, "we have the PR team draft up an apology for your poor choice of language, and you'll issue it as a public statement. It'll go out on all of the team's social media channels, be posted on our website, and you'll post it to your own social media accounts, as well."

Fair enough. I could easily handle that. Grandma would insist on it, actually, whether the team did or not. She'd raised me to be better than this. I nodded my agreement, keeping my eyes on Mr. Sutter. He seemed to be the only person in the room who was on my side in all of this.

Shouldn't surprise me. He'd always acted like a father figure around me, since he'd first brought me to Portland.

"Second," he said, and this time he looked straight at me, "you agree to let the team's public relations department oversee your use of social media for the next six months. You don't post a tweet or anything on Instagram or Facebook without first running it by them and having them approve it. Not even a reply to someone else, whether public or private. *Everything* goes through them first."

That would suck, but even I could see the need for the team's oversight. Maybe they could help rein me in and keep my assholishness in check. Hell, maybe with six months of social media supervision, I'd learn how to self-moderate or something. It was at least worth a shot.

"Fine," I said. Because seriously, so far, I felt like I was getting off easy.

"And finally," he said, "you're going to volunteer every week at a local school. Riley and Mackenzie Jezek were doing it last season, but with Mackenzie's pregnancy, she needs someone to take over for her. That's going to be you."

"That's a really bad fucking idea," I said before I could think better of it. Me, being around kids? Maybe Mr. Sutter didn't realize that my issue was that I didn't have a fucking filter. How the hell would that go over in a school setting?

He kept going, as if he hadn't heard me. "Not only will you read to the kids once a week in the library, but you're going to volunteer in a class of special education students. You're going to work one-on-one with them. You're going to help them see how great they can be—and in return, you're going to learn how great they are."

I groaned out loud—couldn't stop myself. This would never work out well. Once their parents had seen what I'd said...

And if the *kids* knew what I'd said... Fuck, I'd dug myself a massive hole to climb out of this time.

I didn't want them to think I'd meant it. I wasn't a bad guy. Maybe it didn't always seem that way, but deep down, I *wasn't*.

Was I?

Actually, if those words had come out of me, maybe I *was* the piece of shit the whole world probably thought I was.

"Maybe they'll surprise you, Blake," Mr. Sutter said, eyeing me with that fatherly look he sometimes took with a few of the guys. "Maybe those kids will help you learn a lot about yourself. More than you can help them learn."

Fat chance. I already knew everything there was to know about myself.

But no matter what I believed about myself, how could I prove to them—or their parents, or even to myself, the team, the city, hell, the whole league—otherwise? How could I convince anyone I was more than I appeared at first glance? I'd been living with myself for twenty-five fucking years, and I'd never been less certain of my own character than I was in this precise moment in time.

I'd brought this nightmare on myself, though. So I nodded, biting down on all the stupid shit racing through my head. Too much had already escaped my brain and made it out into the world.

I had to make things right.

Bea

Monica Patton, the school's secretary and the one woman who kept all of us teachers sane throughout the school year, held up a finger for me as I was on my way out of the front office, signaling that she needed me to stop. I shifted my stack of files to my left arm and scanned the various notices hanging on the walls of the office while I waited for her to finish her phone call.

They were all for the kids, though, not for the teachers: reminders about permission forms for field trips, notices about loading money onto their lunch cards, overdue fees for library books, and the like. Anything important for the faculty and staff came to our email inboxes if it wasn't delivered to our mail boxes in the office.

Speaking of which… I quickly scanned the stack in my arms. Most of it seemed to be various memos, but one large manila envelope was filled with test prep for statewide standardized testing. I tugged a sticky tab off the pad of them I kept in my pocket and flagged that envelope because I didn't want it to get lost in the shuffle. I tended to be a bit absentminded when it came to these things in the early months of a new school year because there were so many things going on at once, and this wasn't something I wanted to risk forgetting about.

"Absolutely, Mrs. Thompson," Monica said to the parent on the other end of the line. "No, we don't want Susan to come back to school until you're one hundred percent sure she's not contagious any longer. The last thing we need is an outbreak of flu spreading among the students and staff. But she *will* need a doctor's note to be able to return." She paused for a moment, listening. And then, "I'm sorry, Mrs. Thompson. It's district policy. We can't allow her back into her classes until we have that doctor's note on file. You'll just have to find a way to get her to a doctor."

Monica rolled her eyes at me, but not even the slightest hint of her exasperation could be heard in her tone. That was one of the main reasons she was perfectly suited to her job. Plus, she absolutely *adored* the kids, even if she wouldn't take any guff from any of them—or their parents. I couldn't bear the thought of being without her next year, but the woman had more than earned her retirement.

A couple more similar exchanges later, Monica finally ended the call with a sigh. "They never seem to get it. Seem to think that because they have some high-powered corporate job somewhere, they don't have to follow the rules, and their kids shouldn't have to follow them, either."

"Sorry," I said, trying to hide my snicker. I was just glad not to be the only one who had to deal with any number of parents like that, though.

"Don't know what they're thinking. Not how I'd want to raise my kid. You wouldn't, either."

"No, I wouldn't," I agreed, even though there wasn't a snowball's chance in hell I'd ever have kids. But that was neither here nor there.

She waved a hand through the air and shook her head as if trying to clear her mind of the phone call. "That's not what I needed you to stop for. It's because there's been a change in plans. I know you'd asked for Mr. and Mrs. Jezek to come back this term, preferably for your class specifically, if not for the library. And if you couldn't have her, you wanted Mr. Jezek, anyway."

I absolutely *adored* those two. My friend, Dani Williams, had hooked me up with Riley and Mackenzie. They'd come to read to our kids during library time last year, and I was hoping for more of the same this year—specifically only for *my* class, though. Yes, they could come and read to all of the kids in the library, too, if they wanted, but I had something special in mind. But with Mackenzie being well along in her pregnancy, I'd had a feeling something would change.

"But?" I replied, because I could definitely sense a *but* coming on. "Are they sending someone else from the team?" I was distracted, still flipping through my paperwork, because that seemed far more pressing than having a different hockey player coming to read to my kids. Honestly, I wasn't overly fussed about who came. The truth was that my kids would be beyond excited no matter who showed up—didn't matter if they were a pro athlete or married to one, or if they were a police officer or firefighter, or even a grocery store clerk.

What mattered was that someone not connected to the school bothered to take time out of their day to spend some time with my kids. It helped them to feel special, and not in a *special education* sort of way, not in a *short bus* sort of way, but in a truly *special* sort of way.

And that was more important than I could ever put into words.

I got choked up after any visitor left my classroom, because my kids got so excited about the attention they'd received. I didn't even care that it typically took half a day to get them to calm down enough that they could learn again after something like that.

These visits *mattered*.

And it always helped my students to believe they were just as good, just as smart, just as capable, just as deserving as the rest of the kids in the school.

So I didn't care who was coming, just so long as *someone* was coming.

"They sent me," an entirely too familiar masculine voice said from behind me.

A frisson of disgust raced up my spine, and I spun around to see the one man I'd hoped never to clap eyes on again walking into the school's front office, looking as sexy and cocky and rude as ever.

At my glare, a bit of the cockiness fled from his dark, chocolatey-brown eyes, but not enough of it for my taste. "They can send you straight back," I bit off. "I don't want you anywhere near my classroom. *Or* my kids."

Or me. Especially because of how my traitorous body reacted every time I saw him. My head said *stay away from this jerk*. But my libido? She started singing and dancing like a Broadway star every time I saw a picture of him flash by on the TV or internet.

It was a sickness. One I had hoped to be cured of well before now.

No such luck, apparently, despite the fact that he'd once again proven himself to be a cocky bastard of epic proportions.

I'd seen the huge kerfuffle from a couple of days ago over what he'd posted on Twitter. And besides, I would never, no matter how hard I tried, be able to forget what he'd said to me all those months ago. His hurtful words might as well have been imprinted in my brain. I saw them every time I opened my eyes. I heard them in my sleep. They invaded my every thought.

No one, never once in my life, had managed to cut me so deeply with only a single offhand remark.

I wanted nothing to do with this man. Not *ever* again.

I spun around to face Monica so I wouldn't have to look at him, because he made my skin crawl. "Ask the team to send someone else. *Anyone* else," I implored her. "I'm not picky. I'll take one of their wives or girlfriends. Someone from the front office. Anyone." I'd even take the building janitor or the guy who drove the Zamboni at their practice rink.

Just not this jerk.

"No can do," she replied, looking genuinely apologetic. "If you're going to have anyone from the team helping out this year, they've made it clear that it's going to be Mr. Kozlow."

"Then we won't have anyone from the team, because I am *not* allowing this man to step foot inside my classroom." I didn't know if any of my students had seen or heard about what he'd said, but it didn't matter. *I* knew. That was more than enough for all of us.

"You have to," he said then, and he actually sounded a little frantic.

I swung around on him so fast that it sent my thick

hair flying. "I don't *have* to do anything. Not when it comes to you."

But all of the cockiness had fled from his expression, replaced with something that resembled panic bordering on desperation. "Please. Give me a chance."

"And why, exactly, should I give you anything?" I knew there must be daggers shooting from my eyes. My mama and my grandma had perfected that look, and I'd inherited all the same facial expressions. It was our calling card. I used it whenever necessary, but that was typically only when my class had gotten entirely out of hand or when a parent was being unreasonable.

But this jerk didn't quail under my glare, which might just earn him a smidgeon of respect from me. Not much, mind—he wouldn't ever be able to climb out of the hole he'd dug himself when it came to me.

Instead, he turned on a pleading, puppy-dog sort of look mixed with a hint of panic, and he said, "Because if anyone knows what those kids must think after someone says the kinds of things I said, it's me. I was in their shoes growing up."

Certain he was going to say something repulsive like he'd been disadvantaged because his parents could only afford to put him in either hockey or private school but not both, I shoved past him and headed for the door.

"I've got ADHD," he said just as I wrapped my hand around the knob. It was enough to make me stop, for some reason. He took a step closer. "Unmedicated. I couldn't stand how the meds made me feel, so Grandma and I figured out ways for me to cope without them. For a while, they thought I might have some Asperger's, too, but then they said I didn't and

I'm just antisocial, so who the hell knows?"

"What kinds of things do you do to cope?" I found myself asking, even though I didn't want to know. I didn't want to see him as human. I didn't want to think about him being like my students. I wanted to just think of him as a rude, selfish jerk who didn't care how he might hurt other people with his thoughtlessness.

"She put me into hockey, for one thing. Helped me burn off my excess energy so I could focus when I needed to. I do puzzles—word puzzles, Sudoku, anything that makes me think about slowing things down and putting them in the right order. Just started doing yoga before practices and games so I can calm my thoughts. Shit like that."

"*Stuff* like that," Monica cut in, and he shot a look in her direction. "You have to remember you're in a school, and these kids are impressionable. If you say it, they'll repeat it, and then we really *will* have a mess on our hands with the parents."

"Right," he said with a determined nod. "Stuff like that."

Every bone in my body was screaming that I didn't care about his story, that he could be making it up just so that I'd give in, that his own learning and behavioral disabilities weren't enough to make up for the awful things he'd said and done…but there was one other tiny little niggling thought at the back of my mind.

If he was serious, and if he'd really been dealing with ADHD and possibly some Asperger's for his entire life—and he'd become a successful professional athlete in spite of it all—how could I deprive my kids of the opportunity to get to know him and see for themselves what they might be able to do with their own lives? Would I be depriving them of exactly the role model they needed in order to believe in themselves and reach their potential?

I had to take myself and my own hang-ups out of the equation. I had to do what was best for my kids. And maybe, just maybe, this was it.

"All right," I said slowly, turning the full weight of my glare on him. "But we play this by my rules. And if you break any of my rules, this is done. You don't get a second chance. You don't get the opportunity to screw up in front of them multiple times. Got it?"

Relief flooded his features and almost made me *feel* something for him.

Almost. But not quite.

Because I still knew the pain he was capable of inflicting. I'd have to be fully on guard when he was around my students at all times, because I would *not* let him hurt them the way he'd hurt me.

"Got it," he said. "Tell me your rules."

Oh, I'd tell him my rules, all right. But first, I needed to come up with them.

Chapter Two

Blake

"Let's go," she bit off. "We're on the move, and I don't have time to mess around." She shoved her stack of files and envelopes into my hands. Before I could blink, she was barreling out the office door and power-walking through the hallways of the school.

My legs were a good six inches longer than hers, give or take, so I ought to be able to keep up with her without a problem. But Bea Castillo was apparently a woman on a mission, and I almost had to jog to stay apace.

"We in a race or something?" I asked. Because it seemed she was trying to run away from me.

Couldn't say I blamed her, if that was the case. I wouldn't want to be around me, either, knowing myself the way I did.

The moment the school secretary had told me the

name of the teacher whose class I'd be volunteering with (ha-ha, not exactly *volunteering*, but whatever), I'd known my uphill climb would be even steeper than I'd already imagined.

We had a history, Bea Castillo and me.

Not a long history, per se.

But definitely an ugly one.

And once again, the ugliness probably all boiled down to stupid shit flying out of my mouth before I'd had the chance to think things through and realize what I was saying. If I'd taken the time to stop and think, I probably would've kept my mouth shut.

Some things just don't need to be said.

That would apply to roughly seventy-eight percent of the things that fell from my lips, give or take. More if you asked my teammates, maybe a bit less if you asked my grandma, but whatever.

Well, *maybe* I would've kept my trap shut. To be honest, I wasn't sure what I'd said that had irked her so much. One minute, we'd been laughing and joking with one another and everything had seemingly been fine; the next thing I knew, she'd been glaring daggers at me—tear-filled daggers, no less, so I had *known*, without a doubt, that I'd said or done something that had hurt her.

But that had been something like a year ago, and I'd never figured out what I'd done wrong. Didn't appear she'd be filling me in any time soon, either.

Just now, she spared me a glance for long enough to roll her eyes. "I don't have time to waste. There aren't enough hours in the day to do everything I have to do. *Especially* now that I have to deal with you on top of the rest of it."

After a couple of turns I'd never be able to

remember in order to reverse the process, we entered an empty but brightly lit classroom filled with red apple décor covering half the room, while the other half was decorated with pumpkins and fall leaves. She must have been in the midst of changing things over from back-to-school to an autumn theme when she'd gone to the office.

Pointing to a chair better suited to a second grader, she said, "Sit."

I sat, but my knees nearly landed in my armpits because I was about ten times too big for the chair in question.

Ignoring me, she set about sorting through the stack of files and envelopes she'd been carrying, shoving some papers into an in-tray and emptying the contents of other envelopes to file in a drawer of her desk.

Sitting still was not conducive to me being on my best behavior. Especially not if we weren't even talking. I needed to get up. To move around. Already, my feet started bouncing with my overwhelming urge to do *something*. I didn't even care what, at this point. Sitting still was one sure way to land me in hot water, and the water I was already in was hot enough, thank you very much.

"Where are the kids?" I asked after a moment of silence other than the sounds of Bea shuffling her paperwork around.

"We're picking them up from the music room in ten minutes." She didn't even bother to look over at me when she responded, her focus squarely on the work in front of her.

Well, lucky for *her* she had something with which to occupy her mind.

Me, on the other hand? I was liable to go nuts if I

couldn't find something to do with myself. Ten whole fucking minutes. That might as well be an eternity.

Seemed like she ought to be telling me her rules, then. How the hell was I supposed to follow her rules if I didn't know what they were?

But instead of filling me in, she turned to her computer monitor and clicked her mouse a few times, then started typing.

I couldn't just sit still for this long. Especially not in that chair made for miniature humans.

My eyes scanned the room again, almost of their own accord. There was a large bulletin board on the other side of the room. Orange paper had been stapled over it, but the brown, red, orange, and gold leafy border was only half in place. The end of it was dangling, and a stapler was resting on a step stool.

The clatter of her fingernails on the keyboard and her occasional sighs were the only sounds in the classroom. It was enough to make me crazy. Well…crazier than I already was, which was more than enough to be getting on with, thanks. I couldn't freaking deal with the silence and the lack of anything to do with myself, so I got up and crossed over to the partially finished bulletin board. No reason I couldn't finish this up for her while she was working on something else, right?

"What are you doing?" she demanded, but I already had the stapler in hand, and I was shoving her step stool out of my way because I didn't need it. The damned thing would only make me trip.

I didn't bother to answer, because anyone with eyes could see that I was taking over the job she'd left unfinished. Lifting the border into place with one hand, I opened the stapler and pressed it into position, then pushed down hard so it would shoot out a staple.

"You can't just—"

"Are you going to tell me your rules or not?" I demanded, cutting her off and slamming the stapler a bit harder than was necessary.

"Fine," she said. "Rule one: you don't pick up items that could be used as projectiles or weapons unless I give you permission to do so."

"Used as a weapon? Seriously?" I spun around, stapler in my hands, and let the border dangle again. "I'm trying to help you out."

"I didn't ask you to."

"So I'm going to be punished for tackling a job for you? You just told me there aren't enough hours in the day for you to get all your work done. I'm trying to cut down on all the work you have, since you haven't given me anything else to do."

"Doesn't mean I want you to touch anything in my classroom without my permission."

"It's not like I grabbed your ass or anything."

Well, hell. And there I went again, letting my mouth get ahead of my brain.

She glared so hard I was glad the stapler was in my hand and not hers, because I could envision it flying straight for my head. And yet *I* was the one supposedly in danger of launching things as projectiles? Whatever.

But then a timer of some sort started making noise on her desk. She reached for it and pressed a button to make it stop beeping. From a cabinet behind her desk, she took out a pill minder and a protein bar. She tossed back a handful of pills, took a swig of water from a refillable bottle on her desk, and ripped open the bar.

Then she glared at me again. "Put the stapler down where you found it, and let's go." Without waiting for me to comply, she backed away from her desk and headed out the door.

"Time to pick up the kids?" I asked, fumbling to remember where the stapler had been when I'd picked it up. Was it on the table next to the bulletin board, or on the step stool?

Fuck if I knew. I closed it and set it on the table, and then I busted ass to catch up with her since I didn't know where anything was in this school, and I'd never be able to find my way around, otherwise.

Hell, I didn't even remember where she'd said they were. Art? Phys ed? No telling.

Once again, she was power-walking through the halls, this time eating her bar. I couldn't exactly ask her questions now since she had her mouth full. Besides, I doubted she'd give me a straight answer even if she wasn't trying to eat.

I kind of liked walking just a bit behind her, though. Gave me a nice view of her ass. Her pants hugged it in all the right ways, and the bright-orange cardigan she wore didn't hide it completely from my view.

I wanted to squeeze that ass—a thought that had no business cropping up into my thoughts just now. Hell, there was *no* appropriate time for a thought like that.

Because she sure as hell wouldn't ever be allowing me to squeeze her ass or any other part of her. This chick wanted nothing more than to turn me into roadkill.

We arrived at another classroom and she spun around so suddenly that I almost ran into her back. "Wait right there," she demanded, pointing to a spot next to a couple of water fountains. "Don't touch anything. Don't go anywhere. Definitely don't open your mouth to speak to anyone, because I don't know what sort of awful things you'll say. Just *stand there*. Got it?"

"Got it," I bit off, returning her glare in equal measure. I wasn't any happier about this than she was, but I didn't have much choice.

She scowled and then opened the door to the classroom. A cacophony of bells, chimes, and recorders greeted my ears in the few moments until the door closed behind her. Music class, apparently.

Somehow, this was becoming even worse than I'd imagined at first, and that was saying something.

Bea

I knew why he couldn't sit still, so there wasn't any good reason for me to keep snapping at him. It was the ADHD, plain and simple. The man needed something to do, and if I asked him to sit quietly, I was asking for trouble. That meant it was on me if he couldn't follow my simple directions, because I was asking him for something he couldn't give me.

It was the same with my students. I could always tell when it was time for us to switch gears, maybe get them up out of their seats so they could move around a bit, because their inability to sit and focus would have half of them fidgeting—or worse.

Yet, despite my knowledge, I'd tried to force him into doing something I'd *known* he couldn't do, and then I'd snapped at him when he'd tried to use his restless energy to help me.

Did that make me a bitch? Maybe.

Get through today, I thought to myself as Mrs. Cutler

supervised the kids putting their instruments back into their proper homes. *Get through this next hour or so while he's here, and then the rest of the day will be better.* And then tonight, I could call Dani Williams to moan and complain about my predicament. She'd be on board. These early months of her pregnancy had her hormones all out of whack, so she was always down for a good gripe session, just as long as chocolate was involved—and her husband had been making sure to keep her in a fresh supply at all times lately.

Once the kids were in a line, I held one hand straight up in the air, started a countdown of my fingers, and pressed the forefinger of my other hand to my lips. By the time my fingers were all tucked into a fist, my class had quieted down. For it being so early in a new school year, I had to admit, I was impressed. But then again, as soon as they realized we had a guest in the room, all hell would break loose. I'd been mentally preparing myself for a chaotic afternoon since last night.

And that was when I'd still been expecting Riley and Mackenzie Jezek, who were well used to the needs of my students.

"We have a special visitor today," I said once my class was attentively looking my way. "But I need each of you to be on your best behavior so we can all benefit from his visit, all right? Can everybody do that for me?"

Fourteen heads bobbed up and down in answer. I bit down on the inside of my cheek to keep from saying something about the fact that Blake Kozlow hadn't agreed to be on his best behavior, even though my kids had. But that wouldn't help matters, and I needed to present some form of professionalism into the situation.

"All right, then," I said. "Restrooms first. Let's form

two lines, one for the boys and the other for the girls."

The kids sorted themselves out readily enough. But gradually, I felt the weight of fourteen pairs of eyes falling on him, and then the whispering started. And the pointing. At least a few of them knew *exactly* who he was, and their excitement was starting to get the best of them.

But then I caught a glimpse of his response to their reactions. He was shifting in place, alternatively crossing his arms and then trying to hold them straight down at his sides. Something told me someone in his past had constantly told him to keep his arms straight, that putting them in front of him made him seem standoffish. But whatever was behind it, he couldn't handle their scrutiny just now.

I had to wonder what was going through his head and how the kids' excitement and curiosity was striking him. But instead of trying to find out, I sent my students into the restrooms in groups, focusing on *my* job, even if he couldn't focus on anything.

When Tanner Watson came out of the boys' room and went for a sip at the fountain, I couldn't help but notice the awe in his eyes—and the discomfort in Blake's.

"Are you a hockey player like Mr. Jezek?" he asked.

Blake shot a glance over at me, as if asking my permission to speak. Good grief, I had to have been beyond horrible to him if he was scared to even answer a simple question from one of my students. I needed to get myself in check, every bit as much as I needed to keep an eye on *him*. It wouldn't help anyone if the man was too nervous to answer a simple question when asked.

I gave him a curt nod of encouragement, hating

myself for the mingled look of relief and worry that passed through his expression. The man was freaking out about every tiny question, every simple response.

Yeah, I wanted him to be aware of himself and his actions, and of what sort of effect he could have on the other people around him, but I didn't want him to panic.

"I am," he finally croaked out, and I turned my back so I could keep an eye on the rest of my kids while still listening in on their conversation.

"I'm gonna be just like you," Tanner said. "I'm gonna play hockey. For the Storm. Mom said I could. She said I could do anything."

It took a long moment for Blake to respond, which made me wonder what offhand response he was forcing himself to keep inside. But then he said, "Bet you will. And your mom's right. You can do anything."

I couldn't stop myself; I shot a look over my shoulder at him, but for once, it wasn't a glare.

Maybe there was a kernel of a decent human being inside him—somewhere *deep* inside, granted, but it was there.

Didn't mean I was ready to forgive him. And it *definitely* didn't mean I would be leaving him with any of these kids unsupervised.

But for the first time, I had a smidge of hope that this wouldn't turn out to be as awful as I'd first imagined.

Chapter Three

Bea

Admittedly, once I gave him a task to work on, he was fine. Better than fine, actually. He focused in on what I'd assigned him to do and helped the kids, and everything that I caught coming out of his mouth was perfectly acceptable.

That didn't mean I wanted him to ever pick up scissors or staplers or—God forbid—a paper cutter while he was in my classroom. But I had put his chair at a table where he'd be surrounded by some of my students, and I'd shoved him down into it. Then I'd asked the kids to work on coloring some artwork for my walls and assigned him to cut out the leaves and pumpkins the kids had finished shading (using a pair of blunt safety scissors, of course), and then he'd stopped fidgeting quite so much.

Yes, he was still far too large to comfortably fit in

the chair or at the desk. And yes, he reminded me of an overgrown toddler in countless ways. But he had a job to do, and the kids at his table kept asking him questions about playing hockey, and that meant he was occupied and engaged, and everyone was happy. Or at least almost everyone was happy. I wasn't sure I could count myself among them.

Still, I walked among the tables, answering questions occasionally or reminding a couple of my students to stay on task, but mainly I was just keeping an eye on things. Except I kept being drawn back to the table where Blake was seated.

"What color is a pumpkin?" Sasha asked him earnestly, reaching for a green colored pencil.

He looked over at her hand and the manila paper for the briefest of moments—such a quick glance that she probably hadn't noticed—and pointed a finger at the stem and leaves. "These should be green. But the pumpkin itself should be orange, don't you think? Like the one in this picture?" He pointed to a photo I'd placed at the center of the table for the kids to use as their inspiration.

She scanned it, gave him a serious nod, and started shading in the stem with her green pencil.

Then Will passed his paper into Blake's hands. "I'm ready for you to cut it out." Will's *r*s tended to sound like *w*s, as did his *l*s. He'd been working on it in speech therapy, but so far, he hadn't made too much progress.

But Blake didn't seem even remotely fazed by the child's speech impediment, making me wonder how much time in a classroom such as this he might have spent when he was growing up.

He took the sheet of paper from Will and started cutting along the lines, effectively hiding the blemishes of Will's handiwork by removing the places where my student had colored outside the lines.

I bit back something that felt like approval. I didn't want to approve of Blake Kozlow. I wanted to hate him with every fiber of my being, just as I'd been doing for close to a year. It felt good to hate him, didn't it?

Somehow, I wasn't so sure anymore.

"Mrs. Castillo!" Connie said, bouncing in her seat and only remembering to raise her hand once I turned in her direction. "I need to pee."

"Didn't you use the restroom after music class?" I asked, even though I was relatively certain I knew the answer. She had definitely gone into the restroom. What she'd done in there was anyone's guess, though. Connie tended to go in and wash her hands repeatedly but never get down to the business of relieving herself. In fact, this bid for a restroom break might just be another ploy to go in and wash her hands some more. I had tried offering hand sanitizer before, but that wasn't enough to satisfy Connie's obsessive-compulsive need to wash her hands. She needed actual soap from a soap dispenser and the sound and feel of running water.

I wished that my paraprofessional were already here, but Janice Yates split her day between my classroom and that of one of my colleagues—and she wasn't due to join us for another two hours. Which meant I had two choices: I could take the entire class back to the restroom so that Connie could possibly relieve herself and definitely wash her hands a few more times, or I could take her on her own and trust Blake with the rest of my class.

Frankly, neither option was appealing. But disrupting the entire class again just because Connie hadn't relieved herself when she should have would mean it'd take another thirty minutes to get them to settle down again.

I supposed that made up my mind for me.

He was so engrossed in conversation with the students at his table that clearing my throat behind him wasn't enough to catch his attention. Reluctantly, I put my hand on his shoulder.

His head whipped around so fast it caused a breeze. Or maybe the breeze was due to my pulse kicking into high gear because of the way my students were so actively engaged and listening to him tell stories about his teammates (child-appropriate stories, I hoped). Then he flashed a grin up at me that made my heart flutter until I remembered I wasn't supposed to be letting his charms have any effect on me.

I tamped that physical response down, wishing I could stamp it out entirely.

"I have to take Connie to the restroom," I said, forcing my brain back into compliance even if I couldn't do the same for my emotions. "You're in charge until I get back. Don't do or say anything I'll have to explain away later, got it? And don't pick up anything other than what you all have out already." *Nothing sharp* came through in my tone even if I didn't speak the words aloud.

He nodded, a bit of his grin fading under my admonishment, and I felt a twinge of regret for being so short with him. But only a twinge. He'd earned the way I was treating him.

"We'll be back in five minutes. *Do not* say anything that you shouldn't say." I gave him a sharp look, hoping to convey through my expression what I couldn't in words.

"Got it," he said, and his tone was filled with as much irritation and annoyance as I'd been feeling since I'd first laid eyes on him today.

With far more reluctance than I'd care to admit, I guided Connie out of my classroom.

When we returned, I was prepared to encounter World War III being carried out by thirteen small humans and one overgrown man-child—I fully expected the floor to be covered with shreds of paper and for there to be glue all over the desks, and I was almost positive at least three of my kids would be bleeding openly.

Instead, I found things exactly as I'd left them.

I let out a sigh of relief, guided Connie back to her seat, and clapped my hands to get everyone's attention. "So why don't we all come over to the reading spot?" I suggested.

"Is Mr. Kozlow going to read to us like Mr. Jezek did last year?" Tanner asked.

Blake shot a panicked expression over to me.

Would reading to the kids be an issue for him? He hadn't mentioned dyslexia or any other disabilities that might cause problems with reading, but that didn't mean he didn't have them.

"We're not going to read just now," I said, reassuring him and making a mental note to ask him for more specifics about his disabilities later—when we didn't have a classful of students hanging on our every word. "We're going to have a question-and-answer session. I'm sure you've all got lots of questions about playing hockey and being in the NHL, right?"

Fourteen heads bobbed up and down again, and all the anxiety seemed to melt away from Blake's shoulders. He shot me a look as if to say, *Thanks for throwing me a bone.*

I bit back the urge to tell him not to get used to it.

"Everyone settle down, now," I said. "Crisscross applesauce." At my reminder, fourteen children took a seat on the story-time rug and crossed their legs in front of them, sitting attentively.

I guided Blake to the ottoman with a pouf that I usually sat on for story time and nudged him to take a seat. "Language," I reminded him quietly, so the kids couldn't hear. Then I turned to the class and asked, "So who wants to be first? Who's got a question for Mr. Kozlow?"

Fourteen hands shot straight up in the air, while some of the kids attached to those hands virtually bounced up and down in their excitement to pick his brains.

I can do this, I reminded myself. *I can get through today without attempting to rip out his voice box and toss it to the wolves.*

Somehow.

Blake

"**D**o you have all your teeth?" the tiny girl up front asked when Bea called on her. She was the same child who had asked me about using a green pencil to color her pumpkin.

Sasha, I reminded myself. If I was going to be coming back to work with these kids every week—and Mr. Sutter and the rest of the team's bigwigs had made it abundantly clear I would be doing exactly that, for at least the remainder of this season, if not the rest of my tenure with the team—then I needed to make an effort to remember their names. It'd always pissed me off as a kid when adults hadn't remembered who I was.

Maybe I wasn't happy about being here, but I wouldn't take my annoyance out on the kids. They hadn't done anything wrong. *I* was the one who'd fucked up.

I shook my head and opened my mouth wide, reaching in to remove my bridge, which left a gap where my four lower front teeth used to be. Then I gave her a huge, open-mouthed grin, flicking my tongue through the hole so that they'd all crack up.

Sure enough, a mixture of laughter and disgust met my ears.

"Cool!"

"Ew, gross!"

"I can do that, too. Wanna thee?"

It always worked with kids. Kept my teammate's kids in stitches. Most of the guys on the team had at least one or two missing teeth, though, so it wasn't like I was unique. We all tended to have removable bridges, but a few guys around the league chose to go without and simply have a gap in their teeth. Losing teeth was a hazard of the job. We looked like a bunch of little old men. Really fit little old men, but still.

I had to chuckle over the disgust, though. Seeing old people without their dentures used to freak me out, too. But these days, I just rolled with it.

When the laughter died down, I put my bridge back in place. "I usually take that out before a game. Don't want to have to get new teeth made unless I need to fill another hole."

"Did it hurt?" another child asked.

Bea caught my attention and gave a brief shake of

her head, which I took to mean I shouldn't answer. Then she moved into his line of vision and raised her hand into the air, modeling the behavior she wanted him to follow.

Once he did, she gave me the tiniest of nods.

"You have a question?" I said to him.

"Did it hurt when your teeth fell out? Mom said it doesn't hurt, but I got a loose one." He reached into his mouth and wiggled one of his front top teeth.

Now it was my turn to laugh. "It won't hurt when your tooth falls out, but it might bleed a little. That's not bad, though. Those teeth are supposed to fall out, so it doesn't hurt. But when these fell out"—I flipped out my bridge again so they'd see the hole—"yeah, that hurt. They weren't supposed to fall out, you see. These were the ones that I was supposed to have until I was an old man."

"Aren't you already an old man?" one of the kids asked, and most of the rest of them snorted in laughter.

"Maybe so," I agreed. To them, I supposed I was ancient. "But I got whacked in the face with a hockey stick, and it broke them. I was gushing blood all over the place. They had to rush me off for some dental surgery."

"But they'll grow back, right?" a pixie of a child up front asked, looking both horrified and terrified at the same time.

"Yours will," I reassured her, even as Bea caught the girl's eye and modeled raising her hand again. "But you only get two sets of real teeth in your life—the ones you get as a baby, and the ones that grow in when those fall out. After that, if you lose any more teeth, then you've got to get dentures or something, so you need to be sure you take good care of the teeth you've got."

A dark-haired girl near the back raised her hand.

"You have a question, Connie?" Bea said.

"You gotta brush and floss every day," she said matter-of-factly. "Mom said twice a day, but I brush my teeth eight times a day: when I get up in the morning, before and after every meal, and again before I go to bed at night. Sometimes I brush in between those times, too."

"That's a lot of brushing," I replied, doing my best to keep my tone neutral. The last thing I needed was for Connie or anyone else in this classroom to get the impression I was judging her obsessive need for clean teeth.

"Are those dentures?" another boy asked, shooting his hand up into the air.

"It's called a bridge." I took it out again to show the kids, holding it up for a moment before shoving the fake teeth back into place. "If you lose all your teeth, that's when they give you dentures. But if you just lose a few teeth like I did, then they give you a piece that fills the gaps."

"I thought bridges were what you drive on," another boy said thoughtfully.

"That's a different type of bridge, Jason," Bea said. "But both kinds of bridges connect things, right? A bridge that you drive on connects two pieces of land when there's a gap between them, so then you can drive or walk across. And Mr. Kozlow's bridge connects two of his real teeth so he doesn't have a hole in the middle of his mouth."

"Ms. *Castillo*," Connie said dramatically, "*everyone* has a hole in their mouth."

All of the kids burst into laughter, and I barely managed to hold in a snort. "She's got a point," I said, looking over at Bea with a challenge in my eye.

"So she does," she agreed, laughing, too. "I think we all knew what I meant, though, right?"

Most of the kids nodded in quiet agreement. "How about another question? Who has one ready?"

Most of the kids raised their hands eagerly, and Bea called on a boy in the back. "Tony? What's your question?"

"How come you're here instead of Riley Jezek?" Tony asked. "He's better than you."

And now, we reached the crux of the issue. I'd known it was coming and that I wouldn't be able to put it off forever. Didn't mean I was ready to face the music yet, though. I took a moment to clear my thoughts, making sure I chose my words carefully. This was *not* the time to foul up even more than I already had.

"RJ and his wife have a baby on the way," I said slowly. "Did you guys know that?" I paused, waiting for a few of them to nod. "So Mrs. Jezek needed someone else to come and hang out with you guys for a while, and the team thought it'd be good for me— and maybe for you guys, too."

"Why's it good for you?" Connie asked, her hand shooting high in the air halfway through her question.

I shrugged, avoiding meeting Bea's eyes because I didn't want to know what she thought of what I was saying. Something told me she'd find it all wrong, yet again. But this wasn't wrong. This was the only *right* thing I could do in my current position. "Because, believe it or not, I'm a lot like you guys."

"*You?*" one boy near the front of the room said disbelievingly.

"Remember to raise your hands, guys," Bea quietly

but firmly admonished.

But I ignored her, looking straight at those kids, and I said, "Yeah, me. You all know I play hockey, right?" I paused, watching for most of them to nod. "Well, I bet you didn't know I spent my school years in a special education classroom an awful lot like this one."

A chorus of shocked squeals and disbelief flooded the classroom.

"I did," I insisted. "I've got ADHD and maybe a little bit of Asperger's syndrome."

"What's ass burglars?" a cute redhead with tons of freckles asked from the side of the room, and I nearly busted a gut laughing.

But at least Bea was laughing, too.

She pulled herself together before I did, forcing her face into compliance. "Asperger's syndrome is kind of like autism in some ways," she said. "You guys know what autism is, right?"

Several of the kids nodded, and a small girl piped up with, "Like me!"

"Yes, like you, Tabitha," Bea said. "Someone who lives with Asperger's syndrome is usually very, very smart, but they might not be good at interacting with other people. You know how we sometimes talk about social cues? The way you can tell how someone else is feeling without needing them to tell you?"

Most of the kids gave soft sounds of assent.

"Well, someone who lives with Asperger's syndrome doesn't often pick up on those social cues. So they might do or say things that hurt someone else's feelings without realizing they're doing it—or at least not until after the fact, or maybe if someone else fills them in."

As those words fell out of her mouth, I felt the

weight of Bea's stare falling on me, and it was like a light switched on in her head.

About me? Maybe.

Who could know? This woman didn't seem inclined to fill me in on much of anything, so I could only guess.

But still, this little girl deserved an answer from me.

"Asperger's is kind of like autism, yeah," I said. "But it's different, too. It makes it hard for me to understand what other people are thinking and feeling. Like, I bet your parents can always tell if you had a good day or a bad day at school as soon as you get home, right?"

Most of the kids nodded.

"Well, I don't notice those things. It's hard for me. I have to stop myself, slow down and think about it. Like, maybe you say something to your best friend, and it hurts her feelings. How can you tell that she's upset?"

"She looks sad," Tabitha said.

"Yeah." I nodded. "And maybe she cries?"

Her head bobbed up and down.

"For me, I might not realize my friend looks sad or maybe that someone's crying. I don't always realize that the things I'm saying might upset someone—I tend to just say whatever pops into my head, and then I have to apologize if I said something I shouldn't have. One of my buddies is good about telling me when I'm being an as—a jerk," I corrected myself, stealing a quick look at Bea to be sure I wasn't in her doghouse. "I kind of live in my own head a lot, and things like that don't sink in. So I'm always having to make up for saying and doing things I shouldn't have. Anyone else in here like that?"

Most of the kids nodded, and a couple of them raised their hands as if to say *me, too.*

"But you're still smart?" a quiet boy off to the side

asked.

"Please raise your hand before asking questions, Eddie," Bea said, but she didn't try to stop me from answering.

"I think so?" I replied. "I'm good with numbers and puzzles. Not so good with words. Actually, I do a lot of puzzles and number games to help me settle my ADHD, especially when I'm stuck on a long flight or something and there's no outlet for me to use up my energy."

"What kind of puzzles?" someone else asked, and Bea apparently decided to give up on trying to get them to raise their hands, at least for this session.

"Sometimes I do jigsaw puzzles—big ones with lots of itty-bitty pieces. It helps me to slow my thoughts down to a more reasonable pace. And I like Sudoku. Have you guys ever played Sudoku puzzles?"

About a dozen confused stares met my question.

"We've done a couple of small ones," Bea answered. "You guys remember the boxes, and we have to fill in the correct numbers?"

A chorus of "Oh, yeah," and "I don't like those number games," and "They're too easy," came in response.

"There are a lot of things we can do instead of puzzles and number games, though, right?" Bea put in, and a bunch of the kids nodded enthusiastically.

"Yeah, like coloring!" a freckled boy in the back said, bouncing up and down. "Do you color, too?" he asked me.

"Honestly, I haven't colored in a long time."

Bea caught my eye. "Might be something for you to consider, especially for those long flights. It can help keep your mind from wandering too much. They've got a lot of adult coloring books these days—animals and mandala patterns, and all sorts of other things."

"Yeah?" I scanned the room, because the kids looked excited at the prospect of coloring, even though they'd just finished an art project. "You guys think I should try it?"

"Yes!" most of them shouted.

Apparently, I was going to try my hand at coloring for the first time in well over a decade. But I'd need to find something that suited me. Mandalas and animals didn't quite seem to fit the bill.

Time to do a bit of research—once I was done here for the day.

The kinds of coloring books *I* might be interested in pursuing likely wouldn't be appropriate in a school setting—if they even existed, at all.

Chapter Four

Bea

"He was actually a really good fit for my class, better than I'd care to admit. And my kids adore him more than I could adequately say. I think having him around as an example of what they can do with their lives and who they can become if they put in the effort is going to do wonders for their self-confidence. And I'm not even one tiny little fraction of a bit happy about it," I said, all of it coming out in a rush. I was huffing for breath into my phone as I power-walked around my neighborhood later that evening.

Walking was about the only thing I could think of to help me get rid of the irked sensation that had held me in its grips since the moment Blake Kozlow had stepped into the school's front office this morning. Besides, I hadn't gotten anywhere near enough steps in today. My Fitbit might as well be laughing at me for my poor showing.

"Are you ever going to tell me what the heck he did wrong and why we hate him so much?" Dani demanded on the other end of the line. "Because I'm fully on board with hating him—I mean, I was already down with that before I ever introduced you to him— but you two seemed to really hit it off at first." Until recently, Dani had been doing a lot of these walks with me. But her pregnancy had done a serious number on her body, and these days, my friend was beginning to spend more time in bed than out of it—by doctor's orders, no less. No walking and talking for her today, sadly. We'd settled on talking while I walked on my own.

"*Seemed* and *at first* being the key phrases in that observation," I agreed. "Yeah, things were fine between us in the beginning."

Better than fine, actually.

"Hmmph," she said. But she sounded pained— physically pained, not just put out that I'd brushed her off again.

"You okay?" I asked, my concern meter kicking into overdrive as I started doing mental calculations. I was only a few minutes away from my house. If I jogged the last bit, I could be in my car and at her place in fifteen minutes, tops, and we could be on our way to the hospital in another five after that.

"I'll be okay when this bowling ball is on the outside of me instead of on the inside."

"It's not big enough to be a bowling ball yet."

"Getting there."

"You were the one who wanted to make babies right away," I pointed out. "Cody didn't seem overly motivated to jump-start the process of building a family."

"Yeah, but Katie can't have kids, and Luke doesn't have a uterus, nor does Cole, and Luke obviously won't be getting involved with anyone who *does* have a uterus, so I'm the only one of my siblings who can give my parents grandbabies—or at least grandbabies that share their DNA. Doesn't mean I was prepared for bed rest and shit," she grumbled.

I laughed. For as much as she complained, I knew the truth. Dani Williams was beyond ecstatic about her impending motherhood. She just didn't have a non-sarcastic bone in her body, and being confined to bed any amount of time put her on edge.

I knew plenty about being on edge lately. It was the overriding sensation I'd been feeling due to Blake Kozlow walking back into my life.

During that date Dani had mentioned, I'd allowed myself to think, for the span of about an hour, that a sexy-as-hell professional athlete could be interested in me.

Ha-ha. Not so much.

Yeah, the same me who'd once weighed more than three hundred pounds.

The same me who hadn't been able to bring myself to start dating again until Dani had given me a massive nudge in that direction, because no matter what the scale or mirror said, I still saw the three-hundred-twenty-eight-pound version of me, not the one-hundred-sixty-two-pound version of me.

The same me who perpetually saw fat rolls and bulges that no longer existed. And even in those rare moments I didn't see the fat, I couldn't deny the loose, saggy, hanging skin that could only be hidden by formfitting undergarments and lots of outer layers.

The same me who hadn't dated again since that disastrous first outing because it had been so bad that it had essentially confirmed all the negative self-talk that continuously lived in my head.

The same me who only saw jiggly, saggy boobs and flappy, chicken-wing arms and a sad, droopy butt when she looked in the mirror, not the one who looked like a hot *mamacita* in the clothes Dani had created.

And it didn't matter what kind of person lived on the inside—I couldn't seem to see past what had once existed on the outside. And if I couldn't do that, how could anyone else?

Besides, this guy wasn't just a rich, famous athlete—he was younger than me by a good five years. Blake Kozlow had just celebrated his twenty-fifth birthday, according to my internet searches all those months ago, and I'd passed my thirtieth over this past summer break. The idea of a good-looking, uber-successful, young pro hockey player having any sort of interest in me wasn't anything I'd known what to do with or how to handle.

Men had never stopped to look twice at me when I'd been so heavy.

Well, not men like Blake, at least. I'd been on the receiving end of unwelcome leers from creepy old men as far back as when I was a teen and consisted of all boobs and curves, but not after I'd ballooned in weight in college. At that point, I'd resigned myself to being the overweight friend who could always be counted on to provide a shoulder for my thinner female friends to cry on when their boyfriends dumped them.

Yep, I was the DUFF—the Designated Ugly Fat Friend.

And now that I *wasn't* the DUFF any longer? I wasn't sure what to do with myself. I wasn't sure who I was, or even who I wanted to be. In some ways, I missed being able to go unseen in a crowd. Yes, that was a strange thing to think, considering my former weight. But when you're that large, no one sees you. You can blend into the background. You might as well be invisible.

No wonder it had taken so much coaxing for me to wear the clothes Dani had made me—formfitting pieces that hugged my new body and fit me precisely—let alone to go out on a double date with her.

But I'd done it. My imagination had run away with me during that dinner, and I'd started thinking about all sorts of things I hadn't allowed myself to think about in my entire adult life.

Dating.

Kissing.

Hand-holding and other sorts of physical contact.

Sex.

But that one would sure as heck never be happening now. For that matter, none of them would.

Or at least not with Blake Kozlow.

"So what happened?" Dani demanded, interrupting my thoughts. "What changed? I *knew* he was going to make an ass of himself that night. It's why I wanted Cody to find anyone else."

"What happened is we went on another date that I didn't tell you about, and he opened his mouth and said something that he can never unsay." I let out a heavy sigh, turning the corner to return to my own street.

And even if he somehow *could* unsay it, I could never *unhear* those words—or *unfeel* the way they'd made me feel.

Oh, wow. Now that he's seen her eating like that, there's no chance in hell there'll be a second date.

Even though almost a year had passed, I still wasn't ready to tell Dani the words that had come out of Blake's mouth. Because maybe I wasn't prepared to examine what I'd felt and the way I'd reacted.

He'd been looking at a couple a few tables away from us at the restaurant.

The guy was young and good-looking and most likely affluent, based on the way he was dressed.

The woman was a lot like I'd used to be—only not as large by any stretch of the imagination. Curvy. A bit overweight, sure, but I'd considered her to be fluffy more than fat. She'd probably been a bit over two hundred pounds, judging from what I remembered of the various weights I'd been over the years.

I'd watched them for a moment, trying to determine what Blake was seeing. All I'd been able to make out was a woman so engaged in conversation that she was more focused on her companion than she was on the food in front of her. Occasionally, a bite of her food had fallen off her fork and back onto her plate because she was so engrossed in the moment and the conversation and *not* in her food. There'd been a hint of a stain on her blouse, too, so she might have caught some of her food with her chest instead of her plate.

Having been a woman with an overly large chest not so terribly long before that night, I knew the dangers of eating messy foods with a massive bosom all too well, though, so I could sympathize. But she wasn't letting it stop her from enjoying herself with her companion.

Yeah, maybe she'd been eating pasta, which wouldn't be good for her waistline. Yeah, maybe she was going to eat the entire portion the server had set in front of her. But what did that matter?

Blake's insinuation had hit me like a ton of bricks, and then our date couldn't end fast enough to satisfy me. I'd wanted nothing more than to get away from him and never set eyes on him again.

Because if he thought that woman was fat and disgusting and he was sure her date wanted to get out of there ASAP because of it, then what would he think when he found out how big I used to be? Maybe he thought I was a reasonable weight now, but what would happen if he ever saw my chicken-wing arms when they weren't covered by long sleeves? What would he have to say about my droopy butt and floppy thighs when my Spanx weren't holding them in? How would he react to my sad, deflated boobs when my bra wasn't working overtime and they hung down to my waist?

This was why I'd avoided dating—all the what-ifs, the fears about how a man might look at me differently once he saw me naked. To be honest, I wasn't sure I could go there with anyone, but certainly not with a judgmental jerk like Blake Kozlow.

True, I had a better understanding of him now…but I didn't want to forgive him yet. Maybe not ever. I understood enough about his disabilities to know that he likely didn't have a filter—whatever passed through his mind would then fall out of his lips. That didn't change the fact that the thoughts had passed through his mind, though.

But admittedly, he couldn't *make* me feel any particular way. How I had responded to his statement—and how I continued to feel about it— well, that was all on me.

My reaction might say more about me than it did about him in the long run, darn it.

Sometimes, it really sucked to be an adult and to look at the bigger picture. It'd be a heck of a lot easier and make me happier to go on blaming Blake Kozlow for everything I'd felt that night.

I wanted to forget that he was so much like my students, forget that there was a *reason* behind his thoughtlessness and his careless statements even if there could never be a *justification* for them. And then I wanted to banish him from my mind and my life altogether.

I didn't want him taking up any more space in my thoughts.

I didn't want to allow the sharp stab of pain I'd felt that night to creep back up again.

I'd spent too much time and effort trying to see myself, both inside and out, the same way the rest of the world saw me now, and giving Blake Kozlow any sort of power to destroy all the work I'd done wouldn't help anyone—and it wouldn't help me, most of all.

Fat chance of me getting him out of my thoughts anytime soon, though, since he was supposed to be coming back to work with my class at least once or twice a week for the remainder of the school year unless the team was on the road for too long.

"Hello?" Dani said on the other end of the line. "Earth to Bea. Don't tell me you got run over on the street, because then I'll have to get out of bed to come and rescue you, and then you'll have to answer to my husband."

"I'm fine," I reassured her. "Just thinking."

"Thinking about avoiding the subject, apparently."

I laughed, because there was more than just a kernel

of truth to that.

She harrumphed in a way that only Dani Williams could get away with. It was beyond adorable, just like everything else about her. "You're going to tell me one of these days," she grumbled.

"Maybe so," I murmured. But then I let my thoughts trail off, because my driveway came into view, and there was an unfamiliar sports car parked in it.

An unfamiliar sports car with an altogether too familiar man leaning casually against the bumper, his ankles crossed as he stared down at his phone.

Ugh. Not now.

"I have to let you go," I said to Dani.

"You're not getting away with this forever. I will hunt you down and force it out of you."

"Later," I cut in before she could build up a head of steam. "I've got to go."

"Hmph," she said. But then she added, "Fine. Bye. But you owe me dessert. Something full of sugar and fat and all that other good shit the doctors aren't letting me have."

"Fine," I bit off, even though I didn't intend to bring her anything of the sort. I could make her a low-fat, low-carb, low-sugar dessert, and she wouldn't even know it.

By the time I disconnected the call, I'd made it to my driveway and could direct the fullness of my glare straight into Blake Kozlow's eyes. I shoved my phone into my pocket with so much force it was a miracle I didn't rip a hole in the bottom of the fabric.

"What are you doing at my house? And for that matter, how do you know where I live?" When we'd gone on that date, I'd met him there and taken myself home. I hadn't been ready for anything more serious than that.

"Harry told me. Said he brought you Chinese food once or something."

I made a mental note to have Dani rip her husband a new one for giving out that kind of information without asking my permission. "And?" I demanded. "Why are you here?" Having to deal with him in my classroom, surrounded by my students, was one thing. Having him at my house when we were all alone? That was something entirely different. Not to mention completely unacceptable.

He shot a sulky, broody look my way. "And what?"

"And why are you here?"

"I thought you could help me."

Help him? He thought I could freaking *help* him? Wasn't I already doing exactly that by allowing him to come into my class and be around my students? It wasn't exactly my idea, either. And yet he thought I owed him more than I was already giving him, did he?

Not going to happen.

Without sparing him another glance, I headed for my front door.

"Wait," he called out from behind me. "Bea, hold up for a second and talk to me, would you?"

I didn't slow my pace.

Heavy footsteps pounded in my wake, and then his hand landed on my upper arm.

Instinct kicked in. I spun around in a flash, wrapping my fingers around the keychain pepper spray I kept in my pocket when I walked. I whipped it out, holding it up in his face.

He released me and dropped back almost immediately, hands up as if to guard his eyes with them, not that they'd do him any good if I decided to press the button.

"Christ, I'm sorry. All right? I'm sorry."

"You should be."

"Well, I am."

"Good."

"Sorrier than I can ever say."

"And?" I demanded, my thumb still on the button, ready to spray at the slightest provocation.

He looked confused. "And what?"

"And why the heck would you think I would *ever* consider helping you more than I already am? I'm letting you into my classroom so you can do your little PR stunt and get back in your team's good graces. I'm allowing you to *volunteer* with my students, even though I doubt there's a single bone in your body that would come up with this sort of community service project on your own. Isn't that enough? What else do you think I owe you?"

"You don't owe me anything."

"You're right. I don't. I don't owe you a single thing. Good-bye." I turned again, determined to get inside and slam the door in his face if necessary.

But then a pained sound fell from his lips, and I froze despite my good intentions of blocking him from my thoughts and not falling for any sort of emotional ploy he might try to throw at me.

"Please, Bea," he said. "I'm desperate."

He had to go and become all polite on me. A grown man respectfully saying things like *please* and *thank you* and treating others with decency and common courtesy might as well be my personal Kryptonite.

Well, damn it. Damn it all to heck and back.

Damn, damn, damn, damn, crap, shoot, damn.

Without turning to look at him, I paused with one

hand on the doorknob and the other still holding my pepper spray. "What kind of help do you need this time?" I bit off. Not that I intended to help him. But it wouldn't kill me to hear him out.

Would it?

I felt him move up behind me on the steps to my porch, but I refused to turn and look at him. If he tried to give me puppy-dog eyes or something…

No, I was stronger than that. I wouldn't fall for it. I could resist with my students, so I could surely resist with this jerk.

But he didn't respond.

I spun around to glare at him. "Well?" I demanded. "I don't have all day to stand out here waiting for you to give me an answer."

"I need you to help me learn ways to focus, like you do with your kids," he spluttered. "I've tried everything I know to do, and I still end up doing stupid things when I should know better. I don't know who else I can turn to for this."

Yeah, he could have blown me over with a feather this time.

Blake

"Come on, then," she grumbled, holding open the door and looking thoroughly pissed off about it. "I'm not going to stand around all day waiting for you to decide whether you're coming in or not. You don't get to act like an indecisive cat."

I supposed that meant she was willing to help me. Or at least willing to hear me out. Either way, I knew better than to pass up my opportunity. I moved in so I could hold open the door for her to pass inside.

She scowled up at me for a moment, but then she relented.

I closed the door behind us and followed her into her living room.

After tossing her keys on a table, she headed for a large glass cage near the opposite wall. She hadn't exactly invited me over, but my curiosity got the better of me. I crept closer, peering over her shoulder to see what she had in there.

A couple of adorable guinea pigs started moving around and letting out high-pitched squeals.

"Neville and Luna," Bea said to me. "The black one's Luna and the cream one's Neville. They get excited when I come home. And when there are visitors." She reached into a plastic container next to their cage and unloaded some hay to spread in there. "There's a bag of shredded carrots on the shelf in the fridge. Can you grab it? They'll love you forever if you give them their carrots."

I wasn't sure I wanted her guinea pigs to love me forever, but it wouldn't kill me to help her out. And besides, I was trying to get her to do me a favor. The least I could do was help her out with something small like this. I had a hell of a lot of ground to make up.

I headed into the kitchen and found the carrots. But I couldn't seem to stop myself from examining the contents of her refrigerator while I was in there. A couple kinds of cheeses, milk, yogurt, lots of bottled water, a package of chicken breasts, some ground turkey, a couple of plastic containers of what I could only assume were leftovers or lunches ready for her to grab on her way out the door, an entire shelf dedicated to various brands and flavors of premixed protein shakes, and a couple of drawers full of various sorts of fresh vegetables.

To be honest, it looked an awful lot like the contents of my fridge, only with a lot more dairy and less fresh meat and vegetables. For someone who wasn't a professional athlete, though? I was surprised it wasn't full of breads and pastas. In fact, I didn't see anything I'd consider a traditional carb anywhere in her kitchen. Huh.

"You got those carrots yet?" she called out from the living room, reminding me what I was supposed to be doing.

I grabbed the bag and shut the fridge, then headed back into the living room. "Sorry," I said, tearing open the plastic wrapper. "Got distracted."

"Got caught snooping, more like," she muttered, but this time it sounded like she might be amused more than pissed off.

"Maybe a bit," I admitted. "Is that a problem?"

"Depends."

"On what?"

"On why you're snooping."

"Was just curious to see what's in your fridge," I said, deciding honesty would probably serve me best. "You can learn a lot about a person by seeing what they eat. My grandma always told me that."

Bea scowled and took the bag of carrots from my hands, then put a large handful of them in a ceramic bowl situated in one corner of the guinea pigs' cage.

"You don't want me trying to learn about you?" I asked, genuinely trying to figure out what I'd done to piss her off this time.

"I don't like being judged for what I eat," she

snapped. "Or what I don't eat. Or how much I eat or don't eat. Or—"

"Whoa. Don't get your panties twisted up, all right?"

She flashed a murderous glare in my direction, and I held up my hands in surrender.

"I'm not judging you," I said. And I wished I hadn't told her not to get her panties twisted up. That was probably the wrong thing to say, even if she was going way overboard and jumping to conclusions that I wasn't following.

"Aren't you? Isn't that why you felt the need to catalog everything you found in my fridge? Isn't that what you do?"

"I catalog things, sure. I make mental lists. I try to figure people out based on the things I can learn about them." And I still didn't understand why that was such a problem. She worked with kids who had the same sorts of disabilities I had. She ought to understand how our brains worked. Shouldn't she? Or was I expecting too much, just because of a couple of minor things I knew about her?

Now was one of those times I really wished I could read people better.

"And what did you learn about me by poking through my fridge?" Bea demanded, although she didn't sound quite as angry as she had only moments before.

"I learned you eat a lot like I do. You don't have a bunch of junk in there."

"Maybe you should go poke through my pantry. I'm sure you can find something in there that'll help you prove your point."

"What point?" What the hell? I didn't know what

was happening.

"Oh, I don't know. Maybe that I eat too much? That I'm never going to have a guy want to date me because of all the so-called junk I eat? You tell me. You're the one who likes to judge people for the way they eat, Mr. Perfect."

"Judge people for the— What the hell are you talking about?"

"What am I talking about?" she seethed. "*What am I talking about?* Why don't you try this on for size? 'Now that he's seen her eating like that, there's no chance in hell there'll be a second date.' How about that? You remember saying that?"

I stared at her, blinking while I tried to focus my thoughts. It had to be something I'd said during that date I'd taken her on, after the one Harry had dragged me along for. Maybe this was what I'd said to cause everything to go downhill. Things had been great at first, and then out of nowhere, it had all gone to hell.

I racked my brain, trying to remember everything I could about that night, that meal. We'd been having a good time, laughing and joking. Bea had seemed to get my sense of humor, and I'd enjoyed hers.

Hell, I'd enjoyed everything about her. She'd had the most engaging laugh that brightened her eyes and warmed me up from the inside out.

It'd all been going great when I'd noticed another couple in the restaurant. And, me being me, I'd said the first thing that had popped into my head.

"Well, do you?" she demanded.

"Would you give me a second?" I half shouted back at her, trying to figure out what had been so bad about my observation. The chick had been paying so much attention to her date that she'd spilled her dinner all over her shirt.

"You do remember it," Bea said. "I can see it all over your face."

"You seriously decided to hate me for the rest of eternity because I made a comment about how some stranger couldn't eat without staining her fucking clothes?" I shot back.

"Yes, I— Wait, what?" Now, apparently, it was Bea's turn for confusion. "You said he wouldn't take her on another date now that he'd seen how she eats."

"Yeah, I did, but I don't see what the big deal is. She was sloppy as hell. Her food was all down the front of her shirt, and it was like she didn't even realize it. My grandma would've ripped me a new asshole if I'd made a mess of myself like that in public—and that guy was some big corporate bigwig. He needs a society wife, someone he can take to client dinners and fundraising galas without worrying that she'll spill her shrimp cocktail down the front of her evening gown and then try to fish the shrimp out in front of people…"

Bea gawked at me. There wasn't any other way to describe her expression.

"What?" I demanded.

She blinked, still silent.

"*What?*" I nearly snarled. "What the hell did I do now? You've got to explain shit to me, in case you haven't caught on yet. Because I don't get it. I don't have a clue—"

"I thought you were judging her for what she was eating. Not that judging her for spilling her food is much better, but…"

I quirked up a brow in question. "But it's better?" Meaning maybe I wasn't in deep shit with her right now?

Granted, I was bound to do something else to piss her off soon enough. I was still me, after all. But if I had somehow climbed out of her pit of doom…

"It's better for me," Bea finally said. She reached into the guinea pigs' cage and picked up the white one, and then she held him out to me. "Wanna meet him?"

I still didn't know what the hell had just happened, but I took the guinea pig from her hands and held him out in front of my face. He squeaked at me. A lot. Especially when I brushed a single finger down his back.

"He might kinda like you," she said.

I kinda liked him, too.

For that matter, I might even kinda like her. At least when she wasn't mad at me for no fucking good reason.

Chapter Five

Blake

Don't ask me how we ended up in a craft store, but that's exactly where Bea decided to take me. Someplace I'd never stepped foot in before called Michael's, to be precise—which, judging from the items dotting their sidewalk out front, seemed like an oversized warehouse full of bright, colorful things I had no clue how to use or even what they *should* be used for.

Plastic flowers? Seriously? Although now that I thought about it, my grandma would probably like a lot of things in here...

"You do realize that I've probably never stepped foot inside a craft store before in my entire life, right?" I asked in a semi-daze, unfolding my legs to climb out of the vehicle while the bright-red backlit sign filled my eyes.

Bea barely spared me a glance over her shoulder, because she was already bustling toward the doors. "Perfect reason for you to come in one now."

"I don't do crafts."

"Well, maybe you didn't before, but that's going to change if you want my help, like you say you do. You just need to figure out which kind of crafting is right for you."

"But I don't want—"

"There are tons of options in here," she said, effectively cutting me off before the thought had even finished forming.

Crafts. Seriously? I hadn't done anything like this since I was a kid at summer camp, and I hated it then. So I would sure as shit hate it now. What the hell did she think this would accomplish?

Still, I matched my strides to hers and headed into the store—mainly because I wanted to spend more time with her, even though I knew she wasn't so fond of spending time with me. I couldn't change her initial impression of me, but maybe, with time, I could change the way she saw me now.

It was like an explosion of colors as soon as we were inside the front doors. To my left, thousands of silk flowers and ribbons in every style imaginable were spilling over into the aisles in a cacophony of color that would give Grandma heart palpitations. To the right, there were rows and rows of canvases, brushes, and paints. Straight ahead, I could see what appeared to be various types of wall art and decorative pots and other things to scatter throughout a room and make it look homey.

There was no telling what we'd find the deeper we went into the store…and I wasn't sure I wanted to find out. The only thing I felt certain of was that the bright, noisy colors everywhere would be imprinted on the backs of my eyelids and were sure to haunt my sleeping hours.

No doubt, I'd wake up in the middle of the night tonight (if I even managed to get to sleep in the first place) with visions of plastic flowers exploding like confetti all over me. Just the thought of it was enough to make me want to gag in revulsion.

Already, my legs were itching to book it out those doors again—but I'd made the mistake of letting Bea drive me here, so I couldn't leave until she was good and ready to go. I was stuck.

Stuck in my own personal version of hell.

I had to fight back the urge to shudder. It wouldn't be enough to dislodge me from my predicament, so there was no point.

She set her purse in the kiddie seat of a smallish shopping cart and headed toward the back of the store, as if she knew exactly where she was headed and what she'd find there once she arrived. I got the sense that she spent a decent amount of time in this store on a regular basis.

Probably shouldn't surprise me, since she had artsy-crafty things up all over her classroom. She might get her supplies here, and maybe some of her ideas, too.

"Maybe I should just get a pet," I said in the hope that I could convince her we should leave this place, and sooner rather than later. "I could get a guinea pig like you've got."

"Have you ever had a pet before?" she asked, slowing down to scan down an aisle filled with tubes of paints in more colors than I realized existed.

"Nope."

"Maybe you should start with a plant. If it's still alive after six months, you could move up to a fish. And if they're both still alive after another six months, *then* you could possibly graduate to something like a guinea pig. We could get you an ivy. Ivies are hard to kill."

I scowled, not that she could see it with her back to me. But damn. Talk about wounding my pride. "Maybe I should start with a pet rock if I'm really that bad," I grumbled. "I can't exactly kill one of those."

"Hmm," she murmured in a tone that suggested she agreed with me. "So if you haven't lost your rock after six months, then you could move up to getting an ivy or something…"

The sound that left my mouth must have told her exactly how much that stung, because she finally slowed down and looked over her shoulder at me. "I'm teasing you," she said. "I don't really think you're that awful."

"Teasing? Meaning we're good, you and me?" I had to ask because of the whole difficulty-with-understanding-basic-human-interactions thing I had going on. But I was almost positive she understood at least that much about me, which should help both of us.

Shouldn't it?

"I don't know that I'd say we're *good*," she said. "But we're getting better. Okay?"

I groaned. But at least it was a start. "Fine."

Bea gave me a curt nod, and then she turned down another aisle. This one was filled with markers, colored pencils, crayons, and all sorts of coloring books. Halfway down the aisle, she came to a stop in front of a section of books filled with complex mandala designs, complicated animal portraits, and even a few scenic views of nature with so many components I couldn't imagine how to color them properly.

Really? This was what she brought me here for? I shook my head in disbelief. "Coloring books…"

"They're an option," she said, ignoring my dismay. "It works great for most of my students who have ADHD. And if we get you a book or two full of intricate designs, they could possibly provide enough stimulation for your mind to keep you…"

"Out of trouble," I finished for her.

She gave me a sheepish grin while shrugging.

"I'm not taking Scooby Doo coloring books and crayons on road trips to keep me occupied on the team plane."

"No one's suggesting that. These are *adult* coloring books. They're a lot more interesting than Scooby Doo, not to mention they're more complicated, so they'll challenge you. They'll engage your creative brain better, anyway. And you can get colored pencils, art markers…whatever floats your boat."

Without really looking at them, I grabbed three random books off the shelf and tossed them into the cart. Then a little farther down the aisle, I selected a case of art markers with thirty-six colors and added them to the basket, as well. "All right, so is that all we're here for?" Because the sooner I got out of here, the sooner my skin would stop crawling.

"Nope." Bea pushed the cart down the aisle and turned to the left again, heading deeper into the store.

I didn't really have much choice but to follow her.

She power-walked through the aisles, the same way she did at her school. More than that, it seemed she knew exactly where she was headed and what she'd find when she got there. Yeah, she definitely spent a lot of time in this store.

After a few twists and turns I'd never be able to replicate without her leading me, she came to a stop in an aisle filled with puzzles of all sorts—traditional jigsaw puzzles of famous artwork, puzzles with large pieces and famous cartoon characters, 3D puzzles of intricate buildings like Notre Dame in Paris and the White House, and so many others I didn't even recognize.

She moved toward the really complicated ones—a thousand pieces or more with elaborate designs—and pointed. "Pick a couple of puzzles."

"I don't want to pick puzzles."

"Tough. You asked for my help. This is how I'm helping."

"I don't see what puzzles and coloring books are supposed to do for me," I complained.

"They're supposed to help you focus your thoughts. Maybe coloring won't work but puzzles will. Maybe neither will help and you'll need to keep trying other hobbies until we find the right thing. But the point is that you've got to try out a few of these hobbies to see what sticks."

I scowled at her.

She put her hands on her hips and raised a brow in a move that mimicked the school's secretary.

Even though I didn't want to, I grabbed a couple of puzzles off the shelf. One was of a Harley Davidson. If nothing else, I could send it to Grandma. She'd get a kick out of it. The other was a gorgeous white snow leopard or something—to be honest, I wasn't sure what animal was on the design, but I liked the looks of it.

I'd barely tossed the boxes into the cart before Bea

had taken off again, wending her way through the aisles. The next time she stopped, we were surrounded by… Hell, I didn't even know what this shit was.

"Ever try counted cross-stitch?" Bea asked me, scanning the packages hanging from the shelves.

"Never even heard of it."

"Well, you're going to try it." She found one that had an image of a couple of kittens crawling over stacks of books and shoved it toward me. "Here. Instead of getting a pet, you can learn to cross-stitch a pet. You can't kill these cats, even if you forget to feed them. This is a much safer way of going about it. Granted, you could stick yourself with the needle…hmm. On second thought, maybe you shouldn't try cross-stitch, after all."

"You've seriously lost your fucking mind, haven't you?"

In lieu of answering, she shrugged and tossed the package into the shopping cart and took off again. "No skin off my teeth if you stick yourself with a needle, now that I think about it."

"I don't want to do this shit," I called after her, cursing some more beneath my breath as I trailed her.

A couple of gray-haired ladies heading the other way passed annoyed looks in my direction. Apparently, I shouldn't curse while shopping for shit at Michael's.

The only good thing about this shopping trip so far was that I got to stare at Bea's ass a lot since she was constantly about two to five feet in front of me.

"I don't care what you do or don't want to do," she said, not bothering to slow down.

That much was obvious.

"You asked me for help," she said when I had almost caught up to her. "I'm helping." Then she stopped so suddenly that I almost barreled into her.

Hell, maybe I should have. Then I could have steadied myself by putting my hands on her. It'd probably be the only way she'd ever allow me to touch her.

I needed to get all thoughts of that sort out of my head, and for good, because that wasn't what this was about.

This time, we were surrounded by yarn, knitting needles, and books filled with designs.

"Oh, hell no. Not even my grandma knits. I'd never hear the end of it if the guys found out I'm knitting baby blankets or some other shit like that."

"They don't have to know," she said, eyeing the shelves shrewdly. "You can do it in the privacy of your own home. But I don't know how to knit, anyway—I crochet. So that's what I can teach you, or you can find some online videos to help you learn to knit if you'd prefer it."

"I'd prefer to get the hell out of this store before this shit becomes permanently affixed to my retinas and I see it all in my sleep."

She laughed and shook her head, but she was still scanning the shelves. Then she reached for a book called *Simple Crocheted Afghans for the Beginner.* After a couple of minutes of flipping through the pages, she stopped on a page with a cozy-looking green blanket wrapped around the shoulders of someone's mom. She studied the page opposite the picture for a moment and then nodded with a soft, humming sound coming from her lips. "You could absolutely make this one. It'd be a good design to start with. Nice and simple." Then she grabbed a metal thing with a hook on one end from a nearby shelf and headed for another aisle.

I followed, almost bumping into her again when she stopped in front of a bunch of yarn.

"Pick a color," she said.

"I don't see the right green from the picture."

"You don't have to use the color in the book. You can do whatever color you want. What colors do you have in your house?"

"Everything's brown…beige. Neutral."

"Smart," she said, still scanning the shelves full of yarn.

"Smart?" I repeated.

"A lot of colors can be distracting if you've got ADHD. Keeping everything neutral will help calm your mind." Then she reached for a cream-colored yarn and held it up for me. "You like this?"

"Sure?" To be honest, I didn't like anything about being in here, so I'd agree to whatever she wanted, just as long as we could get the hell out of this store as soon as possible.

She glanced back at the book, then at the label on the yarn, and she tossed five of the balls of cream yarn into the shopping cart.

"Can we please get out of here now?" I begged.

Finally, she looked up at me, and then a hint of understanding flooded her expression. "Yeah, we can go. I'm sure a place like this is overwhelming for you, but you won't have to come back often. Just when you need more supplies for whatever activities end up helping you settle your thoughts."

Fat chance of that happening. Even if I found something that helped me out of all of these projects, I could surely find a way to order more supplies online. That was bound to be easier—at least for me—than being swamped by the insanity of a place like this.

We headed for the front and stood in line to check out. I could barely hold still while we waited for our turn. Finally, the cashier got to us and started ringing up my purchases.

"That'll be two hundred forty-two dollars and twenty-seven cents," she said.

Two hundred fifty bucks for a bunch of art projects I doubted I'd ever touch? Damn, this shit was expensive.

But I forked over my credit card and paid, and then we carried three large shopping bags out to Bea's SUV.

"That wasn't too painful, was it?" she said, climbing inside.

Not too painful? Ha. My eyes would likely be burning for days after all of that.

I glared in response, which made her laugh.

Damn, but I did love her laugh, though. Even if she was laughing at me.

Bea

Dani bent her head low over the bowl of ice cream I'd brought her, sniffing it suspiciously. "Is this some of that fake shit you eat all the time? Are you trying to poison me with something? I want oodles of fat and sugar and salt and all the other garbage that makes food taste good."

She didn't need to know that it was Halo Top ice cream—much lower in calories and sugars, and much higher in protein and fiber, and therefore much better for her. So in lieu of answering her, I arched up a brow and said, "Are you going to eat it or not? Because Cody isn't going to give in and bring you anything even remotely resembling ice cream, so you'd better make do with what you can get your hands on."

"So it *is* your healthy, poisonous shit."

"Fine, give it back to me," I said, holding out a hand. I crossed one ankle over my other, making myself comfortable next to her in her bed, where she was propped upright with countless pillows supporting her from every angle. "I'll eat it and you can go without."

She tugged the bowl away from me and tucked it by her side. "Not a chance, *chica*. Hands off my ice cream."

"I'm just trying to be sure you and the baby stay healthy."

"I'd rather you try to be sure I stay sane."

"Might as well be the same thing," I said, winking.

"You're not as funny as you think you are."

"And you're not as scary as you think *you* are."

"Hmph," she muttered, but she started shoving the ice cream into her face, nonetheless. "Oh, God, this is so good," she said around a mouthful.

"Told you." I laughed and filled my own spoon with a bite from her bowl.

She tugged the bowl away. "Hands off. Get your own."

"Good grief. You know I'm only going to eat two or three bites and then I'll stop. And I brought you four different flavors, too, so you're stocked up for a while."

"I don't care. I don't wanna share. I'm already sharing everything with this little leech," she said, fondly rubbing a hand over her ever-increasing belly.

All I could do in response was laugh.

Dani shoved another spoonful in her mouth. "You need to tell Cody exactly where to find this so he can buy me more. What store, which aisle, where on the shelves… I need at least three pints a day from now until this baby is out of me."

"Um, you do realize you need to eat real food, too, right?"

"You do realize you're supposed to be my best friend, and I've already got more than enough people nagging me, between Cody and Mom and my army of doctors. I need you to be on my side."

"I am on your side—which means I want you and your baby to be healthy. Which means I'm going to do everything in my power to be sure you follow doctor's orders."

Instead of responding, she glared and shoved her spoon back into the bowl for another bite, challenging me to take it away with a defiantly raised brow.

"Guess my nasty, healthy, poisonous stuff is okay then," I muttered, holding back more laughter.

"If I can't get my hands on the real deal, this'll do in a pinch. But don't tell Cody how much I like it."

"Why not?"

"Because then he might not be willing to bring me either this *or* the real stuff when I have a craving at two in the morning."

"You're incorrigible."

"And you love me for it." Dani smirked.

She was right about that part, at least.

"So," she said, licking the spoon so as not to miss a single smidgeon of her ice cream, "what's the latest on the Koz situation?"

"Situation?" I had to stifle a snort.

"Have we moved on from it being a situation, then? What is it now?"

"I don't know," I hedged. "It's just…a thing."

"A thing?"

"Yeah."

"An obnoxious thing? A we-want-to-stab-his-eyes-out-with-a-rusty-spork thing? An it's-not-ideal-but-we're-finding-a-way-to-deal-with-it thing?"

"Just a thing," I said.

Dani's eyes nearly bugged out of her head, and her jaw dropped. "You like him," she said, sounding shocked and confused, and maybe a little bit peeved.

"I don't know if I'd say I like him."

"You do," she insisted. "I thought you did before, but then he did a typical Koz thing and we hated him, but now you're back to liking him again." She shoved another bite of ice cream into her mouth. "Damn it. I wanted to keep hating him. I like hating Koz. I don't want to like him."

"You don't have to like him. And you don't have to hate him, either. You don't have to feel anything about him one way or another. This doesn't have anything to do with you, in case you hadn't noticed."

"Whatever. If you like him, I have to like him. If you hate him, I get to hate him like I want to. That's how this shit works."

I snort-laughed. "What shit?"

"This hos-over-bros shit."

"Did you just call me a ho?"

Dani shrugged, shoving another bite into her mouth and practically moaning in pleasure. "Called myself one, too."

"Is that supposed to make it better?"

"Fine, you're not a ho. Actually, if ever I met someone who was the opposite of a ho, it'd be you."

"Exactly."

"We need to change that, and stat, if you're thinking that you might like Koz. You need to go have a wild one-night stand with a rock star or something. I bet we can have Katie help you out there. She's got connections in the business. She knows people."

Dani's sister, Katie Babcock, had worked with some big names in the music industry for years. These days, she was spending most of her time writing songs for some of the hottest acts in the business instead of pursuing her own singing career.

"I don't want a one-night stand with anyone," I argued, struggling to keep my tone serious so Dani would listen to me.

"Oh, please let me set you up with someone. I need to live vicariously through you since I'm stuck in bed."

"You might recall that the last time you tried to set me up with someone was when this whole thing with Blake got started."

Dani groaned. "Don't remind me. But one failure doesn't mean I'm doomed to fail again."

"You're doomed to fail again because I'm not going along with any of your plans."

She pouted and stuffed another large bite of her ice cream into her mouth. "Well," she said, speaking around her dessert, "if you're going to go out with anyone, you'd better dress like a hottie. Even if it's Koz."

"I don't think you need to worry about that," I said.

"Meaning you're going to wear something I made you? Or meaning you're not going out with him?"

Meaning it didn't matter one way or the other. I didn't think he'd be interested in me in that way, so the point was moot.

I shoved my spoon into her ice cream container and stole a bite while she was distracted.

"You're avoiding answering me," she said, pouting.

"Maybe I am."

"Chicken."

"Bock bock bock!" I flapped my arms, making the droopy skin of my biceps and triceps jiggle around. Then I tried to scoop out another bite of Dani's ice cream, but she tugged the bowl away from me so fast she nearly threw herself off the bed. I shot out an arm to stop her progress, barely preventing a fall.

We both laughed like loons, effectively forgetting all about the conversation.

A beep sounded on Dani's phone. She reached for it and swiped the screen. "Game time," she said. "Hand me the remote. You staying or going?"

I needed to work on lesson plans, and I had a stack of papers about half a mile high waiting to be graded. But the temptation to stay was strong.

I shifted a couple of pillows around to prop myself up next to her, settling in for the next little while. "Need to leave by first intermission," I said.

"Mm hmm. Whatever. Next time, you just need to bring your work with you so you can do it while we watch."

"But it'd just sit there, because I'd be watching."

"True, but at least you could pretend to be working. Much like I pretend I'm going to be good about what I eat." Dani reached into her nightstand and pulled out a couple of pieces of individually wrapped dark chocolate, tossing one my way.

I glared at her, but she grinned and winked as she opened the wrapper and put her piece into her mouth.

"Now that I know where your stash is, I'm going to get rid of it," I said.

"I'll just get someone else to hook me up."

"You're a mess, Dani."

"And you *still* love me for it."

Yeah, she was right. I did.

I settled back against the pillows, unwrapping my chocolate and focusing in on the television—because they were doing a pregame segment all about Blake, so his cocky, sexy grin was right in front of me in high definition.

I didn't want to like him, but Dani was right; I did. I wasn't sure it would ever be more than that...but there was something blooming inside me, and I felt powerless to stop it.

Blake Kozlow had worked his way under my skin. Damn it.

Chapter Six

Blake

The puck was on my stick, which was exactly where I liked it, but two Sabres defenders were closing in on me fast.

It was a scoreless game at home even though we were more than halfway through the third period. Something needed to change that. Or *someone*—and I was more than okay with that someone being me. It'd go a long way toward helping me redeem myself in the team's eyes if I could make myself invaluable on the ice.

Whether I was the one to break the ice with a goal or it was another of my teammates, we needed to get on the scoreboard.

I scanned the ice, looking for my options.

One of my linemates, Preston Hutchinson, was all tied up with his defender along the boards and couldn't get free. My other winger, Aaron Ludwiczak, had tried to skirt around his defender, but the guy had tripped him up and none of the refs had called it.

The officials seemed to be trying to stay out of the way, allowing us to settle the game on the scoreboard and not through penalties.

Cole Paxton and Chris Hammond, the two Storm defensemen out on the ice with us, were both relatively free—but they were also my worst-case-scenario options. Those two were a hell of a lot better at playing defense than they were at anything remotely resembling offense.

But now the guy chasing me was zeroing in on me, and he kept getting his stick in my way. Continuing to hold on to the puck wasn't going to help anyone. I needed to find an outlet, someone I could pass it to until I could lose my man.

Another quick glance behind me revealed that Colesy had skated away from the Sabres forward who'd been hounding him, and now he had a clear lane to the net. Apparently that was as good as I was going to get. I took a chance, caught his eye, and passed the puck his way.

One of the guys who'd been tailing me took off to cover Colesy, which was exactly what I needed.

Then I made a beeline straight for the goal, myself, with only one defender chasing me.

Colesy didn't hang on to the puck for long, passing it back to me like it was a hot potato, but my brief time without it was all I required to get a couple of strides away from the Sabres defenseman.

The rubber hit my tape just as Luddy and Hutch both converged on the goal along with me, all of us arriving at virtually the same time.

With a quick wrist shot, I flicked the puck into the mass of humanity in front of the goal. It didn't go in—the Sabres netminder had a clear line of sight on my initial shot—but I hoped the ensuing melee would be enough for us to sneak it past him.

It was a madhouse of flailing skates and sticks, with curses flying in a combination of English, Swedish, Russian, and Czech. I dove into the pile of bodies, too, trying to get my stick on that little rubber fucker.

I'd always had a love-hate relationship with the puck. I loved it when it went off my stick and into the net; I hated it the rest of the time. The hate made it easy for me to hit the shit out of it on a regular basis, which led to the love more often than not.

And then it happened—the puck squirted across the goal line—only no one saw it but me and the Sabres goaltender, who quickly covered it with his glove and inched it back to the other side of the goal line.

"It went in!" I shouted, trying to extricate myself from the sweat-covered pile of smelly hockey equipment and oversized bodies. "It's a fucking goal."

Finally seeing that the Sabres goalie had the puck, the refs blew their whistles and attempted to break up the pile so they could sort through what had happened.

But there was no goal light. No signal from the officials that we'd scored.

I didn't know who they'd credit with scoring it, and for that matter, I didn't care—just so long as they gave us the goal.

The linesmen were still hauling guys apart, but the two refs had skated away toward center ice and were discussing the play with one another. I started to follow them, determined to be sure they saw things my way, but then I thought better of it. I was supposed to be keeping my head down, doing my job but otherwise keeping my nose clean and doing my best to stay out of trouble.

Opening my mouth in front of the officials was probably a bad idea. I was bound to say something I'd regret—and this time, it would hurt my team, not just me. Couldn't allow that to happen, especially since I was still trying to climb my way out of the doghouse I'd created for myself on Twitter.

Instead, I caught Hammer's eye and nudged my head toward the officials, indicating that he should go over and see what they were saying. Then I skated over to the bench, and all of our coaches converged around me.

Bergy bent over the backs of my teammates on the bench so he could hear me. "It went in?" he asked. "It crossed the line?"

"Absolutely. I watched him cover it with his glove and then inch it back out so they wouldn't see it."

"You've gotta challenge if they don't call it our way," Webs said to Bergy.

"We can't afford to lose a challenge at this point," Bergy said. "We might need our time out later."

That was one of the league's rules these days—a team could challenge a call on the ice, but if they lost the challenge, they would also lose the ability to call for a time out. It was a risky call to make in an otherwise scoreless game.

"You won't lose it," I insisted. "The replays will have to show the truth. It was in." At least I hoped the replays would reveal the truth. Sometimes, there just wasn't the right camera angle to prove a goal had happened.

"Whose goal is it?" our head coach asked, raising a

brow. "You looking for the credit?"

I glanced back toward center ice and saw that Hammer had insinuated himself into the conversation along with one of the Sabres players.

"Hell, I don't know who touched it last. I don't care." It wasn't like I was trying to win a league scoring title or anything, and it was still early in the season, anyway, so what did it matter? I glanced up at the jumbotron overhead, watching the replay that the AV team was showing to the whole crowd. "It's in," I insisted, despite the camera angle not revealing anything. "It's a fucking goal."

Hammer skated toward us, looking grim.

The refs finished their huddle, and one of them turned on his mic. "The play is under review," he announced to the arena, and then he skated over to the scorekeeper's bench to put on a headset.

"They're saying no goal," Hammer said when he reached us.

Fuck. That meant the video evidence would have to be definitive in order to overturn the call they'd made on the ice. If they couldn't prove it via some replay or another, then the refs' decision would stand, and we'd still be locked in this scoreless tie.

Around that time, the jumbotron started showing better replays—angles that took us closer to seeing the truth. The crowd went silent while everyone looked overhead to see the truth of what had taken place on the ice.

The first angle was inconclusive. The crossbar was in the way of the puck, and you couldn't tell that the fucker had definitively crossed the goal line.

The next view made it look like the rubber had gone in, but the angle was bad—it could be a camera trick making us *think* it was in when it wasn't.

What we needed was the view I'd had—almost directly overhead but without the stupid crossbar muddying the waters. There'd been a tiny sliver of white ice between the red goal line and the black rubber of the puck. It had *not* been a figment of my imagination or wishful thinking.

Too bad we couldn't wear helmet cams. A camera on the goaltender's glove would be handy right about now. One of these days, once I was retired and bored with life, I'd try to come up with a way to do it. I could make a fortune on something like that.

Granted, I didn't know the first thing about designing cameras or protective gear for use in sports, but that was beside the point. If I put my mind to something, I could make it happen. Grandma had drilled that into my head, and it was one of the few things that had stuck with me.

I kept watching the video, trying to see evidence of what I knew had happened…but it just wasn't there. Bad angles all around. Nothing conclusive. We could only hope that the war room in Toronto had a better angle than the arena's entertainment crew had been able to provide.

Finally, the refs skated back to center ice and conferred with one another before one of them flipped on his microphone. "After video review, the call on the ice stands. No goal."

Our home crowd flipped out, cursing the refs the same way I wanted to. But I couldn't lose my cool, so I bit down on the urge to skate over and tell them exactly what I thought of their garbage refereeing abilities.

"Koz," Bergy said in a tone that allowed me to feel

his glare through the back of my skull.

I turned around to face him.

"Sit." He pointed at the bench.

Sitting was the last thing I needed to do. I needed to move. I needed to burn off the energy that had built up during the time we'd had to wait for the officials to foul up the call. I needed to get back out there and try again to score.

But that wouldn't help me with the coaches, so I sat.

My feet bounced in my skates with the adrenaline that had built up within me. My eyes were jumping around, scanning the ice. I gripped my stick with the need to use it for something more than simply banging it against the boards.

A few of the other guys headed out onto the ice, and Babs shifted down the bench until he was seated next to me.

"Focus," he said.

"I am focused."

"You're focused on being pissed at Bergy and the officials and God only knows who else. You need to focus on the game."

Damn it. I hated it when Babs was right—especially because it happened far too often for my tastes.

Out on the ice, one of the linesmen dropped the puck, and one of our young centermen, Austin Cooper, won the draw—but barely.

"He needs to get lower," I muttered. "The kid doesn't give himself a wide enough base."

"Maybe you should tell him that," Babs said.

"I've told him."

"Tell him again. Most of us need to hear something several times before it sinks in. You're not the only one like that, you know."

I glowered at the ice because I knew he was right.

Babs was always right, damn it. And damn him, too.

But no matter how much I wanted to hate him for it, I couldn't, because he seemed to really *get* me. He understood all my quirks and that I didn't mean to be an asshole all the time, even if I didn't know how to stop myself from doing exactly that. So if there was anyone among my teammates who I needed to try not to piss off, it was Babs.

The clock kept ticking down the time left in the game. We had under five minutes left to score and avoid overtime.

Coop's line came off the ice, Babs and his line went on, and Coop took the seat Babs had just vacated. Which meant maybe I should do what Babs had suggested and tell the kid what he needed to hear.

"You've got to get lower on face-offs," I said, still watching the action on the ice but trusting that Coop could hear me over the crowd. "You're not giving yourself a chance against a guy like O'Reilly."

"I can't get much lower without losing my balance."

"Then you need to stretch and get in the gym more. Need to build up your quads and your core."

"Just don't try to get me to do naked yoga," Coop said, and I almost busted a gut laughing.

I'd started doing naked yoga in the locker room a couple of months back in an effort to ground myself and calm my mind before practices and games. I still liked to do it every now and then. Coop hadn't been in town yet, then, but he'd heard about it as soon as he'd arrived for training camp…and he'd witnessed it any number of times in the interim.

To be fair, the only part of it that had actually been suggested to me was the *yoga* part. Doing it naked—

and in the locker room, no less—had been all my idea. But true yoga aficionados seemed to think that adding the naked element aided in focusing the mind or some shit, and I was determined to do everything possible to clear my mind of all the shit constantly racing through it.

Stripping down in front of the boys? Why the hell not? It wasn't like they'd never seen this shit before.

Besides, I looked good, and I wasn't afraid to show it.

Apparently, some of the guys didn't appreciate the glory of my limp dick dangling in their faces while I maintained a camel pose or whatever.

Tough cookies if you asked me.

They wanted me to be focused in games, so they needed to deal with whatever I required to achieve that level of focus. And lately, focus was even more difficult than normal, for some reason.

So far, practicing yoga (whether naked or otherwise) hadn't helped me too much—as evidenced by my begging for Bea's assistance in any way she'd concede to give it. Still, I liked to do some yoga in the room occasionally before practices and games, but primarily because the rest of the guys freaked out more than because it was helping me to slow down my racing thoughts.

Yeah, I kind of liked being a jerk like that and causing my teammates to flip out. Sue me. It nearly made me giggle like a toddler, seeing some of the guys' reactions. Hammer hadn't looked at me the same way since the first time I'd done it, and I was almost positive that Colesy had been checking me out. Yeah, maybe he was dating Luke Weber these days, but a guy was free to look, right? I was hot, and I didn't care how many people knew it.

Maybe I was a bit of an exhibitionist.

But that was neither here nor there. I shook my head, trying to redirect my thoughts and get it back on the game—and the advice I'd been trying to give to Coop.

The refs had blown the whistle yet again, and now the players on the ice were lining up for another face-off. Bergy sent our top line out to take this one.

"Watch how low RJ gets," I said to Coop. "He'll practically have his nose on the ice. Keeps his weight centered, and he can get more power behind it when he sweeps his stick for the puck."

"You get a taste for teaching after training camp?" Webs asked from behind me, curiosity mingling with approval in his tone.

A taste for teaching? Huh. Maybe I had. Maybe this was more to do with the time I'd been spending with Bea and her students, though. I wasn't sure, to be honest, and I wasn't ready to examine it more closely. I shrugged, focusing on the action.

RJ won the draw and sent the puck flying back to our defense. Keith Burns snagged it and immediately turned the play back up the ice.

"Stick around after practice tomorrow," I said to Coop, watching what Burnzie and the rest of the guys were doing. "I'll work with you for a while. It'll help the whole team if you can win even five or ten percent more draws than you already do. It could mean we end up getting further in the playoffs or something. It's the little things, to be honest."

Coop snorted, but he didn't try to shake me off.

And then our top line worked their magic. Nate Golston finally got us on the scoreboard with about three minutes left in the game following a sick no-look pass from RJ. The way they could do that only further reinforced the idea that they were somehow twins separated at birth, despite the massive differences in their appearances.

Along with everyone else on the bench, I hooted and hollered for Ghost and the rest of that line, slapping my stick on the boards while the home crowd roared in approval.

Once those guys came off the ice, Bergy sent my linemates and me out again. I lined up at center ice to take the draw, not only thinking about all the shit I needed to do to win it but also about how I could use all the things I knew to help Coop improve his game.

Maybe Bea had gotten under my skin in more than one way. Maybe being around her and those kids had gotten me thinking about teaching…using my obsessive need to pore over every minuscule aspect of every single fucking thing I did so I could help other people in my shoes.

And maybe, just maybe, that wasn't such a bad thing.

Bea

It was already too late for me to be up on a school night, since I'd kept Dani company at her house until her husband had come home from the game. That meant it was far, far too late for me to be answering phone calls or text messages.

Yes, I was home and in my pj's, and I'd fed Neville and Luna, so I ought to be going to bed and trying to sleep. But sleep wasn't something I tended to do well during the school year. From September through May, I usually operated on a combination of adrenaline, determination, an abundance of B vitamins, and a decent amount of caffeine. Then I caught up on my sleep over the summer.

I'd barely crawled into bed with a stack of papers to grade, hoping to finish these and tackle a bit more lesson planning before I had to nod off, when my phone started beeping with my text message alert.

Everything in me said to ignore it because someone texting me at almost midnight couldn't mean anything good. But then there was a niggling thought that maybe Dani needed help with something, even though I knew Cody was with her now and he could take care of whatever she might need at this hour.

I should totally ignore this message. It was the only sane, logical thing for me to do.

Despite my reservations, I glanced at the screen. Apparently, I wasn't in the mood to behave in a sane or logical manner. I didn't recognize the number, which was even more reason I should forget it all until morning. But instead, I found myself swiping my thumb across the screen.

Then I really wished I'd followed my instincts. The message was from Blake Kozlow, no less. I really ought to just put the phone down and go back to my work. Or to sleep. Or anything else, but I definitely shouldn't read this message.

I didn't want to think about him any more than I already had been for most of the night while watching the game at Dani's house. It seemed as if the television broadcast had spent an inordinate amount of time focused on him throughout the game. It wasn't as if he'd had an exceptional night—whether good or bad—so there was no reason for them to zoom in on him constantly. Yet every time I'd glanced up, his cocky grin had been filling the TV screen: on the bench, on the ice, during the intermission segments.

I couldn't get away from him.

Apparently not even when I ought to be sleeping.

But since I was a glutton for punishment and I couldn't seem to make myself ignore him the way I knew I ought to do, I read his message.

> Blake: *Since you're still awake, can you start teaching me how to do this crochet shit?*
>
> Me: *I'm not awake. I'm sleeping. This is me snoring.*
>
> Blake: *You sleep with your lights on? And you can send text messages in your sleep? Impressive. That's another skill I need you to teach me.*
>
> Me: *How do you know my lights are on?*
>
> Blake: *Because I'm in your driveway.*
>
> Me: *Why are you in my driveway at this hour?*
>
> Blake: *Because I want you to teach me how to do some of this art shit you made me buy. I've got the yarn and needles with me.*
>
> Me: *Go home and go to bed, Blake. I have to*

work in the morning.

Blake: *So do I. But I can't sleep.*

Me: *Have you even tried?*

Blake: *No point trying. I know myself. Too jacked up after a game. I'll be up until at least four in the morning, so I need something to do.*

I'd already allowed the text conversation to go on too long, and it was driving me crazy to shoot messages back and forth with him. Before I could think it through, I found myself dragging my robe across my shoulders as I headed down the stairs.

I flipped on the porch light and threw open the door.

Blake was standing there, leaning against the wall of my house, looking full of swagger and sexy and fresh out of the shower. His hair was still wet, and he smelled like the most amazing combination of man and soap and a hint of spicy cologne. He had his phone in one hand and a bag full of yarn in the other.

I tugged the edges of my robe tighter and knotted the belt around my waist, trying my best to glare at him. "You're crazy."

"I'm not crazy. I'm restless. Big difference."

A gust of cool wind blew across me, and I shivered.

"You gonna let me come inside, or are we going to stand here all night while you freeze to death?"

"You should really learn to ask permission to come over before you just show up at my place, you know," I muttered, but I stood back and ushered him inside. "Or anyone's house, for that matter. This is becoming a habit. It's rude. And presumptuous. And I don't like it. I doubt your parents would approve of this sort of behavior."

He stared at me for a moment, but then he said, "Grandma wouldn't like it, that's for sure."

"You're close to your grandmother?" I found myself asking, tightening my robe again.

"She raised me," he said matter-of-factly. "My parents weren't around. Anyway, I'm sorry. Thank you for being completely clear with me about what you don't like."

I nodded, silently admonishing myself, and indicated that he should come inside. His arm brushed against mine as he passed through my door, even though I'd pressed my back against the wall to give him space. Despite myself, I shivered so hard I almost shuddered—and I didn't think it had anything to do with being cold this time. If anything, I felt almost hot, which was saying something since I hadn't felt hot once in all the time since I'd had weight-loss surgery.

When we reached my living room, I turned on the lamps on either side of my couch. Then I took a seat and patted the space next to me.

Blake gave me a wary look before sitting, only further emphasizing the reality that I'd been behaving like a bitch toward him.

Time to make up for it.

"So take out a couple of skeins of yarn," I said.

"Skeins?"

"The balls. And we'll need two of the hooks—one for you and one for me."

"Right." He dug around in the bag until he came up with all the things I'd asked for.

At first, he handed me the larger hook, keeping the

smaller one for himself. I shook my head and switched them out. "You'll want a bigger one to start with. Especially with hands the size of yours. It'll be easier to learn with something a bit bigger." Then I found the free end of each skein of yarn and held one out for him. "Right. So hold your hook in your right hand like so"—I modeled the correct hand positioning for him—"and take the yarn in your left hand like this. Then make a little loop with the yarn, slip the hook through it, and tug the end through like this. That's how you make a slip stitch to get started."

"I didn't catch all of that," he muttered, twisting his yarn between his fingers in a way that wouldn't accomplish anything but achieving a knot.

"Try just watching me this time. Then we'll take it step by step."

One tiny bit at a time, I showed him how to make a slip stitch, how to create a chain, and how to move from the initial chain to single crochet stitches.

"Now practice those single crochets for a few rows," I said, once he seemed to have the basic gist of it.

He was studiously staring at the bit of yarn in his hands, so I got up to grab a protein shake from the fridge. If I was already going to be up for a while, as it appeared, I might as well get some fuel for my body. "You need anything from in here?" I called out from the kitchen. "Water? A snack?"

"Got a beer?" he replied.

"Nope."

"Wine? Hard liquor?"

"I don't drink alcohol. Don't keep any in the house as temptation."

"Of course you don't," he muttered, but he seemed

to be laughing about it. Not at me, per se. More at the situation. "Water it is, then."

I grabbed a plastic bottle from the fridge on my way back to the living room, then set it on a coaster on the coffee table since he was otherwise occupied with creating his initial chain.

"It looks messy," he complained after a bit.

"You're tugging too tight on the yarn," I observed. "You need to let it breathe a bit. And it'll look better once you've got a couple of rows, anyway. The stitches will stop curling so much, and your yarn will start to lie flat."

"I want it to lie flat now. Yours did."

"Not quite," I said with a laugh. "Maybe a bit flatter than yours, but I've been doing this a lot longer than you have. I have a feel for how tight to pull on the yarn and how lax I should allow it to be. I couldn't go out on the ice and score a goal on the first try. I probably couldn't even stay upright on my skates."

"That's different."

"Different how? Crochet isn't something you can pick up and do perfectly without practice, any more than hockey is."

He scrunched his brow in concentration, fumbling with the yarn. "I've been playing hockey my whole life."

"Exactly. And you've been crocheting for all of seven minutes, if that. Give yourself a chance to learn something new."

For a moment, he looked up and scowled at me before returning his focus to the yarn in his hands. "How many of these chains do I make?"

"You're just practicing for now, so it doesn't matter. Make it a few inches long, and then I'll teach you to turn it and do a row of single crochets."

I sat next to him again, watching his progress. The hook and yarn seemed delicate in his big hands, but I had no doubt he'd go from awkward and clumsy to focused and proficient in short order.

That was the thing—he needed something to focus on, but then he'd focus so much that he'd master it.

His teammates might be getting crocheted scarves, hats, and blankets as Christmas gifts this year. And maybe he'd make some baby blankets, too, for the ones who had babies on the way. Dani wasn't the only one currently pregnant if I remembered correctly. And on a team that size, the family was always growing.

Well, he'd be making those things for his teammates *if* he could force himself to focus, at least.

After a few more minutes, he had a short chain ready to go. I quickly made one of my own, matching his length, so I could demonstrate how to turn his work and begin his first row of single crochets.

"Practice that for a few rows now, and then I'll teach you the double crochet stitch."

"Can we turn on the TV or something?" he asked after a while, still studiously working on his third row of single crochets. "I need some sound."

I reached for the remote and powered on the television. At this hour, there wasn't much on. I scrolled through the on-screen guide and found a marathon of *Impractical Jokers*. He watched those guys—I remembered him telling me during that disastrous double date—so I felt safe flipping to that show while I observed Blake's efforts.

His focus seemed to improve due to having some sound in the room. I made a mental note for myself—not that I intended to spend any more time with him than was absolutely necessary. But it wouldn't kill me to remember these things that could help him out.

By the first commercial break, Blake had a small sample with three rows of single crochets. Yes, his stitches were uneven, so the edges weren't quite square, but it was a reasonable effort for his first time.

"Ready to move on to double crochets?" I asked as he came to the end of a row.

"I don't know. You tell me."

I tried not to let my grin get too big, because I didn't want him to think I was laughing at him. Then I picked up my own sample and demonstrated the new stitch a few times while he watched. "Your turn," I said once he had seen me do about a dozen double crochets.

His concentration fully on his work, I sat back and watched the comedians on the show making fools of themselves.

About halfway through an episode, I realized that Blake was laughing just as hard as I was. I glanced over. He'd finished a few rows, and his stitches were starting to look more even, but he'd set it aside and was leaning back against the cushions, the same as I was.

He shot a look over at me, as if he sensed my attention on him. "Finished those rows," he said.

"So I noticed. I thought you were going to tell me when you were ready to move on."

"Didn't want to disturb you. I like hearing you laugh. I've missed it."

I blinked in surprise.

"Your eyes get these crinkles around the corners when you laugh," he said. "They're so fucking sexy."

Something warm and unfamiliar and addictive curled within my belly. I had to look away before it completely took control of me.

"Bea," he said, and my pulse shot through the roof.

"Hmm?" I replied, not trusting myself to say more than that.

"Thank you. For teaching me all this shit. For trying to help me."

He reached out his hand, and I had to fight down the urge to flinch, but he was only reaching for his water bottle. He unscrewed the cap and took a sip, then returned the bottle to my coffee table.

"I don't deserve it, but you're helping me anyway. Not too many people would do that."

"You might be wrong about that," I forced myself to say around an overly thick tongue. "A lot of people would help."

"Not when you're someone like me."

Someone like him? Someone rich and famous and seemingly without need for help? Or did he mean something else?

But he didn't elaborate. Instead, he started returning the yarn and other supplies to his bag. "I should let you get some sleep. I shouldn't have come here so late in the first pl—"

"You don't need to apologize for coming over this time," I cut in. "But next time, maybe try texting me first, hmm? Give me a bit of warning?" I'd like to at least have clothes on the next time he showed up at my front door—not that I intended to point out my less-than-dressed state just now.

"Yeah. Yeah, I can do that."

He got up and finished gathering his things. Then I found myself following him to the door—to lock it behind him, or so I told myself. But in truth, there was more to it than that.

When we reached the door, he turned and stared

down at me, an undeniable sort of longing clouding his expression. I told myself he merely wished he'd had a teacher like me back when he'd been in school. That could be the only reasonable explanation for a look like that, at least when it was coming from a man like him and directed toward a woman like me.

But then he bent down and pressed his lips to mine, and everything I thought I knew about him and myself and life flew out the window.

Chapter Seven

Blake

She let out a soft gasp of surprise when I pressed my mouth to hers, but then she rigidly held her body away from me, even though her lips softened against mine.

Surprise? Hell, I was surprised, too. What the fuck was I thinking, kissing Bea Castillo?

Answer: I wasn't.

Or at least I wasn't thinking about anything other than how fucking adorable she was when she glared at me. Yeah, pissing her off seemed to turn me on. Her eyes flashed fire when she was mad, and that fire lit another one that burned inside me. It was a sickness. And one I wasn't overly fussed about curing anytime soon.

She was also insanely adorable in those moments when she decided not to be pissed off at me. The hint of softness that came through in her expression just wrapped around me and refused to let go—much the way I wanted to wrap myself around her and hold on as long as I possibly could. I wanted to dig my fingers into the curve of her hips and waist. I wanted to draw her softness against me and revel in it.

Bea was completely unlike any woman I'd ever been with before.

She was fiery and fierce when it came to her students, but there was also an undeniable layer of caring in there. She was fierce because she loved them and wanted the best for them.

And then she was tough and demanding when it came to me, not letting me get away with anything. Which was good. Obviously, I needed a firm hand in life, helping to guide me through all the shit I fouled up.

Oh, and there was her laugh, too. She had a laugh that turned me on like nobody's business.

She was everything I never knew I wanted until tonight, sitting next to her while she tried to teach me to do some of her crafting shit.

But for now, I supposed I'd have to make do with a kiss. Cautiously, I tested the seam of her lips with my tongue.

She hesitated, making me question my decision again, but then she opened for me. Her arms slipped up around my neck and shoulders, and she fell back against the doorjamb, dragging me along with her.

Hell yes.

I was all too happy to crush her body against mine, leaning in closer so I could feel the supple length of her and all those amazing curves pressing tight against my frame. My dick was happy about it, too. It'd been too damn long since I'd been with a woman. Chicks liked to throw themselves at me because I was a hockey player or something, but once I opened my mouth and said a few things, I tended to scare them off.

Dating was a minefield for me. A one-night stand, sure, I could do that without fucking up too badly. Everyone went in with low expectations, and no one ended up getting hurt when it ended after only a single night.

But I didn't want a one-night stand with Bea. And I didn't think she was the type who'd go in for something like that, anyway.

Her hand slid cautiously up my chest, and she wrapped her fingers around my collar as if to brace herself.

I ached to feel those fingers on my skin. Her fingers. Her lips. Her tongue.

My hips ground against her, almost of their own accord, and I dug my fingers into the softness of her waist. I broke off the kiss so I could taste the column of her throat.

A low whimper rumbled from somewhere in her chest and vibrated through me.

I fisted my hand in the thick waves of her hair and held her head captive so I could kiss her again, taking it deeper so she'd understand what she was doing to me. She clung to me, her body pressed so tightly to mine that I could feel how hard and taut her nipples were through our clothes.

I wanted more.

I wanted to take her back inside her house, push her down onto her couch, strip her naked, and explore all her curves and softness with my hands and tongue and teeth. I wanted to suck her tits until she begged me to fuck her. I wanted to lick her pussy until she came all over my tongue. I wanted to hear the sounds she made when I was buried deep inside her.

And even as all these things I wanted were racing through my brain, I was able to slow down enough to realize I was jumping the gun. Yeah, maybe she was letting me kiss her now, but we still had a long way to go before she'd be ready to bump uglies with me.

She might never be willing to do that, actually. I was already pushing my luck just with this kiss.

So instead of trying to drag her back inside to do all the things I wanted to do, I forced myself to tear my lips away from hers.

"Sorry," I said, my forehead pressed against hers as I tried to catch my breath.

Bea was just as winded as I was. She kept her eyes closed, one hand still clenching my collar, and bit her lower lip. "Why did you do that?"

Well, fuck. I racked my brain for an answer that could excuse my shitty decision-making, but nothing reasonable came to me. "I meant to thank you for helping me," I said.

"You did. You already thanked me. But why did…why did you kiss me?" She sounded wary, like she was searching for an ulterior motive. And she still wouldn't look up and meet my eyes.

I was at a complete loss. Couldn't figure out what the fuck I'd done wrong, because it had seemed like she was as into this as I was. I mean, I hadn't flat out asked her for permission to kiss her first, but she hadn't said no or tried to shove me off or anything. Hell, she'd dragged me closer. Wasn't that a pretty obvious sign that she was into it?

I groaned in frustration. "Does a man really need a

reason to want to kiss a gorgeous woman other than he thinks she's hot and she's been helping him and maybe he wants to thank her? Isn't that enough?"

But she just shook her head and didn't say anything for so long it scared me. "You don't thank someone with a kiss," she finally said.

"Maybe you do if you've got the hots for her," I countered.

"A gorgeous woman?" she said, sounding hurt and dubious. "And you've got the hots for me? You really expect me to believe that?"

"Yeah?"

And then she pushed me away—not hard, but with enough force behind it that there could be no possible way for me to misinterpret what she was doing—and headed for her door. "Knock it off, Blake," she said. "You should go home. And I need to sleep. I've got to work in the morning. Good night."

"Wait," I said, reaching for her arm to stop her, but she slipped her hand out of mine and went inside. "Bea, stop. Please. Tell me what I did wrong."

She tugged her screen door closed, but at least she didn't slam the main door in my face. When she faced me again, she was blinking back tears.

What the fuck had I done to make her cry? I wanted to bash my head against the side of her house in frustration because...*what?*

"Please," I croaked. "You've got to spell shit out for me, remember?"

"I don't appreciate being made a fool of," she bit off.

"Made a fool of?"

"I agreed to help you. I'm trying to do that, and I didn't ask for anything in return. But that doesn't make it okay to toy with me—with my emotions. Just—if you want to thank me, say thanks. Don't go and kiss me or whatever."

"It seemed like you were enjoying it," I complained, dragging a hand down my face in frustration. "And lord knows I was."

"Yeah, you were enjoying making this into a joke. But it's not a joke to me. It's not funny."

"I don't think any of this is a joke," I practically shouted, only remembering to keep my voice down because of how dark it was out. I didn't need to wake up her whole neighborhood. The last thing I needed was to have to explain to the team bigwigs why I'd been arrested in the middle of the night while standing outside a house I didn't live in and shouting at a woman.

"Well, good," she bit off. "Because it's not funny to me."

"Not for me, either. So what are we arguing about?"

"About you treating me like—"

But however she thought I was treating her, she couldn't get the words out because she got choked up. Tears shone in her eyes, the wetness reflected by the streetlights, making me feel like the biggest jackass on the planet.

Fuck, this was all wrong. "So I need to apologize to you?" I asked. "I fucked this up already?"

"You should go home, Blake," she said through sniffles. "It's better if you just go home so we can both sleep on this and look at it with fresh eyes in the morning."

Better for who? Not for me. There wasn't much chance I'd be sleeping any time soon. I'd spend hours lying in bed and trying to figure out what the hell I'd done wrong this time.

I dragged a hand down my face, the scratch of stubble scraping my palm. "Would you please talk to me and explain what I did? I didn't mean to hurt you or upset you. Whatever I did wrong, I swear I didn't mean to hurt you."

"Good night," she repeated firmly. Then she closed the door in my face, and I heard the soft snick of the lock settling into place.

Bea

The cool wood paneling of my front door wasn't enough to calm the heat rushing through my body. Hurt, anger, lust, disappointment…all of it had combined to send me into a tailspin that was bound to keep me up for hours. I might as well not even try getting to sleep for a while, because it'd be an exercise in futility.

I stayed by the door, listening for the sounds of Blake's sports car door closing and his engine starting. It finally did, and then the soft hum drifted down the street and disappeared into the night.

Maybe I shouldn't have kicked him out. Maybe I should've been an adult about the situation and had him come back inside so we could talk about it. But frankly, I was too raw to talk about anything with him just now.

He was toying with me, plain and simple.

There was no other reasonable explanation.

I might be many things, but I was not the kind of woman a professional hockey player in his mid-twenties hit on. So that meant I *definitely* wasn't the sort of woman a man like Blake Kozlow would kiss.

Not unless there was something else behind it.

Was he doing it for a bet? Was it a joke of some sort? Did he think he'd get me to help him more by pretending to be interested in me? If that was the case, once he'd gotten everything he needed from me, he would move on in a heartbeat—and probably have all sorts of jokes to tell his buddies about the fat, old chick who'd thought he'd been interested in her.

Well, he wasn't going to get away with that. Not with me. I had no intention of falling prey to some cruel joke.

I'd already been on the wrong side of those kinds of things too many times when I was a teenager. It wouldn't happen to me again.

Once I could finally peel myself away from the front door, I double-checked the locks and turned off the porch light, then headed into the kitchen. I grabbed a bottle of water and a yogurt out of the fridge for myself, a handful of shredded carrots for Neville and Luna, and I took a spoon from the drawer. I stopped by my guinea pigs' cage and gave them their treats before heading upstairs to sulk with my yogurt.

My phone was blowing up with text messages by the time I made it up to my room, so I took it off the charger and crawled into bed with the phone and my snack.

Several of the messages were from Blake, but I wasn't in the mood to read them just yet. I skipped over those and went to the rest of them.

> Dani: *I think I'm in labor. These pains definitely feel like labor. It's too early for me*

to be going into labor. Tell Cody to take me to the hospital.

Dani, again: *I told Cody I hate him and he's never touching me again because I will not be having another child. We can do like Jamie and Katie and be foster parents or something. Or we can adopt. But I'm never going through this shit again. Don't ever make this mistake. Don't get pregnant. Not worth it, Bea.*

Dani, one more time: *He still hasn't taken me to the hospital. He said I just have gas because of something I ate and it didn't agree with me. He's a lying fucking liar and this is not cool. You need to come and get me and take me to the hospital.*

Dani, yet again: *Okay, so maybe it isn't labor and instead I'm dying. Why aren't you answering me? I'll be dead by the time you respond because Cody isn't doing anything. Except laughing. He's fucking laughing at me, the bastard.*

The next message wasn't from Dani, at all. It was from her husband.

Cody: *I finally got her to take some Gas-X. Suddenly, she's not screaming at me that she's in labor, and now she's not dying any longer…and she's asleep. Crisis averted. Funny how that works. But she fell asleep grumbling about how you had abandoned her in her time of need or some shit, so be forewarned. You're officially on her pregnancy-brain shit list. Welcome to the club. We have meetings every night at 3 am to discuss all the ways she's abusing us and how we can get through the next few months without strangling her in her sleep.*

Chuckling to myself, I debated whether I should respond to either of them tonight. But if Dani was finally asleep, I didn't want to risk waking her up again. Cody would probably murder me. So I made a mental note to check on her at a reasonable hour tomorrow.

But then I didn't have any good excuse not to look at Blake's messages any longer. Bracing myself against the ache of disappointment that had more to do with me and my own unmet expectations than it had to do with him, I opened his message.

Blake: *You're the best thing I've had going on in my life lately. I don't know what I did to upset you. I didn't mean to hurt you. I feel like an ass about it and I don't even know why.*

I sighed in frustration. Apparently, neither of us would be able to let it go until we'd hashed it out.

Sleep? Who needed sleep? I sure wouldn't be getting any tonight.

I propped myself up against my pillows and settled in for the long haul.

Me: *Why did you kiss me?*

Blake: *What the hell kind of question is that?*

I kissed you because you're gorgeous and I'm into you and I wanted to kiss you.

Me: *I'm not the kind of woman a guy like you wants to kiss, Blake. Don't try to pull that with me.*

Blake: *What does that even mean? You're not the kind of woman…? A guy like me? Are you trying to tell me you're trans or something?*

Me: *What? No.*

Blake: *Then what? I mean, I'm cool with that if you are. Whatever. I just like hanging out with you. I let you teach me how to crochet tonight because I wanted to spend time with you. Not for any other reason. I mean, yeah, I need to figure out how to focus and all, but I don't think crocheting is going to do that. I just wanted to be with you tonight. That's all.*

Me: *Get off it already. No man in your position likes hanging out with an old, fat teacher.*

Blake: *Who the hell is this old, fat teacher you're talking about and why are we talking about her?*

Me: *I am. Me. We're talking about me. And about you. And about how you're trying to make a fool out of me.*

Blake: *Can I please come back over? I think this would be easier if we were actually talking in person.*

Me: *No.*

Blake: *Then I'm calling you. Please answer.*

Sure enough, my phone rang. Out of spite, I declined the call. Maybe it was childish and petty of me, but I didn't want to talk to him right now. Not when my mind was still reeling from everything that had happened tonight.

Blake: *Fine. We can't talk. But will you please explain what the hell I did wrong so I can fix it?*

Me: *You can't fix this. I need sleep.*

Blake: *Me too, but I won't be able to sleep unless we sort this out.*

Me: *Sounds like your problem.*

Blake: *Now who's the one being unreasonable, hmm? You're not giving me a chance.*

Me: *Maybe you don't deserve a chance.*

Blake: *Ouch.*

Me: …

Blake: *I'm not okay with this being over after one fucking kiss. Hell, that kiss made me want you more than ever before. I need more, Bea. I need you to be in my life. Maybe you don't want to be with me the way I want to be with you. Maybe I fucked up too badly before and I can't ever make you see past it. But even if you don't want me the way I want you, I still need you to be in my life. I have to make this work.*

Me: *Then you need to back off. You can come and read to my students, but that's it. There's nothing between us other than that. Got it? I'm not willing to be the butt of some joke.*

Blake: *What joke?*

Me: *The one where you go and tell all your buddies how you tricked some dumb, old fat chick into thinking you were into her.*

Blake: *Wait a minute. Old? And who's the fat chick? What the hell are you talking about?*

Me: *I'm the fat chick.*

Blake: *??? You're not fat.*

Me: *Get off it, already.*

Blake: *Maybe you should get off it, not me. Because you're not fat. I don't know who the hell told you you're fat, but they're full of shit.*

Me: *Maybe I'm not fat now, but I was.*

Blake: *And?*

Me: *And guys like you don't want to deal with it.*

Blake: *You sure do seem awfully sure about guys "like me."*

Me: *Because I've been on this side of experiencing what guys like you can do to women like me for my whole life. Men don't look twice at me. Not unless they're into fat chicks because then they can control them or something.*

Blake: *I thought we established that you aren't fat.*

Me: *I used to weigh more than 300 pounds.*

Blake: *And you were probably just as funny and sassy then as you are now.*

Me: *You're not going to make some fat joke? You're not going to run for the hills now that you know what's going on under my clothes?*

Blake: *First, I still don't know what's going*

on under your clothes. In case you hadn't
noticed, we've barely kissed. I definitely
haven't seen anything.

Me: And you won't be seeing anything, either.

Blake: And second, why the hell would I
make fat jokes or run off just because you used
to be bigger? What does that have to do with
anything?

Me: Guys like you should have a skinny
supermodel type on their arms. Not someone
with saggy skin and weird lumpy rolls of fat in
awkward places.

Blake: Damn. Superficial much?

Me: Only as superficial as the world has
taught me to be. Only because that's the way
the world has always treated me.

Blake: Well, in case you hadn't noticed, I'm
not exactly normal. Maybe I'm not like that.
Maybe I want to be with you because you
make me laugh and you challenge me.

Me: And maybe you'll change your mind once
you see what you're dealing with.

Blake: And maybe I won't. You didn't run
off once you found out about my issues. You
could have. You could've told me to take a
fucking hike and not come back. Maybe you

just need to get over yourself and your own insecurities and give someone a chance to see you the way you are. Maybe you're trying to hurt me before I get the chance to hurt you. And maybe, just maybe, I don't have any intention of hurting you, even though you seem bound and determined to think that's exactly what I'll do.

Somewhere through this exchange, I'd started crying—big, wet, frustrated tears. Because there was a lot of truth in what he was saying. My problems with the whole situation seemed to have a lot more to do with me and all the body image issues I'd been dealing with for my entire life than they had to do with him.

I didn't like that revelation. I didn't want him to be right.

Because it meant I'd have to work on *me* and the way I saw myself if I ever wanted to move past this.

It'd probably be the same with any man, if I were being honest with myself. This didn't have anything to do with Blake. It had everything to do with me.

I'd been too scared to let someone in.

My phone rang, and I didn't even have to look through my tears to know that it would be Blake. Despite myself, I swiped my thumb across the screen and answered it.

"Hello?"

"You're crying," he said. "Damn it. I didn't mean to make you cry. I'm seriously trying here, Bea."

"I know you are. And you didn't make me cry. I did."

"You made yourself cry?"

"Because I'm a mess."

"You're not a mess."

"I am. Maybe you've got some issues you need to deal with, but you're not the only one. I've got plenty of my own."

"What kind of issues?" he asked.

"Aren't they obvious?"

"Maybe, but I think you need to say it out loud. You need to talk about it or you'll never be able to deal with it."

Damn him for being right.

I sniffled again and reached for the box of tissues I kept on my nightstand.

"What kind of issues?" he repeated.

"Maybe I've lost a lot of the weight. Maybe I'm healthy now and the world sees me one way…but I still see the fat chick. I still see myself the way I was a few years ago, when I was too big to fasten my seat belt on an airplane and too fat to ride on a roller coaster and so big that no man would ever dream of looking twice at me."

"And you don't think I'd be interested in you if you were still her," he said.

"I am still her."

"You're not fat."

"You wouldn't even see me if I was."

"I'd see you." He sounded sincere. "I would," he insisted. "Because you make me laugh."

"I haven't been making you laugh too much lately," I said through my sniffles.

"No, but you can. And that's beautiful, Bea. You're beautiful."

My tongue was too thick for me to speak. Which was probably for the best, because if I tried to speak right then, I'd most likely burst into a fresh flood of tears.

"I want another chance," he said.

"Another chance?"

"With you. I want to take you out. On a date."

"Oh, no. No, I never should have let Dani—"

"No Dani this time. Just you and me."

"You've lost your mind."

"Maybe, but give me a shot, anyway."

"Why should I?" I asked, reaching for another tissue.

"Because you liked it when I kissed you. You might have even liked it as much as I did."

Darn if he hadn't come up with a reason that I couldn't argue with.

Chapter Eight

Bea

We ended up at an improv comedy show for our date—which might have been an offbeat choice for some, but it turned out to be the perfect fit for the pair of us.

Blake and I, despite our occasional difficulties in the communication department, shared a sense of humor. Slapstick? Sure. Inappropriate? Of course. Bawdy? Just show us where to sign up.

I laughed so hard my sides felt like they'd split in two, and at one point I snorted while taking a sip of water and nearly needed to go to the hospital to get sorted out. Blake laughed even harder than I did because of how hard it was for me to get my coughing fit to settle down. By the time the show came to an end and we were walking back out to his car, we were both holding our bellies from the ab workout.

Or maybe I was the only one feeling the effects on my abs. Something told me his were in impeccable shape.

Well, not something, exactly. My fingers told me that.

Because I'd had my hands on them once…briefly. Too briefly.

I'd always wondered what it would feel like to touch a set of abs like his. Now I knew, and I wanted to know more—and that scared me.

The wind picked up on our brief walk outside, almost blowing my jacket away. Shivering, I reached for the zippered ends and quickly zipped it up all the way to my chin, wishing I'd thought to grab a scarf on our way out the door.

"Cold?" Blake asked, raising a brow in question.

I chuckled, then wished I hadn't because my abs weren't ready for more laughing. "Usually. I'm still not used to being cold all the time."

Blake reached for my hand, almost casually, as we walked to the nearby parking garage. His strong fingers linked with mine. They were so warm, and I could only imagine the rest of him was equally warm. The thought of leaning into him again, pressing my body against his, was a seductive tease.

"That's new?" he asked. "Being cold?"

"When I was heavier," I said, because I was determined to be real and honest with him, even though it scared me, "I was always hot. Everyone around me could be bundled up and shivering, and I'd be wishing I could strip down to nothing because I was sweating. But literally the moment I woke up from my surgery, I was cold. I begged for heated blankets in the hospital. They piled about five of them on me and I was still shivering, and it hasn't changed since. I've had to invest in a lot of electric blankets and have them scattered through the whole house."

"What surgery?" he asked.

I hesitated, but then I remembered that I'd already told him how fat I used to be. No point in trying to hide from reality. "I had gastric bypass a couple of years ago. Weight-loss surgery," I added, in case he didn't know what that meant. And then I braced myself for the lecture or disgust or whatever he felt the need to send my way.

"That's how you lost the weight?"

"Yeah. I literally used to weigh twice what I do now. I was enormous. I wouldn't have been able to fit in those seats in the comedy club tonight. I'd have been spilling over the sides. And then I would have been uncomfortable because I'd be taking up your space, and I'd worry about what you were thinking." It was a never-ending vicious cycle.

"And you get cold a lot now?" he asked.

I shivered just at the sound of the word. Then I shrugged, laughing.

Blake grinned and winked at me, tightening his grip on my hand and sending more warmth shooting up my arm. It spread all through my body. I was almost positive there was more involved in his ability to warm me up than simply the small bit of physical contact.

It was funny how so many people liked to judge others over things they didn't understand. I'd been told that having weight-loss surgery was *cheating* more times than I could count, that I should have just gone on a diet and learned to employ self-control like the rest of the world.

And then there were the others—some of my

family, in particular—who'd tried to convince me that I'd made a huge mistake, one that I could never reverse, and I'd regret it soon and for the rest of my life. Never mind that I was healthy now, and I would have been on my way to an early grave otherwise.

If I'd had plastic surgery to get breast implants or liposuction, or anything else of the sort, no one would have said a word—even though those kinds of surgery were purely for a physical transformation and had no impact on a person's health. But make a life-changing decision to improve your health, and suddenly everyone in your life knows better than you do and is determined to point out what a poor decision you'd made.

At least that was how it often felt to me. Particularly when I refused to eat Mama's tamales and flour tortillas and my *abuelita's tres leches* cake, instead bringing my own foods with me for family gatherings.

But Blake didn't seem to be judging me for it.

He was curious, sure. Most people who found out I used to wear a size-thirty dress and a 50-H bra tended to be curious. It went with the territory. But usually, people looked at me a certain way once they knew I'd decided to have surgery.

He wasn't.

When we reached his car, he waited for me to get in the passenger seat before closing my door. As soon as he went around to the other side, he started the engine and then reached for the center console to press a button.

"Butt warmer," he said, winking. "Give it about thirty seconds, and you'll be nice and toasty."

That was an extravagance I'd never allowed myself. Yeah, I earned more as a special education teacher than a lot of my colleagues did, but I didn't have extra money lying around for fancy features in a car. Everything about my vehicle was utilitarian.

By the time he pulled out into traffic, the seat had warmed up so much that I wasn't shivering any longer. Maybe the next time I upgraded, this would be a feature I should splurge for, despite the cost.

"That's my new favorite thing," I said with a contented sigh, settling back against the seat.

"What? Going out with me?" He waggled a brow suggestively, which only made me roll my eyes and him laugh. "Comedy night? Laughing until your sides hurt?"

I laughed, shaking my head. "Butt warmers."

"I turn mine on when I'm driving in for every practice and game. Even in the warmer months. Helps loosen up my glutes and thighs. It's good before a massage, too. Helps them get in deeper and break up all the knots."

"You get knots in your butt?"

"You can get knots in any muscle you use. Don't you get them?" He turned down a street I didn't recognize instead of getting onto the expressway.

I got the distinct impression that he was taking the long way back to my place. And to be honest, I didn't particularly mind. It meant getting to spend more time talking with him…and despite my reservations, I was enjoying myself.

"I don't know," I hedged. "How do you know if you have knots in your muscles?"

"When your massage therapist finds one, you'll know. Hurts like a motherfucker when they press on them, but then it's so much better afterwards, once they've loosened things up for you. But maybe you don't have a very good therapist."

"I don't get massages, so I wouldn't know if my therapist is any good or not."

"Why don't you get massages?" He sounded shocked almost to the point of being scandalized.

"Can't afford them. And I'm not overly keen on the idea of having someone I don't know touching me and all my loose skin." As soon as I'd mentioned that part, I wished I could take the words back.

He came to a stop at a red light and turned his head to stare at me. Hard. So hard I wanted to shrivel up and disappear into my seat. "When's the last time someone touched you?" he asked.

I rolled my eyes. "About five minutes ago when you reached for my hand."

"Doesn't count."

"A couple of days ago when you mauled me on my front porch."

"You know what I mean," he grumbled, in the most adorable way.

I did know what he meant. And I wasn't in the mood to go there. I shrugged and said, "It's been a while."

"How much of a while? Months? More than a year?"

Not the sort of conversation I wanted to be having with him or anyone just now. I stared out the window on my side.

His hand came down over mine. Warm. Strong. A seductive tease of things that both called to me and terrified me.

"How long?" he demanded, quietly but insistently.

"I don't want to talk about this."

"*Bea.*"

"What?"

"You're avoiding the question."

"If you want to know how long it's been since I've had sex with a man, then the answer is never. I've never had sex. Not with a man. Not with a woman. Not with a goat. Not on a train or in the dark or on a plane. Never."

"How old are you?" he asked, putting his foot to the gas pedal again since the light had turned green.

"Thirty," I bit off. "And if you make one single crack about me being a thirty-year-old virgin—"

"I'm not making jokes about it," he cut in. "I'm not making jokes about *you*."

Not yet. I couldn't seem to stop the dark thoughts from invading my mind.

"Is it a religious thing? Or you just don't want to have sex before marriage or something?"

"It's a men-don't-look-twice-at-the-fat-chick-because-she's-invisible-to-them thing."

"Well, since we've already established that you're not a fat chick anymore, that no longer applies. If it ever did to begin with. Might have just been in your head." He stopped at another light.

"It wasn't just in my head."

"Maybe it was. Like you said, you didn't want to be seen. Maybe you were doing your best to be invisible, and you did too good a job of it."

He could be right about that.

I enjoyed being invisible. I felt safe when I was invisible.

But that safety was just a mirage. I knew it now. Maybe, by isolating and insulating myself like this, I wasn't going to get hurt by loving someone who didn't love me back, but I still ended up getting hurt. I got hurt because I never allowed anyone to love me. I wouldn't let them close enough to hurt me, which meant I didn't let them close enough to care, either…which meant I ended up getting hurt very badly, even though it was the very thing I was doing my damnedest to avoid.

"Either way," Blake said, seemingly oblivious to the war going on inside my head, "I can promise you, men look twice now. Or at least this man does." The heat in his expression did a serious number on me.

A series of tingles shot through my belly and up my spine. I was glad when this traffic light turned green so he had to focus on the road again.

Within a few minutes, he was pulling into my driveway…and I was experiencing another war inside my head. I wanted to dart out of his car and race into my house and lock the door while he was still on the other side of it, but I also wanted to stay right where I was for a little longer—and it wasn't just the lure of the butt warmers.

The truth was, I liked the sensation of his hand resting on mine, his powerful arm brushing up against me. I liked the way his cologne tickled my nostrils. I liked the chills he elicited in my body and the way they turned to an all-encompassing heat a moment later, kind of like Icy Hot for my insides.

I liked an awful lot about him, and I didn't know what to do with that.

"Can I walk you inside?" he asked, and it might have been a casual, maybe even chivalrous, question if I hadn't just told him I'd never slept with a man before. But my admission seemed to change everything about our dynamic.

Or maybe it was only changing things in my head.

My pulse was so loud it was deafening. I nodded and unfastened my seat belt. By the time my fumbling fingers had managed that task, Blake had shut off his engine, gotten out, and come around to open my car door for me. He even offered his hand to assist me out of his car, as if he knew how wobbly my legs must be.

"Hey," he said, and he tipped my chin up with his free hand until I lifted my eyes and looked up at him.

"Hmm?"

"I just want to take you inside tonight. I mean, maybe I *want* more, but that's all I intend to do. It's all I expect."

"And maybe a good-night kiss?" I suggested. Heat flooded my cheeks, making me glad it was dark outside so my embarrassment wasn't obvious.

"I'd never turn down a good-night kiss."

"Good."

"Or any kiss from you."

"You'd better not."

I didn't know where the boldness had come from. But I liked it. I liked this new side of me a lot, and I hoped I could keep it up.

If I could, Dani would be proud.

Well, she'd be proud if she could get over the fact that Blake Kozlow was the one bringing it out in me. But that was neither here nor there, because she wasn't involved.

This was just me and Blake.

I fumbled around in my purse, digging for my keys and dropping them on the ground once I'd finally wrapped my fingers around them.

Blake bent to retrieve them, and instead of handing them back to me, he tugged me toward my front door and unlocked it so I wouldn't have to.

I brushed past him on my way inside, every nerve ending in my body on high alert, my thoughts whirling at breakneck speed. The slight skim of my arm against his chest as I slipped by him made goose bumps pop up all over my body. I shivered, but not from cold.

He closed the door and hung my keychain on the hook where I kept my keys.

Then, before my nerves could get the best of me and I could scurry away, he took my hand in one of his, linking our fingers together, and backed me up against the wall. He did the same with my other hand.

I looked up and met his eyes.

But I wished I hadn't.

Because the heat in his gaze had me locked in place, and I doubted I'd ever be able to move a muscle again.

Blake

Bea was such a contradiction in so many ways. She was bubbly, fiery, and fierce most of the time. But in the next breath, she could become as timid and unsure of herself as anyone I'd ever come across.

I wanted to see that fire come out in her more often. It killed me to see her retreating into her shell, trying to be invisible. There was probably a hell of a lot of truth in what she'd said about people not seeing her when she'd been heavier—but most likely it was because she'd done everything possible to avoid being seen.

But I definitely saw her now.

She'd been helping me with my ADHD and repairing my relationship with the fans and the team…but maybe there was something I could help her with, too.

There were still a few inches between us, other than where our hands met. My fingers were twined with hers, our palms pressed together, but that was the only contact between our bodies. But I could *feel* her nerves, and maybe a hint of her longing, and even a tiny bit of fear.

I didn't get the sense that she was scared of me, per se. It seemed to have more to do with the unknown. Maybe she feared the way she felt at the moment— about me or about what she'd told me or about what we were about to do. Whatever it was, I didn't want her to be nervous or anxious right now.

I wanted her turned on. I wanted her to be as hot and bothered as I was.

But to accomplish that without potentially sending her running like a skittish rabbit or hissing at me like a cornered alley cat, I'd need to take my time.

Going slow might just kill me, but boo fucking hoo, too bad for me.

"This is okay?" I asked, just to be sure.

And even though her eyes were wide enough they could be saucers, she nodded, keeping them locked to mine.

I lowered my head, angling it to the side so I could nibble on her jaw and neck.

She sucked in a sharp breath before releasing it, and her pulse pounded against my tongue when I licked her there. Hell, her response was turning me on like I never could have imagined. Most of the women I'd been with were experienced. They knew what they wanted and they weren't afraid to ask for it. For that matter, a lot of them just plain demanded it.

But for Bea, this was all new. I couldn't afford to forget that. If I fucked this up, not only would she never let me near her again, but she might not ever let *any* man have a chance.

That was a lot of pressure, and I tended to go one of two ways with pressure: either I exceeded all expectations or I fucked up royally. There was no in-between.

But I didn't want any old guy touching her. Only me. No clue where the hell that thought had come from, but it was there, and I didn't think it'd be going away any time soon.

I wanted Bea Castillo more than I'd ever wanted a woman before, and I wanted her all to myself.

"I need to touch you, Bea," I said, trailing my tongue over the hollow in her neck as I made my way back up to her mouth. "I want to put my hands on you. Can I?"

"Yes," came out as a strangled sound.

I'd barely let go of her hands and started to move them toward her waist when she grabbed hold of my wrists with a grip that surprised me in its strength.

"What?" I asked, trying to figure out how I'd already fucked up.

She took a couple of deep breaths, her eyes wide and wild. "Over my clothes," she insisted. "Only over them."

"Okay. Whatever you say, Bea. Over your clothes." I felt the need to repeat her words—not for me, but so she'd know I completely understood and agreed.

She nodded, her eyes closed tight.

Fuck, she was still so scared and unsure of it all. Unsure of me. I hoped she wasn't scared of me, but just scared of the unknown.

I started by brushing only the tips of my fingers along her jaw and then down her neck, planting soft kisses over her cheeks and nose until I felt her shudder. "This okay so far?" I murmured between whisper-soft pecks and tiny tastes with my tongue.

"Mm hmm."

The pulse in her throat throbbed against my thumb. It was going wild, the realization of which was enough to make me crazy with need. My dick was pure steel behind my zipper. Throbbing. Painful. Desperate. I couldn't remember the last time I'd wanted a woman as much as I wanted her.

This was going to be torture. Pure, utter torture. But hopefully torture that would pay off—eventually.

"If you don't like something or you want me to stop, you just say the word," I said, and I felt her nod as I dipped my head in to suckle the lobe of one ear. "I'll stop. Or I'll change to what you want. You just say the word, okay?"

"Mm hmm." The sound was barely a vibration beneath my lips.

I licked her where the vibrations had just been.

She sucked in a sharp breath, which pushed her breasts toward my chest. I bit back a groan of longing because I was dying to get my hands on those tits. And my mouth.

Patience, I reminded myself. If I could be patient enough, it would be rewarded—eventually. Maybe. Hopefully.

Tentative hands splayed over my chest. I let out a growl of approval that got swallowed by her lips as she unexpectedly grabbed hold of my collar and tugged me closer.

An inch at a time, I moved my exploration along her

neck, over her collarbone, down until I could fill one hand with her breast. It was soft and full, and her tit pebbled like a rock against my palm when I gently squeezed. She nipped my lower lip in surprise, which prompted me to squeeze a bit harder.

"Oh my God," she murmured against my mouth.

"More?" I asked.

She nodded, so I moved my other hand to her free breast and deepened the kiss, taking long, slow drags of her tongue as I rolled her nipples between my thumbs and forefingers.

Bea ground her hips against me, and my dick almost whimpered from the combination of ecstasy and torture.

I wanted to strip off all her clothes and screw her against the wall. I wanted to sink inside her and lose myself. I wanted to drive into her until she was shaking and limp and calling my name. I wanted it so much I was practically desperate from it.

But instead, I took what she was willing to give, and I gave her as much as she was willing to accept, and I told myself to be happy with it.

Soft, surprised sounds kept coming from the back of her throat, which only turned me on more. Her body was on fire, just as much as mine. I had no doubt she was slick with need.

She was ready.

Scratch that—her body was ready. Her mind hadn't caught up yet.

So after long minutes of kissing her like there might be no tomorrow, I forced myself to separate from her. Her lips were pink and swollen from my kisses, her eyes almost black with longing and fully glazed with lust.

"I should go home," I rasped, planting another chaste kiss on her forehead.

"You should." She nodded, her hands still clasping my collar and holding me close.

"Yeah. I should."

But neither of us made any move to release the other. We were both still gulping air, our hearts pounding.

I forced myself to relax and pressed my forehead against hers, my hands resting on her ribs so I could casually brush my thumbs along the undersides of her breasts. "I want to do this again, Bea."

"A date?"

"All of it."

"All of…?"

"A date. Driving you home. Laughing with you. Making out until we're both horny as hell and desperate for more and we can't catch our breaths. Everything."

"Everything?" she repeated, still winded. Or maybe it was what I'd said that had stolen her breath this time.

"Yeah. Everything. I want it all with you."

It was an admission that should have terrified me. But instead, it did the opposite. For the first time in as long as I could remember, I felt an immense lightness spread through my entire body, a warmth that had nothing to do with the lust still raging through my blood.

I wanted this woman more than I wanted my next breath. And I was willing to do whatever it took to make her want me just as badly.

Never woulda seen this one coming.

Chapter Nine

Bea

"That's it," Dani said emphatically, propping herself up against the pillows. "You're not allowed to make decisions about your love life anymore."

I rolled my eyes and shifted my body in her bed, crossing my left ankle over my right instead of the other way around. My legs and feet were going numb from being in the same uncomfortable position for too long—I shuddered to think how uncomfortable she must be by now, which was all the more reason I kept bringing her goodies. "Hate to break it to you," I said, "but you don't exactly get a say in this. And I don't know that I'd call it a *love life*, anyway. I wouldn't say I have one of those. Besides, Blake and I have only been on one date. *One.*"

"Two." She scowled spectacularly. My homegirl was

nothing if not dramatic. "And the fact that you're calling him *Blake* now speaks volumes."

"I'm not counting the first one. It was a huge flop due to a misunderstanding. We're starting from scratch."

"Scratch sounds good. As in if he does anything to hurt you or if he comes near me, I'll scratch his eyeballs out."

"Good thing he won't be coming near you, then."

"Are you scared to bring him near me? I think you are. And I think it's because you know he doesn't deserve you."

"And it's even better that you're stuck in bed so you can't do anything to him," I added, ignoring what she'd said about him not deserving me. If anything, I was starting to think it might be the other way around. I'd thought nothing but the worst of him for so long, and most of it was due to a misunderstanding. He had his fair share of flaws, sure. But who didn't? I definitely hadn't been giving him enough credit when it came to his ability to see past *my* flaws—and my own inability to do exactly that.

"I will cut off his balls with a rusty spork if he does anything to hurt you," Dani said fiercely. "I notice you conveniently neglected commenting on that part of my statement."

"He can't hurt me unless I let him." And I wouldn't be allowing him close enough to hurt me. Would I? Hmm. Didn't think so. But still… "And to cut off his balls, you'd have to be close enough to reach them. And you'd have to get your hands on a rusty spork. No one in your life is going to give you access to either of those anytime soon."

"I can get my hands on one," Dani insisted.

"And I can inform Cody and everyone in your family of your plans and make sure it doesn't happen," I countered. "Between them, I'd guess your father, Cody, Jamie, Luke, and now Cole can restrain you."

She harrumphed. "All sorts of places will deliver. Some of them even deliver within an hour. I've got an app on my phone for that."

Further proof that there truly *was* an app for everything.

I chuckled. "And you're stuck in bed, so how are you going to accept your delivery?"

"Just because I'm *supposed* to stay in bed as much as possible doesn't mean I'm completely *incapable* of getting out of it. I have to get up to use the bathroom and other crap every now and then, you know."

"Doesn't mean you should be going up and down stairs. Especially not on your own. That sounds like an accident waiting to happen."

"I can hold on to the rails."

I lifted a dubious brow. "So you'd put your baby at risk over this? You'd take the chance of falling down the stairs just to prove a point or get revenge for a slight when you don't even know the full story?"

Dani gave me a pout that could put all other pouts in the history of the world to shame. Apparently, I'd finally struck the right nerve.

"What kind of misunderstanding?" she demanded, making me do a double take.

"Huh?"

"You said it was just a misunderstanding on that first date."

"The date that we've agreed wasn't a date?"

She waved a dismissive hand through the air. "I haven't agreed to anything."

Wasn't that the truth? I sighed. "He said something that I took to mean one thing when really, it was about something else entirely."

"Maybe he's just trying to save face by claiming that. Maybe he really did mean the other thing and he just wants to get back on your good side. I mean, the guy has no filter. He says everything he's thinking—but that means he has to be thinking it to begin with, or it wouldn't come out of his mouth."

I chose to ignore the niggling bits of doubt that wanted to creep back into my mind. She had a point, no matter how much I wanted to believe what Blake had told me. I didn't want Dani to be right. For some reason, I *wanted* to believe in Blake and his pure intentions.

Was it lust talking, though? Was I only having a change of heart because of the sensations he'd roused in my body when he'd kissed and touched me? It was hard to know, because I'd never been involved in any relationship of this sort before now, and so I had nothing to gauge my response against other than the ways I felt when I read certain books or watched certain movies.

But I wasn't ready to give in to that sort of thinking so soon. I wanted to believe—not only in him but in my skills sensing ulterior motives. "You can think whatever you want, Dani. I can't change that. All I know is what I believe to be the truth."

She pouted. In defeat? I could only hope that she would give up so easily. She never had before. My *chica* liked to dig in her heels, especially when she was sure to lose.

"Seriously, though?" she said. "Koz? Of all the men in Portland that you could have possibly started a relationship with, why does it have to be Koz?"

"I don't know that I'd call it a relationship. Not yet, at least."

"Meaning you want it to be one."

"I don't know what I want." More than that, I wasn't sure what my fears would allow me to go after. He'd had a point about my insecurities, and I had to be ready to confront them or else this would all blow up in my face in the worst possible way.

"You let him kiss you."

"We don't choose who we're attracted to," I said, shrugging.

"Looks aren't everything."

"I never said it was about looks. Attraction isn't solely based on that." Lord knew the attraction on *his* side couldn't possibly be physical. I was moving forward with this on the belief that he was so attracted to my personality that he could look past the physical. For now, at least. I was sure things would change if and when I ever let him see what was going on beneath my clothes.

But Dani had just started to work up a head of steam. "That's it. You're just blinded by lust. You just need to get laid by some other hottie and then you can get Koz out of your system."

"First off, I have no intention of getting laid by some random guy—"

"You totally should," she said, interrupting me with an adamant nod. "A hot, sweaty screw will do a body good. Besides, it's great exercise. You could walk a bit less and just do some boinking for your workout that day. And then you can tell me all about it, and I can live vicariously through you because Cody is bound and determined to make me follow doctor's orders to a T, and my OB-gyn seems to think that sex would be a bit too vigorous due to my stupid complications or something, and I'm horny as hell and as big as a boat and I can't get any action."

"What makes you think I'd tell you all the gory details?" Emphasis on *gory*, since that's all it could be once my saggy, baggy skin was involved. Was it possible to have sex fully clothed? Doubtful, but I'd have to research the possibilities.

And if I was thinking about that, it meant I also needed to see my doctor. And sooner rather than later.

Dani didn't seem inclined to go along with my reasoning. "Because I'll beg and plead and annoy the ever-loving shit out of you until you do."

"And that's different from the way you behave all the time *how*, exactly?"

She tossed a pillow at my head.

I grabbed it and stuffed it behind my back.

"*Please* let me arrange for some hottie to screw you into oblivion and remove Koz from your life," she begged.

"Not going to happen."

"Oh, come on. You're such a spoilsport."

"Nope. I'm a pragmatist. And I don't have any intention of letting *anyone* 'screw me into oblivion,' as you put it. Not Blake and not anyone else."

"Chicken."

I tucked my thumbs in my underarms, flapped my arms, and *bocked*.

"How come you're calling him Blake?"

"It's his name, isn't it?"

She let out an aggravated sound.

"You might be surprised. He's not so bad once you get to know him."

"Once you get to know… You like him!" She shouted it as an accusation, not an observation.

"So what if I do?"

Dani let out a sound of disgust, wrinkling her nose at me. "One of these days, Bea. One of these days, I'm going to set you up with the man who'll get you out of your funk once and for all, and then you'll owe me big-time."

I had to bite back the urge to tell her I'd already found someone who could do exactly that.

And maybe he'd be willing.

But was I? Not sure.

I laughed and shook my head to brush her off. But now, I couldn't stop thinking about letting Blake *screw me into oblivion*, as Dani had so callously put it, or *get me out of my funk*…and I doubted the thought would go away easily.

Would I be ready for it if and when the time came?

......

I arranged for a substitute teacher to fill in for me one afternoon a few days later while Blake and the Storm were gone for a long road trip—because I decided to bump up my annual appointment with my surgeon by a couple of months. For…well, for *reasons*. Or for one reason, in particular. But this one was a doozy.

"Looking good," Dr. Dennison said, scanning the numbers on my chart. "Your blood work is excellent. Still no problems with getting all your vitamins or your protein? You're not missing doses or skipping meals?"

"No more problems than normal. I might forget a dose of vitamins about once a month or so, but for the most part, I take them on schedule. And eating every two to three hours is just a habit now. I don't have to think about it. If I ever go too long without a meal or a snack, I get cranky—and I have a few good friends I can always count on to point out if I'm being a witch and tell me I need to eat something."

"A witch?" His laugh was unexpected.

"To put it politely. I get irritable when I need some protein, apparently."

He winked. "Your weight is holding nice and steady. Looks like you're down about three pounds from your last visit."

"Today it might be down, but yesterday I was up by about two pounds. It fluctuates but stays within about a six-pound range."

"That's fairly normal for anyone, whether they've had weight-loss surgery or not. It's just how the human body works. Water weight, what you had to eat, how much exercise you got, whether you're retaining water due to your menstrual cycle…"

"How close we are to the full moon and whether I danced naked around a fire…"

He chuckled. "The actual number on any particular day isn't what matters." Then he faced his computer again and eyed some more of the numbers and results. "Are you comfortable at this weight?"

"I wouldn't mind losing another ten pounds, but I'm fine being where I am. My body feels comfortable at this weight." And frankly, I didn't relish the thought of losing *too* much weight. As it was, my grandmother was always bemoaning how skinny I was and that I wouldn't eat her cooking anymore. Abuelita didn't know and didn't care about the differences between carbs and proteins and fats. To her, food was food was food—and if she made it for me, I should eat it. It could be tough trying to be healthy when the people in your life didn't respect your decisions, but that was neither here nor there.

"Comfortable, hmm?" the doctor said. "Bet you never thought you'd say those words."

I grinned. "Never. Not in a million years. But I like being able to say them, and more than that, I like being able to mean them."

"And how are you feeling about your excess skin? We talked about it a bit last year, but you still weren't done losing weight at that point."

I shrugged. "Resigned?"

"You could probably get some of it removed," he pointed out. "There are plastic surgeons who specialize in this sort of operation these days. You've been at a steady weight for long enough that a good plastic surgeon would consider you an excellent candidate for surgery. There are a couple in this practice, even. I could refer you…"

"I could get some of the excess skin removed *if* I could afford it," I pointed out. "But on a teacher's salary, that's not going to happen, whether a surgeon would take me on or not. So I'm just going to have to deal with it."

"Is any of it causing you health problems? Because you could maybe get your insurance to cover it if there's a medical reason behind it. Rashes? Does it pull you over sometimes? Cause back pain?"

"It just annoys me. I don't have anything like that going on."

"All right, then. I'd say all in all, you're doing better than anyone could have predicted or expected. You're a model example of what bariatric surgery can do for someone. I feel comfortable saying I'll see you again in a year, unless you have something come up before then, or if you need anything else from me."

"There is *one* other thing I wanted to talk to you about on this visit," I said, my nerves suddenly getting the best of me. Not that there was a good reason for me to be nervous about this. Dr. Dennison had seen me at my absolute lowest points, the heaviest I'd ever been in my life, and he'd been by my side through every step of this massive transformation. There would be no judgment coming from him. Not now and not ever.

In fact, he'd been my biggest cheerleader for the past couple of years, encouraging me when I struggled and cheering me up every time I hit a setback in my weight loss or energy level.

"Why do I get the sense you're having problems asking me whatever you need to ask me?" he asked.

"Because I don't know how to tackle this particular subject matter. It's not something I've ever felt the need to talk to anyone about before, doctor or otherwise."

"Out with it, whatever it is. There haven't been any secrets or subjects that were off limits between us, not through this whole process. We've talked about everything from exercise to poop. You've told me the nitty gritty, and I've seen your insides. No point being anything less than up-front and open about it all, whatever it is. Right?"

He was right. And more than that, we both knew it.

I took a deep breath and spit it all out in a rush. "You told me to come to you if I ever changed my mind about birth control and so I need you to prescribe something because this might not happen, but it might, and I need to be prepared for it, right?"

He gave me a sly wink, then turned back to face his computer and scan my chart. "I had a feeling it might be something like that. You finally dipped your toes into the dating pool, hmm?"

"Something like that," I mumbled.

"Any chance you're already pregnant?"

"Unless I'm the second coming of the Virgin Mary…"

"I've got to perform a pregnancy test, just to be sure. To be safe."

"There's really no point."

"Other than the fact that your insurance won't pay for your birth control unless I do the test."

Well, then. "That's fine." One more poke wouldn't kill me. And I had no intention of getting pregnant accidentally. Particularly not if I could do something to prevent it. Otherwise, I would never have brought up the idea of birth control in the first place, after all.

"Do you feel comfortable taking a daily pill and not forgetting a dose? Or would you prefer to go with something like an IUD or a shot?"

"I already take my bariatric vitamins every day. A daily birth control pill wouldn't be any different."

"The pills are very effective, but so are the other methods. You do have options."

I shook my head. "I think I'd prefer to stick with pills."

He typed a few things into my chart. "Same pharmacy as before?"

"Hasn't changed."

"It'll be ready for you to pick up later today. Shoot me an email or call my office if you have any questions about how best to take the pills. You can take them at the same time as one of your other daily doses so you won't forget. And it'll be more effective if you take it at the same time each day, within about an hour or two."

Taking pills on a schedule was something I was already well used to. "No problem."

"You'll need to start this first pack on the Sunday after your next period. Same day your period starts if you begin on Sunday."

"Got it," I said. "What if I want to start them sooner?"

"Can't wait?"

I shrugged. "Just in case."

"You'll be protected within two days of starting the pills on this one. But it'll mess with your regular cycle. You might have some spotting."

"Spotting isn't the end of the world."

"And be sure you use a backup method of contraception until then. And save the informational packet so you'll know what to do if you miss a dose."

"Thanks, Dr. Dennison," I said, gathering up my things.

"That's what I'm here for." He printed off the notes from today's visit and then handed them to me, as well as another slip of paper with the orders for me to take to the lab. "And if you ever decide you want to have babies, that can be in your cards, too, now. You're more than healthy enough to have a successful pregnancy. And you're plenty young enough, too."

Thoughts of Dani's current misery rushed through my mind, and I shook my head. "Doubtful. Seriously doubtful."

"Mm hmm. I seem to remember you saying the same thing about how you'd never need a prescription for contraception…"

He was right, but having children was a completely different idea than having sex.

Wasn't it?

Had to be.

Blake

About two months into the season, we had a long road trip with several stops along the East Coast. The games were grueling, mainly because of the travel and being three time zones away from where we lived.

Although we had to play against every team in the league, we didn't face these Eastern Conference teams often. The lack of familiarity with their playing styles could have proven to be problematic, yet we had come away with wins against Pittsburgh, Philadelphia, and Tampa already. We still had two more games to go before flying home: one tonight against Carolina, and another in two days against Florida.

This was our longest road swing of the season—the longest we'd be away from Portland at any one point—and I was shocked by how much I was missing home.

I'd never been overly attached to Portland before now. I mean, yeah, Jim Sutter and the coaching staff had been great to take a chance on me after I'd made an ass of myself in my first NHL stop in Anaheim. And for the most part, my teammates tended to put up with me—some more than others, but still. Hell, a couple of them might actually like me, like Babs. Most of them just tolerated me, but that was a crap-ton better than I'd experienced in other places.

But despite my comfort level with the team and the familiarity I'd developed with my surroundings, Portland had never truly felt like *home* to me before.

Home was with my Grandma in Upstate New York.

Or it had been. She was still there, along with an enormous chunk of my heart, but another piece of my heart was somewhere else.

For the first time ever, I missed Portland. I missed it like crazy.

It wasn't the city so much as who I'd left behind: Bea.

She had the sweetest, sexiest laugh. It was one of those full-bodied laughs that made your sides hurt because it was just so fucking good. And the more I was around her, and the more she laughed, the more she made me laugh, too.

I'd texted her a couple of times on this trip, the first time claiming I needed her assistance with my current crocheting project and the second time asking for her color recommendations for one of the stupid coloring books I'd taken with me.

She'd rattled off the directions for crocheting by rote, as if she hadn't even needed to take the time to think about it. That hadn't been the case at all for coloring; she'd flat out refused to tell me what colors to use.

"That's the beauty of art," she'd said adamantly. "There's no right or wrong. If you want to make your sky pink and the grass blue, you can do it."

"But this isn't grass and sky. It's a mandala," I'd argued.

"Even more reason I won't tell you what colors to use. You can do *anything* you want, and it'll be great."

No matter how vehemently I'd argued, she'd refused to budge. That was what led me to Googling color combinations from my Raleigh hotel room at three in the morning instead of resting up for tomorrow's game.

Apparently, teal and orange went really well together, so I had already colored four different mandala designs with various combinations of teal and orange shades. But now I was getting bored with that pairing, so I needed to come up with a new set of contrasting colors to use. My orange and teal markers would run out of ink, and I'd still have tons of ink left in the other markers—and that would probably set off my ADHD, and I'd flip out.

Also there was the fact that I was getting bored with mandalas. It didn't matter how complex the designs were—they were monotonous. Which, I supposed, was the point. Repeating patterns. Soothing designs. Some shit like that.

I took my laptop out and connected it to the hotel's WiFi, and I started Googling adult coloring books. Maybe I couldn't get anything better while we were on the road, but I could probably order some books and have them waiting for me at home by the time we returned to Portland.

I typed in *adult coloring books* in the search bar and got all sorts of hits. Most of them were the same mandala and landscape types of books I'd already bought, but after a few pages of search results, I started finding books that were *much* more interesting.

Or at least more interesting to me.

Some of them were curse word coloring books, full of flowery lettering that spelled out words like *fuckwad*, *dipshit*, *twatnozzle*, *fucktrumpet*, *douchecanoe*, *cumbucket*, and even a few curse words I'd never encountered before. And then after a couple of pages full of books like those, I found some coloring books filled with designs of pinup girls and other almost naked chicks with massive tits and tiny waists.

Fuck. Yes.

I whipped out my credit card and picked out a few of both types of books that had good reviews, and I placed an order so they'd be waiting for me at home by the time we returned to Portland. If I could add a bit of spice to this coloring shit, it might just work out for me.

For now, I needed to content myself with the mandalas, though. I went back to coloring and hoped it would lull me into sleep at some point.

......

The next day, I ended up doing more of the same. I pulled up the color wheel I'd saved on my phone, which showed me which colors contrasted with one another. Red and green was too much like Christmas. Nope. Not going there. Purple and yellow seemed like an okay option, so I selected all my variations of those colors from my marker kit and settled in to work.

Yeah, maybe I was supposed to be napping before the game, but since when had I ever managed to nap?

Since never, that's when.

I was halfway through shading the meticulous design when my phone lit up with a text message. Habit had me peeking at the screen just in case it was from Bea—because she consumed most of my conscious thoughts these days, and even a few of my subconscious thoughts.

But it wasn't from Bea.

Grandma: *Call me later. AFTER your game, not before it. I need to talk to you.*

Well, fuck. She never sent me cryptic messages like that. *Never.* Grandma was as straightforward and to the point as they came. She knew what this kind of shit would do to me. She knew I'd never be able to think about anything else until I found out what she needed to talk to me about.

If she was messaging me and asking me to call her after the game, there was only one thing this could possibly be about.

God damn it all. Her motherfucking cancer was back.

Chapter Ten

Bea

I still had about a dozen of my students' spelling tests to finish grading, but I couldn't seem to focus on my work. And this time, I couldn't even blame my lack of focus on Dani and her pregnancy issues or the way she was trying to stick her nose where it didn't belong. Tonight, my distraction was entirely due to having the Storm game on while I was trying to work. Every time the commentators mentioned Blake, I looked up to see what was happening with him.

To say he'd been having a rough night so far would be an understatement, although his mistakes hadn't cost the team on the scoreboard—yet.

He'd only won three face-offs the whole game, which was so far below his average as to be laughable if it weren't such a serious issue for the team. Every time he sent a pass toward a teammate, it got picked off by an opponent that he had apparently not seen. His shots all sailed well wide of the goal or soared so high that they hit the netting over the boards that protected the spectators. He even seemed to be skating slower than usual.

To cap it off, he'd already been sent to the penalty box for three minor penalties plus a fighting major, and it was only halfway through the second period.

Following yet another Hurricanes shot that Storm goalie Nicklas Ericsson managed to fend off and cover, one of the refs finally blew his whistle for a TV time out.

I realized I'd been biting down on my tongue due to the anxiety of watching Blake struggle so much, so I forced myself to loosen my jaw. It ached. A lot. I couldn't let myself stress out over him and his game—it wouldn't do either of us any good.

Ninety seconds. The commercial break meant I had ninety seconds to grade three papers before the game would return. I could do this.

I buried my nose in my work and quickly powered through my marking, making a mental note to spend more time with my students tomorrow going over some of the exceptions to traditional spelling rules. Almost every paper I had graded so far had a variety of misspellings for words like *eight* and *thought*. The silent *gh* was tripping them up, and the fact that *ei* could sound like a long *a* hadn't seeped in for a few of my kids yet, either.

I was just finishing up the third student's paper when the game returned, so I set my marking aside and switched focus.

"That's right, Storm fans," the commentator said.

"Blake Kozlow is in the penalty box again, and we're going to show you why."

Then they proceeded to air some footage that had taken place during the TV time out.

It seemed harmless enough at first. The play came to a stop, just as I'd remembered it happening. But as the players on the ice headed toward the benches and the arena's crew came out to shovel the ice shavings, Blake was straggling behind the rest of his teammates.

For some reason known only to Blake, he stopped before reaching the bench. He was blocking the arena's crew. It looked like the man asked him to get out of the way so he could finish doing his job in a timely manner, and Blake just…lost it. There wasn't any other way to describe his response. He yelled so much that the poor man was cringing away from him, as if maybe he feared Blake would go postal and use his stick as a weapon or something.

Two of Blake's teammates came over and literally hauled him onto the bench, but the damage was already done, and one of the refs had his arm in the air while skating toward the Storm's bench.

That was where the replay ended, and then the broadcast's cameras zoomed in on Blake sitting in the penalty box. He looked livid, but something told me his anger was fully directed at himself.

But now I *really* had to wonder—what had gotten into him tonight?

This wasn't normal. Yes, sometimes he lost his cool. And more often than he'd probably care to admit, he ended up doing and saying things he wished he could take back, as evidenced by the Twitter debacle that had landed him in my classroom.

But this seemed to go beyond his usual sort of mess

up—similar to the Twitter debacle, only this time it was in a game situation instead of being a social media faux pas. This directly affected his career, whereas the other was less tangible.

My gut clenched as I watched his expression change every time the camera panned over to him again during the Hurricanes' power play. And when the horn sounded and the goal light flashed, he skated back across the ice to rejoin his teammates with his head hanging low. One of the commentators said something about it being the "skate of shame," and I wanted to punch the guy through the TV screen.

It was probably a good thing that the broadcast team didn't have any microphones on the Storm's bench, because the coaching staff appeared to be ripping into Blake so badly I could almost feel him shrinking away.

After that, I couldn't look anywhere else but at the TV. Certainly not at the spelling tests I was supposed to be grading. I shoved them aside and watched the rest of the game, mainly to see two things: what would happen with Blake, and how would he respond to it?

Answers: he was glued to the bench for the rest of the game, and badly. By the time the game finally—mercifully—ended, the Storm had lost by a score of five to one, and Blake hadn't been allowed back on the ice for even a second. The coaches had benched him through the rest of the second period and for every moment of the third.

He'd been practically vibrating with the need to burn off some energy, to get out on the ice and fix the problems he'd created. It was visible and obvious, at least to me, but I knew the danger signs for someone with ADHD. But instead of allowing him to use all of that pent-up energy and frustration by channeling it into something with the potential to go either way on the ice, they'd forced him to wallow on the bench in the misery of his own making.

Blake had always had a tendency to lose it sometimes—I'd realized that about him before I'd ever met him, and the things he'd said and done since we'd gotten to know one another had only further proved the point—but this seemed to be more. It was bigger somehow.

Even though I ought to turn off the game and finish grading these papers, I found myself reaching for my cell phone and shooting off a text message.

> *Call me later once you're allowed to use your phone. I'll be up. You need to talk about whatever it is that's bugging you.*

I thought about telling him I missed him before deciding against it. This wasn't about me—it was about him.

But sending him a message wasn't enough to help me regain my focus. It was now directed squarely on Blake, so attempting to grade more spelling tests or do some lesson planning would be an exercise in futility. I set all my work aside to finish tomorrow, and I waited by my phone.

Having him in my life was proving to be like passing a car wreck: no matter how gruesome it got, I couldn't look away.

Blake

I was about to board the team plane for our flight down to Florida when Webs caught me securely around the shoulders with a grip brimming with old-man strength, and he hauled me off to the side, well away from the rest of the guys.

"Bergy's seriously talking about benching you next game," he said.

I shrugged, even though that wasn't the sort of thing I could just shrug off. This was my fucking career, and I could feel it slipping through my fingers, but there didn't seem to be any way to stop it. I was caught in a downward spiral, much like I'd experienced in my first stop in the NHL.

Hell, until the Storm traded for me, I'd thought that my career was already over. I thought I'd already burned up all my chances.

Jim Sutter had given me one more shot, though, and now it seemed as if I was squandering it. Everything I did was wrong, even when I was trying to make it right again.

I couldn't get my head on straight. Couldn't find my footing. I'd been tossed into the deep end and it was either sink or swim—but I had lead weights on my ankles, pulling me under. No chance to swim.

"Guess he's going to bench me then," I muttered. "He's the coach. It's his call."

"That's it?" he growled at me. "You're just going to shrug and say it's his call like you don't even give a fuck?"

"I give a fuck," I bit off.

Maybe I gave too many fucks. That was probably my biggest issue in all of this.

"You're already walking a fine line with him after

your Twitter shenanigans. You can't afford to lose your shit in a game like you did tonight. Not again, Koz. You've got to get your head on straight."

"I know it. I just don't know…"

"What?" he asked when I didn't finish my thought.

"I'm trying, okay? But the shit in my head is getting to me."

"What kind of shit in your head?"

"Doesn't matter. It's my problem to figure out."

Webs gave me a look that made me think of the ones Grandma used to give me when I'd fucked something up and wouldn't let her help me set things right again.

That look made my skin crawl, especially coming from Webs.

"What kind of shit?" he demanded again.

He was usually the member of the coaching staff that guys would go to when they had a problem and wanted advice on how to tackle it. He'd been one of us back in the day, and he still felt like a bit of a go-between for us and the rest of the coaches—someone who could see our side even if he had to make us see their side. He was kind of like a dad in that way—or at least he'd been the closest thing to a dad that I'd ever had.

I doubted he knew that, but it was the truth.

Still, I wanted nothing more than to get away from his scrutiny right now, because the last thing I needed was something else making me think about Grandma, who was the only parent I'd ever known—my real parents had spent the majority of my life in and out of prison and drug treatment facilities.

I hadn't called her yet. I couldn't bring myself to do it just now. Besides, I'd rather wait to hear the news when I was alone in my hotel room. Didn't want the rest of the guys to see me fall apart, and that was exactly what would happen once she told me the news.

Maybe I already *knew* it, but it didn't seem real yet since I hadn't heard her say the words.

Some small part of me seemed to be under the impression that if I put off making that call for long enough, if I waited to hear it come from her mouth, then maybe I could avoid the inevitable. Ridiculous and unlikely, sure, but there was a bit of hope lingering somewhere near my stomach.

Webs pinned me with the same sort of glare he'd given Babs years ago whenever Katie had been around. The same glare he sometimes *still* gave Harry. The same glare I'd seen him giving Colesy recently—since our D-man had started openly dating Luke Weber, our assistant coach's only son.

"Don't know why you're giving me the don't-be-an-asswipe look when I'm not chasing after one of your kids," I grumbled, wishing I could somehow avoid the heat of that stare.

"Well, you're still being an asswipe, and it's my job to tell you that you need to knock that shit off."

"I won't take so many penalties next game," I argued.

"That's not what I mean."

It wasn't? I shrugged, not following. I glanced over to where the rest of the team had almost finished boarding the plane, wishing I was already in my seat so I could put on some headphones and attempt to disappear.

"Something's getting to you," he said. "That's why you were a loose cannon out there."

"And?" I hated that I sounded so defensive.

"And I'm trying to help you out," Webs said. He glanced behind me and quickly returned his gaze to me, but the furrow to his brow had me curious.

I took a look over my shoulder and caught sight of Bergy shooting a glare in my direction. Yeah, I was pretty sure between my Twitter debacle and tonight's craptastic performance, I'd be in Bergy's doghouse for the rest of the season. No chance of me climbing my way out of that hole.

"Help me out how?" I forced myself to ask, once more looking over at Webs.

"I know you've never really had any sort of father figure in your life—"

"What, you aren't getting enough father-son time with Babs, Harry, Colesy, and Luke?" I butted in. "Did Babs put you up to this? Or Harry? Maybe Harry's threatening not to let you have time with your grandkid if you don't get me in line?"

As soon as the words were out of my mouth, I wished I could take them back. Because the truth was he was trying to help me out. I just couldn't control myself—especially not with my brain going crazy with worrying about Grandma.

Webs didn't deserve me treating him like this. He was trying to act like the father figure I'd always seen him as, and I was biting his head off.

"I just thought you should know you've got people in your life who care," he said. "That's all."

Grudgingly, I nodded, unsure what to say. He grunted and headed for the plane.

"I think my grandma's cancer is back," I called out after him. But then I wasn't sure why I'd done it, and I wished I could take the words back.

Especially since they caused him to stop in his

tracks.

But they were out there, and my throat felt as if it were closing in on me. To be honest, I wished it would. I wanted it to close off so I couldn't breathe anymore. Because I didn't want to think about a world without my grandma in it.

She'd already kicked cancer's ass once. But it had taken a hell of a lot out of her. I wasn't sure she could do it again, and that scared the shit out of me.

Webs slowly turned around, an inscrutable expression clouding his eyes.

I swallowed hard, but the lump in my throat wouldn't budge. My eyes stung. Fucking cancer. And fucking tears.

"You think?" Webs finally said, his voice gravelly.

"She told me to call her after the game. Wouldn't say why."

"Have you called her yet?"

I shook my head.

"Why not?"

I shrugged again.

"Whatever she needs to tell you, you need to hear it," he said.

"Don't want to."

"But you need to." He closed the distance between us, draping an arm across my shoulders in a father-like gesture I'd seen him use with kids so many times I could probably see it in my sleep.

It made the lump in my throat even bigger.

"Come on," he said. "Let's call her now."

I took my phone out of my pocket and powered it on. I pulled up her number from the contacts list. But then I couldn't make myself press the button. "I'd rather do it in my room once we get to the hotel later.

Sometime when I'm alone."

"That's not the kind of phone call you make when you're alone," Webs grumbled. Then he took the phone from me and pressed Send before shoving the phone up against my ear.

Well, hell.

"You can't be in Miami yet," Grandma said almost before the phone had finished ringing.

"Coaches thought I should call you now. Before the flight leaves." My tongue felt too thick to belong to me. I wasn't sure how I was managing to get any words out at all. "So what's up?" I asked, my tone much lighter than I felt.

"Just wondering if you might be able to carve out some time to come and visit me when your team comes up this way in a couple of weeks." She sounded winded.

In a couple of weeks? That sounded…ominous. She'd never asked me to come for a visit during the season other than maybe over the All-Star break. But she'd only done that once. This couldn't be good.

"Grandma, are you sick again? Because if you are, I need you to just tell me."

"The doctors found some more cancer," she said slowly.

"When? And where? Is it the same as before?"

"It's breast cancer again."

"But you already had a mastectomy."

"Well…it spread."

The words felt like an anvil falling on my skull. "Spread where?"

"To my lungs. And my brain. And they found some in my bones, too."

A wave of nausea hit me and nearly took my legs

out from under me. The only reason I remained on my feet was because Webs tightened his arm around my shoulders and hauled me up against him, lending me his strength because mine was gone.

Grandma was my strength. She was the reason behind anything good in me. If I lost her, I'd lose everything.

"Are you telling me you're dying?" I choked out.

"You think I'm gonna let a little cancer keep me down?" She laughed, but it wasn't as full and robust as her normal laughter. "What do we do when cancer comes knocking on the door?"

"We give it the finger and tell it to go fuck itself," I said by rote, thinking of the matching tattoos we'd gotten the first time she'd been sick.

"Well, that's what I'm doing. But if you can come to visit…"

"I'll find a way," I said. "I'll talk to…" Hell, I didn't know who I needed to talk to about it. Couldn't think clearly enough to figure it out.

"We'll work it out," Webs said, with a hell of a lot more confidence than I felt. I doubted he even knew what he was promising to work out, but right now, he was the only thing holding me together. His arm around my shoulders was my lifeline to reality.

"I'll work it out," I said to Grandma.

"That's good. But don't you go playing like you did tonight in that next game. Got it? Too many penalties."

"I always take too many penalties," I said, and I couldn't stop the grin from coming through. It was the first time I'd felt like smiling in hours—and I wasn't even sure why it was happening now.

"Got to clean up your act, Blake. You need someone to keep you in line."

"That's your job."

"Yes, that's my job. For now."

Chapter Eleven

Bea

Blake didn't call me that night. Or the next day. He didn't respond to any of my text messages, either, which had me really worried about him. But nothing concerned me more than the fact that he wasn't on the bench for the Storm's next game against Florida.

I couldn't think of a single game I'd watched with Dani over the last couple of years when he hadn't played. Sick, injured, whatever—Blake would be on the ice. Now that I knew about his ADHD, I realized activity was something that he actually *needed*, not just something he enjoyed. For him to miss a game…this couldn't be good.

Or was I just reading too much into the situation? Was I making it into a bigger problem than it truly was? Quite possible, although I had a sinking feeling in my stomach that I was right, and this was a huge issue. The commentators simply said he was a healthy scratch and left it at that. No reason was given for his absence.

Had the coaches benched him because he'd fouled up and taken too many penalties in the last game? I doubted it, because a couple of times they showed the other healthy scratches up in the press box, and he wasn't with them. That meant something else was going on—something he didn't want to talk about, if I took his lack of response to my messages at face value. And the fact that he didn't want to talk about it likely meant it was exactly what he *needed* to talk about.

Then again, there was a decent possibility that he might just not want to talk to *me* about it. If I kept trying to call and text him, would he see that as me nagging?

We weren't quite what I'd call a couple. Not yet, at least, and I wasn't sure we ever would be.

So far, we'd only gone on a date. Yes, he'd kissed me like I'd never been kissed before. But considering my lack of experience in that area, that wasn't exactly saying much.

Maybe I'd jumped the gun by getting my doctor to prescribe contraception. Maybe, now that he'd been close enough to kiss me, he'd also been able to feel my loose skin and lumpy, bumpy spots, all my flaws that my clothes tended to disguise, and he didn't want to have anything else to do with me, but he just didn't want to tell me so. Saying something like that to a person's face wasn't easy for anyone, and for someone like Blake, who already struggled with tact... He'd probably just want to cut me off without another word.

But he hadn't seemed disgusted by me. Had he? Was I just blinded by my own lust and therefore incapable of seeing the truth of the situation? That was a distinct possibility. My Male Interest Radar had never been trained to function properly, and it was a bit late in life to give it a tune-up.

Honestly, I needed to talk to someone like Dani about this. Dating and relationships—these weren't areas of strength for me. I mean, I'd had a date to my senior prom in high school, but we'd gone as friends—two outcasts who wouldn't have gone otherwise. Since then? Nothing until Blake.

Only, now that I thought about it, maybe Dani wasn't my best option for that sort of advice. She'd likely flip out if I let her know that he'd kissed me.

But who, then?

I tended to keep my relationships with my coworkers strictly professional. We might ask one another how our families were after a long holiday weekend, or sometimes a few teachers would get together on a Friday for happy hour drinks and appetizers at a chain restaurant near the school before heading home for the weekend—but we never talked about anything serious beyond work-related issues: the latest testing requirements, our upcoming in-service training, a book that someone had read with great ideas for changes to disciplinary structure.

Not anything *real*. Not anything about life. It was all about work.

Before I could second-guess myself, I was reaching for my phone and dialing my mother's number.

"Beatriz," she said, an admonishment in her tone. Like everyone in my family, she called me by my full name, pronouncing it in the traditional way. My friends and coworkers tended to shorten it and Americanize it. "You weren't here for your brother's birthday last week."

"I called him and wished him a happy birthday. I

explained that I had to work. He understood." And frankly, they should *all* understand. I lived and worked in Portland. I couldn't just head down to San Bernardino in the middle of the week any old time I wanted.

"Your abuelita expects you to be here next month for Paola's *quinceañera.*"

I rolled my eyes since Mama couldn't see me do it through the phone. "I'll be there. But you can let Abuelita know now that I won't be eating any of her tamales, or any of her *trés léchés*, or anything else she makes. I'm going to bring my own food." It'd be much safer that way—much less chance of me making myself sick by eating too much sugar or carbs or fat. I'd rather risk my grandmother's wrath any day than suffer a bout of dumping syndrome in the midst of my niece's big day. "But that's not what I'm calling about," I said, trying to shift the conversation in a (slightly) more favorable direction. Mom might not be on my side when it came to dealing with the family, but in the end, they all wanted the best for me. Or so I had to believe, and I did my best to convince myself of this on the regular. We just didn't always see eye to eye as far as what that might look like and how I should go about getting there. "I had something I wanted to ask you," I said.

"Hmm?" she replied. She sounded distracted more than miffed.

Understandable since she was planning my niece's quinceañera.

"I've started…dating someone, I guess," I hedged.

"Dating?" Suddenly, Mama's tone was sharp and clear, and in my mind's eye I could picture her sitting up straight and setting aside all the papers she'd been shuffling through. "Who is he? Have we met him? Your father and brother will need to approve of him."

Once again, I didn't bother trying to stop my eyes from rolling. "My father doesn't need to approve of anyone. And if he doesn't get to do that, there's no chance I'd let Miguel involve himself in my private life. None of you get any say in this, one way or another. I'm not a child."

"But—"

"But nothing, Mama. That's not what I'm calling you about, anyway, and if you intend to try to go there, I'll hang up and call someone else for my advice."

She took a moment to respond, and I could practically feel the wheels spinning in her mind. Finally, she said, "Advice? What sort of advice do you need?" Her query was filled with the sort of curiosity that meant she was fishing for fuel to start gossiping about my private life with the rest of the family as soon as we hung up the phone.

Which meant that now I needed to figure out how to word it…

"He has to travel a lot for his work," I started, avoiding the reason for his travel. Telling her that he was a professional athlete would be akin to inviting her disbelief and ridicule. Heck, even *I* had a hard time believing it, and I was the one experiencing it. "And something happened during his current work trip. I don't know what. But he's not at work anymore, and he's not answering me."

"Men don't like to be nagged, *mija*. They need their space. You know how your papa is when I try to remind him about mowing the lawn or raking the leaves."

"This isn't— This is different."

"Nagging is nagging is nagging. Doesn't matter what you're nagging about—the fact is you're doing it."

"But I'm worried that something is wrong."

"Men don't like to tell their women about their problems, *mija*. They like to think they can handle them all on their own."

"But I want to help him with whatever it is," I said. "I just don't know what it is, so I don't know how to help him."

"That's when you have to use your feminine wiles. You've got to figure out the problem. And then you have to find a way to help him without him realizing you're helping him. He needs to think he's strong. He needs to believe he can fix everything himself—including you. But really, you'll be taking care of him. That's how these things work. Men think they're taking the whole world on their shoulders, but women are the ones holding them up and keeping them from losing their grip."

"I don't know how to do that," I said. Especially not if I couldn't deal with my own issues. And we'd already established that, no matter how healthy I might be physically, I still had a world of problems to deal with on the emotional front. How could I be there for Blake—even if he finally answered—if I couldn't deal with my own crap?

But if he wouldn't answer, I supposed the point was moot.

"You'll find a way. That's what we do. We figure it out and make it happen, right? You need to come for a dress fitting this weekend," my mother said, already putting my problems to the side and moving back into the realm of my niece's quinceañera. "Paola wants all the women in the family to have dresses in the same color and the same fabric as her dress."

I groaned. "I'd rather have my friend make my dress." Dani might be confined to bed, but having a project like this to work on would give her something to do—and I could be sure it would be something more appropriate for my age and body than whatever the women of the Castillo family came up with when left to their own devices.

"You're coming," Mama said adamantly. "And you need to bring your man to the quinceañera. Your father needs to meet him. And so does your brother."

That could only be a disaster. Maybe it was for the best that Blake wouldn't answer me, after all. I could save him the horrors of meeting my entire extended family and having to navigate those waters.

Considering his ADHD and other issues, avoiding my family for as long as possible seemed like the best conceivable idea. I would be the only person in the bunch who had a tiny smidgeon of tact.

It was a disaster waiting to happen.

I had no intention of ruining Paola's quinceañera in that way. My own quinceañera had been enough of a disaster to fuel the family gossip mill for decades.

Blake

"You ever gonna answer all those calls and messages you keep getting?" Grandma demanded. It wasn't a question even if she worded it as one. That wasn't her style. Besides, she had always known she needed to take a firm hand with me, and that didn't seem to be fading even though her health was.

"They don't matter right now. The only thing that matters is you."

"Could be your team."

"They know where I am and why I'm here. They were the ones who approved it and made this happen. It's fine."

But that was a massive lie, whether Grandma knew it or not.

The truth was that nothing was fine, but Webs and Jim Sutter had both promised me that going to sit with my grandma for a few days when she was this sick wasn't going to cost me my place on the team. Webs had sworn he'd find a way to smooth things over with Bergy, even, but I wasn't going to hold my breath on that score. Our head coach had decided I was pond scum, and there wasn't anything I could do to change his mind.

Grandma hmphed. "I'm not going to die any quicker or slower if you ignore the rest of your life just because I'm sick, you know."

I'd been here for two days, sitting by her hospital bed, laughing at her awful jokes and the way she kept flirting with her favorite male nurse, holding her hand while they dug around in her arms to try to get in a new line after one of her veins gave out, and silently begging her to hold on just a little longer every time she failed to eat more than three bites of any meal they offered her.

"Don't make a joke of that, okay?" I said.

"Of what? Dying?"

"That's not a joke."

"Death is the biggest joke of them all. Everybody's going to die. God's going to get the last laugh."

"Yeah, but you're not allowed to die just yet. And it's not funny to me."

"Funniest thing going on in this room."

"No, the funniest thing going on in here is the way you keep yelling at your nurses because you hope they'll think you're a mean old lady so they'll send Brett back in here to deal with you."

"It works, doesn't it? Can't blame an old, dying lady for wanting a pretty face to look at while she gets her ass wiped."

"Stop saying that."

"What? You don't like hearing about Brett wiping my ass?"

"Stop saying you're dying," I begged.

"I need to say it. Because you need to hear it."

I scowled to fend off the stinging sensation that was clawing at the backs of my eyes. "You can't see his face when he's wiping your ass, anyway," I muttered, hoping to deflect her attention away from me.

"Sure I can. I can see it in my mind's eye. And he's pretty nice to look at no matter what he's doing."

"You're a mess."

"Takes one to know one."

I shot a look at her—the same sort of look she used to give me any time I was acting like a smartass around her. "Where do you think I got it?"

"Who's going to look after you when I'm gone?" she asked, flipping the subject again so fast I got whiplash from the speed of it.

"You're not going to be gone. You're not allowed to die."

"I'd say you should take that up with God, but I don't think He's going to make any exceptions to His rules just because I'm worried about you."

"Why the hell are you worried about me?" I almost choked on the words. "You're the one with cancer."

"And you're the one I'm leaving all alone when I go."

"I'm not a child."

"No, but everyone needs a parent sometimes. Even when they're all grown up. Even when they think they've got it all figured out. Hell, *especially* when they think they've got it all figured out, because that's when it all falls apart."

"The only thing falling apart around here is you."

"Liar."

The single word was full of so much love and heartbreak that I had to look away or else I'd fall to pieces and prove her point. I got up and crossed over to the other side of her bed and looked out the window, staring blankly at the season's first snow falling softly on the bare trees outside her room.

"You never have been able to lie to me, Blake. I'm glad that hasn't changed."

"Nothing's changed."

"Almost everything's changed. And it's all changing again. But you haven't."

Neither had she, nor her ability to see straight through me and get to the heart of whatever troubled me.

"I just want to know that you're going to be okay when I'm gone."

"How the hell am I supposed to be okay in a world without you in it?"

"You'll have to find a way." She reached for my hand and squeezed it with a surprising amount of strength, considering how frail and weak she'd become. "And maybe some of those people who keep calling you and sending you messages can help. Seems like you've got someone who cares. Maybe a lot of someones."

I shrugged, but I found myself facing her again, my back to the window, as I took out my phone and unlocked the screen.

There were several text messages and missed calls from a handful of my teammates, and one from Jim Sutter. I should probably listen to his message soon if nothing else. After all, whether Grandma lived or died, I needed to do whatever the hell I had to in order to keep my spot on the team.

But the only messages I seemed inclined to listen to or look at were those from Bea. And there were a lot of them. She'd called and left me two voice messages, and there was a long stream of text messages from her. They'd started out with her being concerned and asking me if I was all right. But somewhere along the line, her tone had gone from concerned to downright pissed off. The most recent one had her threatening to hunt me down and cut off my balls with a rusty spork courtesy of Dani Williams if I didn't respond to her soon, at least to tell her I was alive.

For some reason, that instantly warmed me up and made me laugh.

"What's got you smiling?" Grandma asked.

"Just a message from this woman I've been kind of seeing."

"One of your groupies?"

I raised a brow.

"You know. Your groupies. Don't you have any? I was sure you would."

"You mean puck bunnies? Chicks who want me just because I play hockey?" I did a double take. "What do you know about all that?"

"I wasn't born yesterday, if you haven't noticed. I might have been a groupie, once upon a time."

"If you're going to tell me you went on tour with the Beach Boys or some shi—"

"Led Zeppelin," she cut in. "But that was a long time ago."

I shuddered, thinking about my grandma getting on some skeevy tour bus. But then again, that sounded like exactly the sort of thing she might have done, once upon a time.

"Bea's not like that," I said. "She's different."

"Different how?" Grandma asked.

Different in all the best possible ways. But all I said was, "She's not chasing after me. I'm chasing after her."

Grandma narrowed her eyes and nodded. "I like the sounds of her already."

"You'd like her a lot, I think." I sat on the edge of Grandma's bed. The need to be as close to her as possible, for as long as I could, was heavy in my gut.

"And why's that?"

"Because she doesn't take any shit from me. She puts me in my place."

Grandma burst out laughing, long and full. She laughed so hard that she was gasping for air, and it set off several of her beeping machines, and the nurses rushed back into the room to make sure she wasn't dying. She shooed them away once she'd recovered and they managed to get the machines under control again.

One of them gave me a nasty look on her way out the door.

"Ignore that bitch," Grandma said. "She thinks that

since I'm dying, I shouldn't have any fun. But that's bullshit. I want to go out having fun. I want to live every minute of the rest of my life the way I've always lived it."

"Yeah, but the point is they're trying to keep you *alive*."

She waved a dismissive hand. "Back to you. So if you're getting messages from this woman, and she makes you smile, and she's not a groupie or a puck bunny, and you think I'd like her…why aren't you calling her back? Why haven't you talked to her since you got here? Did you even bother to tell her what's going on, or did you just zero in on getting here to sit by my sick bed and nag me about listening to the nurses?"

I glowered at Grandma even as I took out my phone and pulled up Bea's number to call her. I thought about leaving the room to make my call, but Grandma would just dig it all out of me afterward, anyway. No point trying to hide anything from that woman. She knew all the right buttons to push and when to push them to get her way.

"Hey," Bea said breathlessly into the phone the moment she answered. "Sorry about the rusty spork thing, but I was running out of ideas for how to get you to respond, and I've been worried. Dani suggested it and I didn't take the time to come up with anything better even though that was probably a bad idea. But I thought I'd done something to upset you. I didn't—"

"You didn't do anything," I cut in, and already my throat started to close on me. But if I didn't get it out now, I wasn't sure I'd ever be able to, so I pressed on. "I'm in New York. My grandma's sick, and I— I just— I can't."

"She's sick?" Bea said. "Sick how?"

"Cancer." The word was like gravel in my throat. "Her cancer's back."

"Oh, God, Blake. I'm sorry. Is there anything I can do? Is there anything you need?"

"You," I said before I could think better of it. "I need you."

Chapter Twelve

Bea

In all my years of teaching, I'd never used any of the vacation time I'd accumulated, and I'd only used a handful of my sick days over that same span. Since my gastric bypass was an elective procedure, I'd been able to schedule it over my summer vacation. I did my best to schedule all of my follow-up appointments on days that school was out or after school hours so that I wouldn't have to miss any more time with my students than was absolutely necessary. Because of my stinginess with taking time off, I had a lot of paid leave waiting to be used, and I had a good excuse in my arsenal for getting the time off approved.

Before I could think better of it, I'd arranged for a neighbor to take care of Neville and Luna for a while and I was on a flight to the East Coast without a clue as to what I'd do with myself once I arrived. But once Blake had said he needed me, it hadn't even crossed my mind to stay home.

This was the first time I'd flown anywhere since my weight loss. I wasn't prepared for the elation at being able to fasten the safety belt without requiring an extender; it was nice to forgo the uncomfortable process of requesting one from the flight attendants.

I spent the majority of the flight working on marking papers and lesson planning, because I didn't know how much time I'd be able to devote to work once I arrived in New York. My inclination was that once I arrived, I would devote as many of my waking hours as possible to keeping Blake calm and helping him with caring for his grandma as well as I could. Any work I could do on the plane would quite possibly be the only work I'd get done until I returned to Portland.

I barely noticed the passage of time on the flight because I was so consumed by my work, and before I knew it, we were landing.

Blake was waiting by the baggage carousel, looking haggard and exhausted. I headed straight for him, letting go of my grip on my carry-on suitcase as I reached for him.

He wrapped me up in his arms and lifted me off my feet in his enthusiasm to see me—which was a first for me. Or at least the first time any man had lifted me off my feet since I was a little girl. I'd been too large—and too self-conscious—to allow any man to do anything of the sort for a very long time.

I felt guilty over the thrill I experienced at the sensation, because this wasn't supposed to be about me at all. I was here to comfort him. Nothing more than that. But the thrill was there, nonetheless, washing over me and leaving me breathless and tingling in all sorts of uncomfortable and private places.

He buried his face against my neck, holding me tight around the waist, and kept the length of my body pressed alongside him so that I couldn't help but feel all his muscles, his strength. It was a sharp contrast to my soft rolls and bulges. For a moment, self-consciousness threatened to overwhelm me. But then he let out a choking sound that had to be a stifled sob, and I forgot all about myself.

"Hey," I said, my voice dry and husky after the flight. I loosened my grip on his shoulders, wrapping my arms fully around his neck in an effort to soothe him. "It'll be okay. You're going to be okay."

"I'm not. Not if I lose her."

"You will. Because you won't ever lose her if you remember everything she taught you and all the ways she's loved you. But you've still got her now, anyway."

"I do. For now. But it won't be for much longer."

"The doctors don't think there's any hope?"

He finally released his grip on me. Instantly, I felt the loss of his arms and his presence. It seeped through my body and left me feeling as heavy as I'd been years ago as I settled back on my own feet.

"She's got months. Maybe only weeks. Hard to say for sure, but it's not enough time no matter how long it is."

I nodded, at a loss. There were no words appropriate for a time like this. "We should get you back to the hospital, then. You should be with her as much as you can."

He nodded, hugging me tight again, the scratch of stubble thick against my neck. This time, he didn't release me for long moments. When he finally did, he picked up my carryon bag and took my hand firmly in his, and he led me out to a waiting cab.

......

Blake's grandmother was asleep when we arrived at the hospital, so we opted not to wake her. Blake took up a chair next to her bed, so he could be right by her side if she woke and needed anything; I took out some work and sat next to the window, giving them as much privacy as I could while still sneaking the occasional surreptitious glance to catch him holding her hand even as they both dozed. Needless to say, my efforts at working weren't going very well. I couldn't concentrate. I couldn't focus on *anything* other than Blake and the way he worried over his grandmother.

This was a side of him I'd never seen before. She brought out a sweetness in him that was lacking in most areas of his life—or at least in those that I'd seen. The only experience I'd had with him that came close was when he'd been with my students, but even that was on a much different playing field than this.

Watching them this way made my heart ache for him. It was obvious that she was the best thing he had going in his life. Yes, he had a dream job and all the money he could ever need, but work and money weren't terribly important when it came down to the nitty gritty. If anyone knew that, it was me. I loved my job. I adored my kids. But that wasn't enough to fulfill the deepest longings in my heart.

Family, friends—love. Those were the big things. The ones that mattered.

Blake's grandmother was his heart. And he was about to lose her.

After a while, the soft hum of his snoring joined the beeping and whirring machines as the only sounds in the room. He was bent over the side of her bed, resting his head on his folded arms, much as some of my students would do during nap time. It looked uncomfortable, but I didn't have the heart to wake him and encourage him to move.

With any luck, he wouldn't have too many aches and pains later. Something told me the ache in his heart would be a thousand times worse than any crick in his neck, anyway, and he needed these moments to be close to her regardless of the personal cost to himself.

But when I glanced back up at his grandmother's face, I found dark eyes—his eyes in her face—blinking at me. She lifted one hand to her mouth and held a single finger to her lips, saying, "Shh," and then pointing down at her sleeping grandson.

I nodded, a smile coming unbidden to my own face. That was such a motherly move. Maybe he hadn't come from her womb, and maybe she was technically his grandmother, but in all the important ways, she was his mother. Their bond was as plain as day.

"He hasn't slept in two days," she said softly. "Don't want to wake him just yet."

"He's been too worried about you."

"You're Bea? You're the non-groupie?"

"Non-groupie?" I spluttered, trying to keep my amusement down since he was still sleeping.

"He said you're the real deal, not a puck bunny or something."

"I don't even know what a puck bunny is."

"Then you probably aren't one. That's good. He needs someone stable in his life. You're stable? You've got a good job, a family, that sort of thing?"

"I'm a teacher—"

"Then you know all about hard work," she cut in.

"Yes, ma'am."

"I'm not a ma'am. That makes me feel old. I don't

like feeling old."

I stifled a laugh because I didn't want risk her wrath if I accidentally woke Blake. "Then what should I call you?"

"Lil is fine. Or Lillian if you want to be formal, but I don't go in for formal. Not enough time for that shit."

"All right, Lil it is."

We'd only known one another for a few minutes, but I could already see so much of her in Blake. She'd obviously played a huge role in shaping him into the man he was.

"He tell you much about his parents?"

I shook my head. "Only that you raised him."

"They're in prison. Drug stuff. His mother was using while she was pregnant with him. When the authorities came in to arrest them, they found Blake crawling around with the stuff all over the floor. He had to go through detox when he was just a baby. It's why he is the way he is."

"But you've loved him anyway."

"Course I do. He's my grandson. It's not his fault he was born to parents who were addicts. I love his mother, too, even though she doesn't recognize it. She thinks love is letting her do all the shit she wants to do, even if it kills her. But I loved her better by forcing her to get clean through sending her to prison. They never see things that way, though. It's one of the symptoms of the disease. Addiction," she added, in case I hadn't followed. Then she narrowed her eyes at me, and for a moment I thought she was about to nod off and sleep again. But finally, she spoke again. "You think you can love him? You think you can see through the surface shit he does and understand who he is underneath it all?"

I blinked back my surprise at her frankness. But I had to admit, her direct path to the heart of the matter, and her honesty, were refreshing. "I have my own issues I'm trying to sort through," I admitted, because she deserved nothing less than the full truth.

"Everyone's got crap to deal with. Means you're human."

"True," I said with a grin.

"And?"

"But I think we're working on becoming…something."

"Something," she repeated with an arched brow that turned her statement into a question.

"I don't know what we're doing. I don't know what I want it to be. It's all new for me."

"You haven't ever been married before?"

I shook my head. "Never even dated anyone, to be honest. Not until Blake."

"Why not?"

"Because I was always fat before and I didn't think anyone could love me that way," I found myself saying, without any understanding of why I would say these things to a complete stranger. But the truth was she was dying. If ever there was someone to whom it would be safe to spill my guts, it would be her.

"Didn't think you deserved it?" she demanded.

I shook my head, hot tears springing to my eyes. "I didn't even love myself, so how could anyone else love me?"

"They couldn't. You wouldn't let them."

"I suppose I wouldn't."

"But do you love yourself now?"

"I'm trying to."

"He'll love you to pieces if you'll let him," she said.

"He hasn't had many people to love in his life, and even fewer have taken the time and effort required to see past the surface. But when he loves someone, it's full tilt. He can't turn it off. He'll give it everything he has and more than he should sometimes, forgetting to take care of himself in the process. If he's going to love you like that, you'd better be ready to believe you deserve it. Because I won't be around much longer. He's going to devote it all to someone else soon. And he wants that someone to be you. Do you think he's made a good choice?"

"I'm not sure. I hope so."

"Hmph. Why the hell did you come here if you weren't already all in? Maybe you don't realize it yet. Maybe you just need a nudge. And maybe this is your nudge."

Maybe indeed.

Blake

I woke with a start, then wished I hadn't jerked myself awake because I had a crick in my neck and the sudden movement made it hurt like hell.

I moaned, but then I wished I hadn't, because it seemed to disturb Grandma's sleep. She twitched, and her eyes started moving fast behind her closed eyelids.

"She finally nodded off again about ten minutes ago," Bea said quietly. "The nurse came in and gave her some more meds through the IV."

"You should've woke me up."

"She wanted you to sleep. She said it's almost the only sleep you've had in days."

"I don't need to sleep."

"You do if you're going to be any good for her."

She had a point, but I didn't want to concede it. I glowered over at her.

"When's the last time you had anything to eat?" she asked.

I shrugged, but my stomach growled.

"That's what I thought. Come on." She stood up and set her work on the chair she'd been sitting in, and then she held out a hand for me. "You've got to take care of yourself or you won't be able to support her."

"I don't know how to take care of myself. That's her job."

"You've been taking care of yourself for as long as you've been in the NHL. She already taught you everything she can teach you. Now it's time for you to use all the things you've learned from her."

"I don't want to."

"Life doesn't ask you what you want or what you think you can handle. Life just throws a bunch of things at us and we have to find a way to dodge the worst of the blows and to survive the ones we can't avoid." Bea reached down and grabbed my hand since I still hadn't taken hers, and she tugged me to my feet with a surprising amount of strength. "You've got to eat. You won't be any good to her if you don't take care of yourself."

Begrudgingly, I found myself walking beside her through the halls of the hospital. It was a good thing she was paying attention to where she was going, because I sure as hell wasn't. Within a few minutes, she led me into the cafeteria and took me straight to the salad bar. When I didn't immediately start building a salad, she placed a plate in my hands and gave me a pointed look before picking up another one for herself and piling it high with fresh spinach, ham, and chopped egg.

I wasn't capable of deciding what I wanted to eat just now, so I copied what she was doing, filling my own plate with the same things she'd selected. Once we'd added salad dressing and grabbed bottles of water from a fridge case, she took me to the counter so we could pay for our meals.

She started to reach into her purse, but I managed to regain my focus just in time to dig my wallet out of my pocket and press a credit card into the cashier's hands.

"I'll pay for your flights, too," I said when she shot a questioning look up at me. "And hotel. You wouldn't be here if I wasn't a basket case."

"You're not a basket case."

"Close enough. But either way, I'm paying."

She nodded as the cashier finished ringing up our purchases. Then we carried them to a table and sat down to eat.

"Thanks," she murmured.

"Thank *you*," I said. "I can't go through this alone."

"You don't have to. You're not alone, Blake."

"I know. I just…" I shrugged because the words got stuck in my throat and refused to move either up or down. They just lodged themselves there.

"You feel alone. You feel like you've got the whole world on your shoulders and you don't know how you're going to manage it."

I nodded, staring at my salad even though I couldn't take a bite.

"You're not alone. I'm here with you. And you've got your team to help out, too." She reached across the table and took my hand, squeezing it. "You're not alone," she repeated.

Maybe if she said it enough times, the words would sink in. Maybe I'd start to believe them. Doubtful, but it was worth hoping for.

"Should I get an Uber to take me to a hotel in a bit? I haven't reserved a room yet since I just booked the flights and came straight out, but—"

"You don't need to get a room," I cut in.

"But…" She blinked at me.

"You can stay with me. Or I'll pay for your room if you don't want to do that," I amended because I suddenly realized that was really presumptuous. "I mean, I'd like you to stay with me, but I understand if you—"

"I'll stay with you," she said.

"You don't have to."

"I know that. But I want to."

"Good," I said, but what I really meant was *thank fuck* because I didn't know if I could get through another night on my own when I was so worried about Grandma. I really meant what I'd said in that call: I needed Bea. I needed her now, and I knew I'd still need her in my life later on—especially after Grandma died. And it wasn't just because I was a fucking wreck and didn't know how to take care of myself.

I needed Bea because I was falling in love with her, and there weren't too fucking many people in my life I could say I loved.

There were even fewer who would say it in return. Probably just Grandma, to be honest. But considering Bea had dropped everything and jumped on a plane across the country to be with me, I had a bit of hope that maybe she could fall in love with me someday, too.

We didn't talk much for the rest of our meal. Didn't really need to. Usually, I'd be cracking jokes right and left, but I just didn't have it in me right now. But Bea didn't seem to mind. She just stayed by my side, solid as a rock, her presence keeping me calm when my mind was like a tempest.

When we returned to Grandma's room a bit later, she was awake again—probably because they were taking her vitals, changing out her IV bag, and shooting her up with more medications.

"You two need to get the hell out of here," she barked as soon as she saw me walk through the door to her room. "You look like death warmed over. Got a bit more color than you did earlier. I guess she fed you?"

"She did," I admitted.

"Good. Then she's got more sense than you. Now go sleep. That's all I'm going to be doing anyway. At least I will be once they stop poking me."

"I'd rather stay here with you," I argued, but it was only a feeble attempt on my part. And it wasn't entirely true. There was a very large part of me that wanted to spend every possible moment I could with Grandma. But there was another part of me that realized she was right, and I needed some rest in order to make the most of those moments I had with her.

"Do what you came here for, Bea," Grandma said pointedly. "Take care of my boy."

I shot a look in Bea's direction. She shrugged it off. Apparently I wouldn't be getting any answers from her.

But I was practically dead on my feet, and if I didn't get some decent rest soon, I wouldn't be any use to anyone. The meal had helped, but it had also forced me to recognize I was nearing the boundaries of my own limitations.

I bent over Grandma's bed and kissed her on the cheek. "We'll be back in the morning. Call me if you need anything."

"I need that male nurse to come back. Can you arrange for that to happen? He needs to help me with my bed pan or something."

Bea chuckled, and I couldn't seem to stop myself from laughing, too. I narrowed my eyes at Grandma. "I'm being serious here."

"So am I."

"Mm hmm." I straightened away from her bed, stretching my back. "I'm going to stop by the nurse's station on our way out of here and tell them to keep him away from you because you're going to sexually harass him and I don't want to deal with a lawsuit."

"You go right ahead and do that, Blakey. That might just get him to come see me more often."

I grabbed the handle of Bea's suitcase in one hand, took hold of her hand with my other, and led her out of Grandma's hospital room, the sound of Grandma's gleeful cackle following us all the way to the elevator bay.

"I like her," Bea said softly once the elevator doors closed us in.

"I love her," I replied, my voice cracking. "And she's all I've got."

"She's not all you've got," Bea said, reaching for my hand.

There was a part of me that hoped I could believe her.

But there was a bigger part of me that knew the truth: only Grandma had ever loved me before—no one else. I didn't see that changing any time soon. It didn't matter whether I loved Bea or not. That just wasn't the way my life worked.

Chapter Thirteen

Bea

Blake was so exhausted—probably both from a lack-of-sleep standpoint and an emotional one—that he fell asleep almost as soon as we arrived at the hotel room, collapsing on top of the blankets instead of tucking himself in. I did my best to make him comfortable, taking off his shoes and wrapping one of the blankets around him, but I didn't want to do too much and disturb his nap. The thing he needed most now was rest, even if he wasn't in an ideal position to get it.

Then I turned off most of the lights in the room and drew the curtains closed to block the light coming in from the street lamps and cars passing by. I always slept better in the dark, so I assumed he would, as well.

While he slept, I set myself up at the desk and lit a single lamp near me, primarily using the light of my laptop screen, and I knocked out some lesson planning for next week. Since I wasn't sure how long I'd be staying with Blake, I needed to design lessons that a substitute could easily follow, while still making sure they would be beneficial to my students—but also something I could modify to suit my own teaching strengths in case I returned soon enough to present the lessons myself.

The school secretary had assured me that they'd arranged for an experienced, quality substitute teacher, but I wasn't so sure about all of that. Most of my colleagues complained about the lack of instruction their subs could provide while they were out. How much of that was due to their students thinking they could goof off and how much was due to the substitutes' inability to control a classroom was debatable.

I'd planned three days' worth of lessons and emailed them in to the school by the time I found Blake blinking at me from the bed. The heavy sounds of his breathing had slowed so gradually that I hadn't noticed the change to recognize that he was awake until I found those dark eyes fixated on me.

"How long have you been awake?" I asked, saving my work and closing my laptop.

He shrugged, which shifted the blankets until they fell off his upper body, revealing the rippling muscles of his chest and forearms tugging against his T-shirt. Then he rolled over onto his side to face me. "Didn't want to bother you. You looked busy. And I know you had to drop everything to be here with me."

"I wouldn't mind the distraction, to be honest. Work can wait."

"You look cute when you work. You scrunch up

your face when you're thinking. Makes me want to kiss the tip of your nose."

An unexpected thrill shot through my body, settling heavily in my belly. I couldn't quite catch my breath.

"You need to keep working?" he asked.

"I can take a break." My whole body started tingling with anticipation—but I wasn't sure what I was anticipating.

Shifting his body in the bed, he inched back and patted the space where he'd been, in a clear invitation to join him.

My stomach jumped into my throat, but I set my laptop aside and crossed over to sit on the edge of the mattress. The space he'd vacated was warm from his body, seductively urging me closer to his heat. But my unease wouldn't allow me to settle in or get too comfortable. I held myself rigidly away from him, forcing myself into an unnaturally straight posture.

"Closer," he said. "I want you to lie down with me."

"I'm nervous." The truth rushed from my lips before I could stop it, and I shivered even though I wasn't cold.

"I won't bite," he teased. Then he winked, lacing the strong fingers of one of his hands through mine. "Unless you ask me to. If you want that sort of thing, I'm game."

I studied the joining of our hands. His grip was so solid and sure. My hand seemed small and weak, further emphasized by my clammy palm. But I had to give myself a mental shake to break out of the stupor that had suddenly claimed me from the realization that I'd never looked at any part of my body before and found it to be small.

"I don't know what I want," I said, but it was a lie.

"What do you want?"

The crease between his brows when I glanced up at his face again told me he knew it for the lie it was. His dark eyes were so serious as he studied me. "Guess it's a good thing for both of us that I know what I want."

"What?" My voice cracked, and the word was almost inaudible.

"I want you."

His admission reverberated in my mind, banging against the walls of my brain like a pinball bouncing in an arcade game. But even though I was desperate for it to be the truth, as he slipped a hand behind my neck and drew me closer, there was a voice in the back of my mind shouting that it was a lie.

That didn't stop me from wanting him, though.

But a moment of clarity washed over me, and I put a hand on his chest to stop him. "I got birth control, but it's not effective yet," I found myself saying, heat rushing all over my body and especially to my cheeks. "We can't— We need condoms. Do you have any here?"

He shook his head.

"Then we can't—"

"I don't need a condom to make you come. Let me make you come."

"Oh," I said, a wispy sound that was mostly breath.

As his tongue teased the seam of my lips, begging entry, the voice yelled that no man could ever truly want me like that. No man could want to give me pleasure unless he was getting something out of it, too. And what could Blake possibly be getting out of this? As I opened and gave in to the heady pleasure of his tongue gliding against mine and his powerful hand inching up my rib cage and tugging the fabric of my shirt along with it, his fingers dusting my bare skin, the voice turned shrill and panicky.

"Stop." I grabbed hold of his wrist, halting his progress before he uncovered any more of my loose, sagging skin. "Hold on for a minute."

"I'm sorry." His apology was out before he even knew what the problem was, as if by rote, as though he assumed that he'd done something wrong.

But this wasn't anything he'd done. This was all me. All my own insecurities and fears. "Don't be sorry," I choked out.

Confusion clouded his eyes.

"The lights," I explained. "I just need to turn out the lights."

"I want to see you."

Hot tears of shame sprang to my eyes. I didn't even know why I should feel ashamed, but I did. My mortification slogged through my veins like cooling tar. "I can't. I need it to be— Please." The whispered words crackled with an electric sort of ache in the silence.

For far too long, he studied me, his dark brow creased with a combination of concern and confusion that made me want to get up and rush from the room without looking back. But then he kissed the bridge of my nose before reaching for the switch next to the bed, cloaking us in darkness. "Better?" he asked.

A hint of light peeked in through the curtains, but I could only make out shadows—nothing solid or substantial. Almost immediately, my unease started to dissipate. "Better," I replied, my nerves still going haywire but no longer threatening to send me into full-blown panic.

He touched his lips softly to mine, a tender,

featherlight brush of warm flesh that was gone before I could adjust. "Can I touch you now?" he murmured. "I want to touch you. I want to make you come. Is that all right?"

"Yes." I could barely hear my reply over the pounding of my pulse, so I reached for his hand and guided it back to where it'd been before I'd had my minor freak-out.

The heat of his palm seared my skin, working better than any of Dani's warming fabrics had ever done. He splayed his fingers along my ribs, slowly inching toward my breast. I moaned against his lips when he squeezed me through the stretchy fabric of my bra. I couldn't breathe at all when his thumb and fingers found my hard nipple and gave it a pinch. There was a hint of pain, but it wasn't much and I welcomed it because of the heady pleasure that followed soon afterward; my entire body leaned in toward him almost of its own volition, silently begging for more.

"I want to take your clothes off," he murmured, his lips pressed to my forehead. "I want to taste you everywhere. I want to suck your tits and rub your clit and make you come all over my hand. All over my tongue."

For whatever reason, those words had my body thrumming with an unfamiliar ache. Some unknown force had me reaching for the hem of my shirt and lifting it up and over my head.

Blake helped me free the shirt from my arms. He tossed the fabric to the floor and leaned over me until my back and shoulders hit the mattress, and he licked a path from my jaw to my collarbone that left me shuddering.

"You taste good," he murmured, and his fingers

were unhooking the clasp of my bra. "Your skin's so fucking sweet."

As soon as the fabric was free from my body, my breasts slumped to the sides and my hyperaware self-consciousness returned full force. I tried to contain them, to cover them up, but Blake was faster than I was. He took one in each hand, gently cupping them as my nipples drew up and hardened against his palms.

Thank God I'd insisted on keeping the lights off. I couldn't bear the thought of him witnessing my embarrassment. The idea of him seeing the way they flopped around was just— I couldn't even let myself go there.

He kept kissing my collarbone, gradually moving lower, alternately suckling and nibbling and licking my skin until I was tingling all over, my body straining up for more of his touch. When his tongue circled one of my nipples, a moan fell from my lips that made it sound like it'd been ripped from the dead.

"Oh, God," I cried. "I didn't know it could feel like that." I'd touched myself before—I mean, who hadn't?—but this was different than anything I'd ever done on my own, or anything I'd ever dreamed of, for that matter. Nothing could have prepared me for the sensations roaring through my body.

But he didn't back off at all, chuckling against my skin as he suckled my tit between his lips until I was squirming to get away even though I was frantic for more.

With lips and teeth and tongue, he made a trail down my belly, stopping at my waistband. "Can I take these off?" he asked, his fingers hovering over the button and zipper of my jeans.

Agreeing, I lifted my hips to help him in removing

them before my nerves could kick in to stop me.

It only took him a couple of quick tugs to have my jeans and panties all the way down my legs. He tossed them somewhere and bent over me, and then his hot mouth and authoritative hands were on me.

He pushed my thighs up and spread them apart, leaving me completely open. But he had to be able to feel the loose skin drooping all over the place. I wanted to shove him away, but he swirled a pointed tongue over my clit, and I forgot all about my unease.

He used his lips and tongue in sinful ways.

I was lost. A total goner.

Whatever mortification I had been feeling dissipated almost as quickly as it had built, because Blake's wicked tongue took over my brain.

My toes curled, and I made a fist in the sheets because I thought I might come up off the bed if he didn't stop soon, but I didn't want him to stop. He slipped a finger inside me, then added a second, curling them up and brushing them gently against some wonderful, unknown spot. The suction of his lips on my clitoris was more than I could take. My hips rocked up off the bed, as if seeking something elusive of their own accord, and then it hit me like a firecracker of sensation down below. A zing of electricity followed by boneless weightlessness.

I was well and truly spent.

I'd never felt weightless before. I was always overly conscious of my weight, my body.

After a minute, Blake shifted his body up mine to lie next to me. I was limp and slack everywhere, all my recently discovered muscles having had enough for now, but he dragged me up against him. I wrapped my limbs around him and held on with all the strength I could muster.

His warmth was addictive. His scent was a drug.

He trailed the fingers of one hand lazily through the thick waves of my hair while I tried to remember how to breathe. I was a lot more active these days than I ever used to be, but even though I'd been lying down through the whole thing, that had been one heck of a workout. I needed time to catch my breath.

"You ever make yourself come like that before?" he asked after a couple of minutes.

Good thing the lights were out so he couldn't see my embarrassment. "Not quite like that," I hedged.

He chuckled, a deep, rich, cocky sound that made me want to give him cause for a laugh like that more often. He tugged me closer until I was practically halfway on top of him. His body was all muscle beneath me. Solid, hot, addictive muscle—so completely different from my body of mush.

"I want to make it happen more often," he said into the dark. "I could get addicted to making you come."

Our intimate proximity made me self-conscious, particularly since I was naked and covered in sweat and he was still fully clothed. I shifted, angling myself away from him slightly, but Blake only tugged me closer. He dragged me all the way on top of him. The heat of his very hard erection pulsed against my belly. I felt guilty that he hadn't found any relief yet, but I wasn't sure what I should do about it.

I licked my lips for courage. "Tell me what to do."

"Hmm?"

He brushed my hair back from my face, so I propped my head up and looked down into his eyes.

"Tell me what you want. What you want me to do," I repeated.

"You don't have to do anything."

"But I want to…help you," I said for want of a better word.

It was hard to be sure in the dark, but it seemed like the hint of a smug smile crossed his features.

"You have no idea how fucking hot it is to hear you talking like that."

Yet again, I was glad of the dark. "So? Where do I start?"

"Will you touch me?"

"How?"

He held out a hand. "Give me your hand."

Trying not to shake, I put mine in his. He guided it down to the bulge in his pants. He was a lot harder than I'd expected, and there was so much heat warming my palm.

I trailed my fingertips over the smooth fabric.

"Fuck, baby," he murmured, burying his face in my hair. "I can't even begin to tell you how bad I've been wanting you to touch me."

"Like this?" I asked.

"Harder. Squeeze me."

I added more pressure, and he groaned against the side of my head.

"I want—" I cut myself off, not sure how to ask. "Can you take off your pants?" I finally spluttered.

"Fuck yes." In about three seconds flat, he'd whipped off his clothes, underwear and all, and tossed them onto the floor, barely dislodging me in the process.

As soon as he resettled on the bed, he wrapped an arm around my waist and dragged me up against him, my totally bare flesh to his essentially-bare flesh. But now my nerves were going haywire. I was naked. He might as well be, because his shirt wasn't doing much to cover him.

"Show me what you want," I said.

"You don't have to do any—"

"I want to," I cut in. "I want this. But I need you to show me. Take my hand and show me."

I was sure he was going to get frustrated by my inexperience and roll away from me or something, but he surprised me by taking my hand in his and guiding it to his erection. He closed my fingers around his length. The heat and smoothness of his skin surprised me.

"Now what?" I asked.

"Squeeze me a little—not too hard."

"Like this?" I added a bit of pressure.

He groaned. "A little more. And then stroke me up and down."

His skin moved like hot, satiny velvet beneath my touch, gliding over the firmness beneath the surface. I still wasn't sure what I'd been expecting him to feel like, but this definitely wasn't it. This was…nice.

"Tell me if I hurt you," I said.

"Baby, you're hurting me, but it's the best kind of pain. You can always hurt me like this. Anytime you want to."

For some reason, that sent a tingle of excitement up my spine. I stroked his length a few times, my boldness growing every time he made a sound. And there were so many sounds—sharp intakes of breath, unintelligible moans, guttural requests for me to stroke him faster. Within a couple of minutes, there was a sheen of sweat covering him, and his hips were rocking up into my hand.

His hand locked into a knot of my thick curls, he

kissed me hard; I tasted my own musk on his tongue.

"Faster," he murmured against my lips, so I stroked him faster. He dove into my hair with both hands, holding my head captive as he kissed me like no man had ever kissed me before. "You're driving me crazy in the best possible way." And then he let out a muffled shout and went still.

Warm, sticky fluid coated my palm.

"Sorry," he said after a moment. "I should've warned you I was coming. Should've gotten a tissue or something."

But I shook my head and disengaged from him, getting up from the bed. "It's all right. I just need to…" The thought trailed off, but he didn't need me to finish it. Did he? But whether he did or not, I couldn't speak anymore. The simple act of finding my voice would require more dignity than I had left.

After gathering up my clothes, I headed into the bathroom. I shut the door behind me before turning on the lights, because I didn't want to risk him seeing any part of my naked body. After rinsing my hand in the sink, I turned on the shower, cranking it up almost as hot as it would go, as if the heat could wash away all the crap going on in my head.

One thing no one ever told me was how messy sex was. And this wasn't even true sex—just a hand job and some oral.

But the physical mess was nothing compared to the chaos taking place in my mind.

I'd let him touch me. I'd allowed him to feel all my loose skin, the permanent, sagging, disgusting reminder of how huge and repulsive I'd once been.

And at least in my own mind, the way I looked without my clothes on now was even more hideous than the way I'd looked at my heaviest. I was like a bald cat—ugly and creepy, but no one would ever be able to look away due to sheer fascination about how skin could droop and hang like that. Their curiosity about the folds and wrinkles and whatnot would eventually outweigh their disgust, and they'd stare.

He would stare.

Never again would I be able to sense his eyes on me and believe he was looking for any reason other than disgust, or maybe some sick sense of fascination. But certainly never with any semblance of desire.

I stood beneath the hot spray of water, my eyes closed, allowing it to wash away the tears I'd been holding in.

How would I ever look him in the eye again now that he *knew* and it wasn't just something he kind of understood but not really? The state of my body wasn't the sort of thing anyone could grasp until they'd witnessed it with their own eyes or touched it with their own hands.

Now he knew.

But I probably didn't need to worry about facing him, because I doubted he'd even attempt to look in my eyes again. Even now, he was probably packing away my things and calling down to the front desk to arrange for another room for me.

If Dani ever found out about any part of this whole debacle, she'd be saying "I told you so," for years.

Nothing to worry about, Dani, I thought to myself as the water did what little it could to cleanse the awful thoughts from my mind. *He won't have a chance to hurt me. I'll take care of that well enough on my own.*

I always did, after all.

Chapter Fourteen

Blake

I'd gone and fucked up again, and I didn't have the first clue what I'd done wrong this time. Bea had been almost in tears when she'd scurried off to the bathroom—I could sense her distress in the air between us even if I couldn't see the shimmering evidence of it for myself.

The temptation to follow her into the bathroom and refuse to leave until she filled me in as to how I'd screwed myself over nearly overwhelmed me, but I forced myself to give her some privacy. I owed her that much and so, so much more.

I flipped on the lights, dragged on a pair of shorts, and tried to tidy up the room a bit while she was in the bathroom, attempting to distract myself by keeping busy. It didn't take me very long to clean up the random pieces of clothing we'd tossed, though, and soon I was wishing I had something to do with myself again—maybe one of the coloring books or some crocheting—*something*. But all I had was my phone.

I'd left the coloring books I'd brought with on the road trip in Grandma's room in the hospital, thinking they'd be of more use to me there while I sat by her bed and she slept. Should've brought them with me, even though I hadn't realized it at the time.

Just served as further proof that I was an idiot. Not that there'd been any lack of evidence on that score.

Taking out my phone, I pulled up a mind-numbing game app to try to waste some time and entertain myself for a bit, but it didn't help much. None of these games required enough thought to be a true distraction. I closed that first one down and opened up a nine-by-nine Sudoku puzzle, hoping that would do the trick until Bea returned and I could apologize for being an ass.

She was in the bathroom for a long time—well after the water had shut off and I'd completed probably twenty or more Sudoku puzzles, because they didn't present enough of a challenge to me anymore. I had to fight off the urge to barge into the bathroom and demand answers, but obviously acting on my impulses was a bad idea, especially when it came to this relationship.

I only ended up getting myself into trouble when I did things like that.

When she finally came out again, I tossed my phone on the bed and tried to prepare myself for the tongue-lashing I'd earned.

But she didn't give me one.

"You should shower and get dressed so we can get you something to eat," she said without bothering to look at me. She started folding up the clothes I'd set on the foot of the bed, tidying things up beyond what I'd already done while she showered. "And then tomorrow we can go back to the hospital to see your grandmother again. Unless you want to go back tonight? What time are visitation hours over? I'm sure she'd like that, now that you've gotten a bit of rest. Does this hotel have a restaurant downstairs, or—"

"Bea," I cut in. I wasn't even sure what I wanted to say—just that I needed to say something to dig myself out of the hole I'd apparently buried myself in.

"Hmm?" She folded my shirt into a tidy square and fastidiously set it on top of my already folded jeans, studiously avoiding my gaze.

"Do I need to apologize?" I asked. "Because it definitely feels that way."

"You don't need to apologize."

I only wished I could believe her.

The hollow tone she'd used and the fact that she still wouldn't look at me, though? Between those two things, there wasn't a chance in hell I'd believe her words.

Especially not once she turned away from the bed and started packing up the clothes she'd been wearing earlier, stowing them in her suitcase when she ought to be emptying its contents into the drawers.

My stomach jumped into my throat. "Are you leaving?" I croaked.

"I'm going down to the front desk to see if I can get another room."

"What? No." I jumped off the bed but didn't know what I intended to do with myself now that I was up.

In lieu of answering, she slipped her laptop into a sleeve and tucked it into the protective pocket of her carry-on bag.

"Why?" I demanded.

"Because I think it's better this way."

"Better for who? Because it won't be better for me." Which could only mean it was better for her. I'd fucked up well beyond anything I could have imagined if she was refusing to stay here with me.

She didn't respond to this. A couple more items got placed into her bag, and then she zipped it up and headed for the door, slinging the strap of her purse over her shoulder.

I jumped into action without thinking, darting past her and blocking her exit.

Bea's glare did a number on my nerves, but I refused to budge. If she wanted to get past me, she was going to have to move me out of her way.

"Tell me what I did wrong," I demanded. "Did you not want…?" The thought that I'd pushed her into anything she wasn't ready for made me sick to my stomach. I mean, I wanted to get laid as much as the next guy, but Grandma had instilled in me a healthy respect for boundaries. Over the years, I'd happily fucked plenty of women who'd offered themselves up for the taking, but they'd always been the ones to initiate, not me.

And when it came to the women who had a permanent position in my life, those boundaries were even more important. Granted, until recently, Grandma had been the only woman I'd consider to be *in my life* and not just on the outskirts of it, but that was neither here nor there.

But Bea wouldn't answer me.

Hell, she wouldn't even look at me.

After prying her bag from her hands and setting it

next to the door, I reached over and tipped her chin, hating myself for the tears glistening in her eyes. She shook her head, dislodging my hand, and tried to sidestep me.

"What?" I repeated, refusing to let her past me just yet. "I thought we agreed that you'd explain shit to me when I don't understand something."

Her eyes closed, as if she couldn't bear to even look at me while we spoke. Her voice cracked as she said, "I just thought that you'd want to rethink things. You know, now that you know."

No wonder so many marriages failed if people were always talking in riddles to each other. "Now that I know what?"

"What I'm like," she whispered.

"I already know what you're like. You're funny as shit, and you're not afraid to bust my balls—"

"Underneath my clothes," she cut in, trying to back away from me.

I reached for her wrist and locked my hand around it, preventing her from going too far. A risk, sure—she might not take too kindly to my interference, but I had to do something. "The only thing I'm rethinking," I said cautiously, "is that I should've made sure I had condoms on hand for whenever you were ready."

She shook her head, like she was refusing to believe me.

"Bea," I said, but she tried to tug her wrist free. She was surprisingly strong, but I was stronger. I tightened my grip, being careful not to hurt her. But then I waited until she glanced up and met my eyes again. "I want you more than I know how to handle," I admitted, because the truth seemed to be called for. "Touching you earlier—getting a taste of you—that only made my want for you even stronger than it already was."

"But…" And for once, she didn't seem to have a ready comeback waiting to bust my balls.

"Come with me," I said, and I tugged her into the bathroom. She stumbled slightly, thrown off by the shift in gears, but she followed without putting up a fight. I flipped on the light and faced the mirror, standing her in front of me. "Tell me what you see."

She rolled her eyes, so I pinched her upper arm lightly before settling both of my hands on her shoulders, anchoring her in place.

"You really don't want me to tell you," she muttered.

"Do it. What do you see?"

"Too much of me and not enough of you."

Yeah, so maybe she was right. I definitely did *not* like hearing that shit.

"Know what I see?"

"Are we playing Twenty Questions or something?"

"I see a gorgeous woman who's scared to look at herself, so she won't let anyone else look at her."

"I can't stop you from looking."

"Bullshit. You won't let me have the lights on. You won't let me see you."

She scowled, shrugging my hands off her shoulders, and then left the bathroom. "We should get going," she said with finality, effectively putting an end to the conversation. "Get showered, Blake."

"Are you going to take your things and get another room as soon as I get undressed and can't chase you out in the hall?"

She didn't answer me with words, but eventually she gave me the tiniest shake of her head.

It might take me a while, but eventually, I did learn

from my mistakes. So instead of arguing with her further, I did what she'd asked—I got into the shower, hoping that she would still be in my room when I was done and not down at the front desk or already established in some other room without me.

Bea

"Shouldn't you be getting back to your team soon?" Lillian demanded in lieu of a traditional greeting when the two of us returned to her hospital room the next morning.

"They know why I'm here. They know this is more important."

"Watching an old lady die is more important than living your life, hmm?" But despite her barking at him, she couldn't stop herself from smiling at the bouquet of tulips he'd brought in. "Where'd you find tulips like that at this time of year?"

He handed them off to me, and I arranged them in a vase I'd found down in the gift shop, filling it with water before positioning each stem carefully.

"You can buy flowers of all sorts at any time of year these days," Blake said. "I'd think you'd remember that from the last time you had cancer."

"I'm an old lady. I don't remember shit I don't want to remember. And that is definitely something I'd rather forget."

"You don't want to remember flowers?" he shot back.

"I want to forget being sick before. Hell, I want to forget being sick now. You should help me out with that."

I snorted but tried to cover my laugh with a fake cough.

When I surreptitiously glanced over, I found Lillian eyeing me, but Blake didn't seem to notice. He was scanning the dry erase board on the wall where the nurses noted items about his grandmother's care. He was studying it so intently that it seemed he was trying to memorize every detail or detect if she'd been neglected in some way while we were gone.

I kept myself busy on the other side of the room, fussing with the flowers even though they already looked perfect other than being slightly droopy—but they'd perk up soon, now that they were in water.

"Blake, I need you to go hunt down that male nurse for me," his grandmother said.

"I can do that for you," I volunteered.

"I want Blake to do it," she bit off, not even looking in my direction.

"Can't you just press your call button?" he asked.

"I can but they keep sending Nurse Ratched. I want Brett."

"There isn't a Nurse Ratched on your team," he said, scanning the board once more. "Looks like you've got Emily and Samantha today."

"Emily is Nurse Ratched. Hell, so is Samantha."

"They've both got the same name?"

"I want Brett."

I snickered.

He grumbled a few things about her getting sued for molestation or harassment, but he left the room.

"He doesn't take hints well," Lillian said to me.

"He also doesn't appear to be familiar with *One Flew Over the Cuckoo's Nest.*"

"No one's perfect."

"You should've just told him you wanted a word with me."

"I could've. But then he would have wanted to know what it was about, and I thought this should be just between the two of us."

"Sounds serious."

"I don't have time to be anything less than serious, so if you don't get that impression, we have problems. And I don't want to have problems with you."

"Fair enough."

"Have you thought any more about what we talked about before?" she demanded. "About whether you can let him love you?"

After everything that had happened between us at the hotel, I wasn't sure how to answer her question. And even though my skin wasn't prone to revealing a blush, I felt my cheeks heat.

"You have thought about it," she said definitively.

"I haven't— There's just—" I cut myself off, stumbling over my own words.

"He's not always thoughtful."

"That's not the problem, Lil. I am."

"What does that mean?"

"I don't even know. I just— I can't let him see me."

"He already sees you," she barked. "He's not blind."

"I think you know what I mean." Having finished arranging the tulips in the vase, I placed it on a table near the window so the sun would hit them.

"I do. And I also know it's horseshit." She scowled so fiercely I felt it in my toes. Her expression made me think of Blake, to be honest. "He knows you used to be fat, right?"

I nodded.

"Well, he's not an idiot. Might not always seem that way, but he's got a hell of a brain on him. You got stretch marks and shit you think he won't like—"

"It isn't just stretch marks," I cut in, taking small sips from my bottle of water that I always carried with me. "That's not even the half of it."

"Well, everybody has something. I've got old, wrinkly skin. And I don't have any tits anymore. Cancer took 'em. But shit like that never stopped me from knocking boots with the mailman."

I spluttered on my water, almost spraying her. "The mailman?" I choked.

"Once or twice. But he wasn't perfect, either. Had a massive beer belly and hairy balls. Don't like getting pubes in my teeth when I give oral. Makes me choke, and I do that well enough on my own these days without any help."

I was about to choke, myself, but mine was due to surprised laughter.

"Point is, Blake's got enough sense to know it isn't all about superficial shit. He's had to deal with more than his fair share of that kind of thinking over the years—because of his ADHD and shit. But he's not gonna give a rat's ass what you look like, as long as he likes you and you like him. He just wants to be with you. So maybe you need to figure that out, too."

Blinking in surprise at her frankness, I said, "Maybe I do."

"So see to it. Because I don't think I've got that much time left, and I need to know he's got someone looking out for him when I'm gone. If it's not going to be you, I need to help him figure something else out, without letting him onto the fact that I'm interfering."

Before I could respond, Blake had returned, toting

a nurse who very clearly did *not* look like she could be named Brett.

"I thought I told you I didn't want Nurse Ratched," Lil groused.

"Mm hmm," the nurse replied. She headed for the bed and pulled a curtain, shutting Blake and me out.

He reached for my hand and nudged his head toward the hall.

A series of tingles raced up my spine when the warmth of his palm met mine. I felt an urge to inch closer to him and allow his warmth to seep all through my body, but I didn't want to use him, and that was exactly how it would feel. At least to me, it would. Maybe not to him.

Had I used him earlier? Again, he probably didn't think so, but I was starting to think I had—especially since I'd almost immediately shut him out afterward.

"She give you a hard time?" he asked once the door to her hospital room closed behind us. "She can be kind of blunt. I love that about her—I need blunt— but some people don't get it."

"Maybe I need a dose of bluntness, too."

He snorted in laughter.

"She wasn't any harder on me than I deserved."

"Stop that, all right?"

"Stop what?"

We were wandering through the halls of the hospital without any true destination in mind as far as I could tell—neither of us had any need to eat, and we'd already been to the gift shop today. Before long, I realized we were heading toward the pediatric ICU and oncology units. That probably wasn't the best destination for us, but we kept walking, Blake guiding me as though he knew exactly where he was going and why.

"Stop beating yourself up," he said. "And maybe stop pushing me away without telling me what I've done to deserve it."

"You didn't do anything wrong," I insisted. "You don't deserve me treating you the way I have been."

"Hmm."

I tried to turn us down a different hallway, but Blake tightened his grip on my hand and tugged me through the double doors.

"What are we doing? Where are we going?"

"There's someone I want to see in here," he said.

A woman at the nurse's station looked up when we came in, and she smiled at him. "Back again?"

"Grandma sent us away so she could yell at her nurse, so I thought we could come and say hello to Christopher."

"Christopher?" I asked Blake softly, but he didn't react. Maybe he hadn't heard me at all.

The nurse grinned, oblivious to my query, her eyes glued to Blake. "They didn't send her boy toy this time?"

"If they're smart, they've reassigned him to a different ward for as long as Grandma's in this hospital. Maybe they can prevent a lawsuit. So is it all right if I check in on Christopher?"

"Absolutely. You know where to find him. He'll be thrilled. He hasn't had any guests all day—hardly any all week." She walked around to the front of the desk to join us and bent her head close to mine. "Both parents are working two jobs just to be able to pay for his treatments, and his grandparents don't live in the state. Sometimes his friends from school stop by, but no one's been here all week other than his parents for overnight stays, and he's usually sleeping then."

She waved us back through the halls, and Blake took off as if he knew exactly where he was headed.

He knocked on a partially closed door, poking his head into the room.

"Koz!" a crackling child's voice shouted with unbridled glee.

"Mind if I bring my girlfriend in to see you?" Blake asked, drawing me into the room alongside him without waiting for the boy's response.

"I didn't know you had a girlfriend," Christopher replied as we slipped inside the room.

He had the face of a gaunt ten-year-old but the body of a seven-year-old, with protruding bones visible everywhere. Not a hair was to be found on him, but he more than made up for that with IVs and hospital bracelets galore. A bulletin board hung on the wall next to his bed, covered in get-well-soon cards and artwork that I imagined his classmates had created for him.

My heart did a flip, but not because this little boy thought I was Blake's girlfriend; it was because Blake had taken it upon himself to spend time with a sick child. For all the faults he had—and they were numerous—he truly was a good man underneath it all.

His grandmother was right. He had a good heart, if you could learn to see past his issues. And who the heck didn't have issues? Lil had made it perfectly clear that my own issues were easily as big as Blake's, if not bigger.

"I haven't had a girlfriend for very long," Blake replied, squeezing my hand. "Not too many girls would know what to do with me. But Bea does." Then he faced me again and dropped his voice so that only I could hear him say, "At least, I think you do. Do you?"

This time, my heart flipped so hard that it almost stopped beating and I wasn't sure it would recover. But somehow I managed to nod.

And then I hoped he was right.

I smiled for Christopher's benefit and took a seat near the window so he could have Blake all to himself for this visit. Blake dragged one of the chairs closer to the little boy's bed, and in no time, they were deep in conversation. They started off talking about hockey, and then they moved to football and the Bills' chances at getting to the Super Bowl this year. Before long, I lost track of their discussion, my thoughts returning to everything Lil had said.

If she could be believed—and I saw no reason to doubt her—then Blake just wanted to be with me.

Which meant somehow I had to get over myself.

Because, whether he was ready for it or not, he was going to need someone in his corner sooner rather than later.

He wasn't alone in that regard, though. I needed someone in mine, too.

And I wanted that someone to be him.

Chapter Fifteen

Blake

That evening, Bea found a quiet waiting area not too far from Grandma's room, and she took her laptop with her to do some work and give me some time alone with my grandmother.

I recognized the opportunity to get some advice, and I jumped on it as soon as Grandma was awake and lucid enough to carry on a conversation.

"I need ideas," I said, dragging my chair closer so I could hold her frail hand in mine.

"What kind of ideas? You've always had plenty of those, but usually the sort that'll get you into trouble."

I chose not to give her the satisfaction of admitting she was right; Grandma already knew she was, anyway.

"Ideas for how to get Bea more comfortable with me," I said.

"You mean sex?"

"Not sex, exactly. More with letting me see her."

Grandma stared. "It's not you she's uncomfortable with."

"But—"

"It's her," Grandma cut in, and she pierced me with a hard gaze. "She needs to be more comfortable with herself. With her body."

"But how do I make that happen?"

"*You* don't. Only she can." At my grumble of annoyance, Grandma added, "You can't make a person think anything or feel anything they don't want to think or feel. Life doesn't work that way. All you can do is encourage her. Maybe help her see herself the way you see her."

"But how do I do that?"

"You've got a brain between your ears. You've got all sorts of ideas going on in there all the time. Figure it out, Blake."

Figure it out. Yeah. If only it were so simple.

......

Later, while Grandma napped and Bea was still in some waiting room where she could work in peace and quiet, I searched my brain to come up with something that would help Bea feel more at home in her own skin.

The only thing that came to me was to call Brie Burns.

She was married to one of my teammates, and she'd struggled with her weight for as long as I'd known her, up and down and up and down again. But she'd never seemed to lack confidence, at least outwardly in my presence, so I hoped she could be a decent starting point if nothing else.

I made sure my ringer was on silent so it wouldn't disturb Grandma's sleep and shot off a quick text message.

> Me: *Suggestions for how to get a woman more comfortable in her own skin?*

> Brie, responding almost as soon as I'd sent the message: *I would think your grandmother has larger concerns on her mind right now…*

> Me: *Not Grandma. A woman I'm dating.*

> Brie: *Didn't think you were there for dating…*

> Me: *She lives in Portland. Just came out because of Grandma. Anyway, she used to be heavy. Won't let me see her naked. Barely lets me touch her. Did you have issues like that?*

> Brie: *Not exactly. Kind of, though. I'd say it was similar but still different. But body image is a big deal for a lot of women. Works itself out in unique ways for each of us. And it's hard to feel sexy if you're worried about your man staring at stretch marks or whatever.*

> Me: *So how do I help her get past that?*

> Brie: *Depends on the woman.*

> Me: *What helped you?*

> Brie: *I needed to learn to see myself the way*

Keith sees me. Help her with that.

Me: …

Brie: *I don't know who you're talking about, so I don't know what it'll take. She might not know what she needs, either. She might not ever be able to see herself the way you see her. Our brains are evil that way. We're predisposed to see the worst in ourselves. Especially women. It's one of the curses of being born without a Y chromosome. Pretty sure it's genetically hardwired into our brains.*

Me: *Yeah, tell me about it. So ideas on how I can help her see what I see?*

Brie: *Maybe take her to a lingerie store? Have her try some things on, and maybe let you see her in them? I don't know… Ooh! And then do a photo shoot? I've seen a few online lately. Sexy ones—women of all shapes and sizes, sometimes with their partners, maybe in some slinky lingerie, which you could get her when you take her shopping first…*

Me: *Now there's a thought. But would she think that was about me and not about her?*

Brie: *Depends on her, I guess. And on how you present the idea.*

Me: *So I'm screwed. That's what you're saying, right? I'm screwed?*

Brie: *Use some tact. Maybe ask Babs how to phrase things...*

Me: *Tact has never been a strength of mine. Not even with Babs helping me. And I don't want him to get involved, anyway, because he might say something to Katie, who would probably say something to Dani, and I don't want Dani involved in this.*

Brie: *???*

Me: *Let's just say Dani and my girlfriend are friends and Dani doesn't approve of me.*

Brie: *Hmmm...*

Brie again: *Hey! You're near Buffalo, right? Somewhere in upstate NY?*

Me: *Yeah. Why?*

Brie: *Q and Mia are there.*

Me: *And...?*

Brie: *And Mia is a photographer, dummy.*

Me: *Oh. That's right. I forgot.*

Brie: *Is your girlfriend with you now?*

Me: *Yeah, she's here. Not right beside me at*

the moment, but she's here in NY.

Brie: *Call Mia. I bet she'd be all over doing a shoot like that as long as she's got the time. She loves capturing people—real people, not models. She's been doing shoots lately for women who've had mastectomies and stuff like that. She's awesome. And she's good enough that she'll be able to get all the angles and lighting right so that your girlfriend can see herself in a new way. She can help you figure something out and find a way to present it to your girl without sounding like you're a jackass. I mean, you kind of are, but…*

It was the truth, so I couldn't even be mad at her for bringing it up.

Brie, again: *And say hi to her kids from all of us.*

Me: *Sure. Will do.*

In reality, though, I had no intention of calling Mia Quincey. Maybe she was married to a former teammate of mine, but I doubted she'd want to help me with anything.

I could be a tough pill to swallow, and I knew it.

Brie: *Any idea when you'll be back? The guys will want to get together…*

Me: *Why? They doing okay on the ice?*

This conversation made me realize that I hadn't even bothered looking at the scores since I'd left. I had no earthly idea how the team had been doing without me. Fuck. I should probably do something about that... What sort of hole had I left them in? They could've gone on a massive losing streak without me, and I wouldn't have the first clue.

> Brie: *Because you're part of the team and you're having a hard time, and they want to show you support, dumbass.*

> Me: *Oh. Yeah, I guess that makes sense. Well...not sure yet. A week or so? Two weeks? Depends what the doctors say, I guess.*

> Brie: *Tell us once you know. Keith wants to have everyone over at the house. He says it's been too long since we had a party, even if it's about you. And tell me what Mia says once you've asked her about the shoot. And what your girlfriend says about the shoot. What's her name, BTW?*

> Me: *Bea.*

> Brie: *Bea, as in Dani's friend, Bea?*

> Me: *I don't want Dani involved in this...*

> Brie: *Mm hmm...*

> Brie, again: *Anyway, I want to see the pictures. If Bea's okay with that. Make sure*

she's okay with that because I want to see them but I don't want her to be pissed that you shared them with me.

Brie, apparently still not finished: *And if they're half as awesome as I imagine they will be, since I know Mia's talents, then I'll probably need to get some done, too. I'd imagine Mia is probably about to get a whole lot busier. Hope she's ready for this.*

Brie, one more time: *Actually, now you've given me an idea. I might have to call Mia, myself, to see if she'd be game… I think we should do a Storm WAGs charity calendar or something. We're hot. We could raise money for the Light the Lamp Foundation…*

Me: *I should really go now or something.*

Brie: *Wait. How's your grandmother doing?*

Me: *Not good. Really bad.*

Brie: *Really, really bad?*

Me: *Dying. They said there's not really any hope. Just trying to keep her as comfortable as they can, now.*

Brie: *I'm so sorry. Let us know if we can do anything to help.*

Me: *Thanks. So what's Mia's number?*

While I appreciated the thought, there wasn't anything anyone could do. Pretty sure Brie knew that, too, but offering to help was what people tended to do at times like this. She sent me Mia's number a moment later with another note about how she'd be contacting her soon about the calendar idea.

If Brie was going to call Mia, too, I supposed that I'd have to at least give her a shout to see what she had to say. With any luck, she'd be too busy and have to decline.

I had to admit, though, the idea of a photo shoot *was* intriguing. Especially if it could potentially have the sort of effect on Bea that Brie seemed to think it could.

Next thing I knew I was calling Mia Quincey for the first time ever and hoping that it wouldn't lead to Bea walking out of my life for good.

Bea

When I returned to Lil's room, I found it jam-packed with people, and none of them appeared to be employees of the hospital.

Blake was seated in his customary chair next to her bed, close enough that he could hold her hand. But a gorgeous blonde woman was seated across from him, and a man with an athletic build was standing near the window, a nurse was changing out Lil's IV bag, and there were two kids—a bit younger than most of my students—on the floor playing a game on an iPad.

Everyone but the nurse looked up at me when I entered the room, making me uncomfortable. Blake's nervous grin helped, though.

But then I had to wonder why he was nervous. I was the intruder…

"You must be Bea," the blonde woman said, getting to her feet and crossing over to me with a warm smile and a hand outstretched to shake mine. She had a camera in her other hand—not just a cheap digital one that anyone could buy at Target, either, but a professional camera with detachable lenses and the whole shebang.

"Hi," I said warily.

Blake got up and came over to my side. "This is Mia Quincey and her husband and kids. Mitch used to be one of my teammates."

Nodding but still confused, I asked, "Are you here to take pictures of Lil?"

Maybe Blake wanted some pictures of the two of them together. Something he could keep long after she was gone? I honestly wasn't sure, but that was the only thing that made sense.

"She's taking pictures of you, smarty pants," Lil said from her bed.

"Me? No." I was already shaking my head and trying to back out of the room, but Blake reached for my hand as if anticipating my reaction.

"Let's go out in the hall and talk for a minute," he said, and he nudged me hard enough that I stumbled and followed, with Mia not far behind us.

"What's this all about?" I demanded in a whisper, because the halls were more crowded than usual. It seemed like there was something big going on and we were probably in the way. I moved closer to the walls so we wouldn't obstruct the path, folded my arms in front of me, and glared at Blake so he'd know I wasn't amused.

"It's about— I just—"

"He thought you might want to do a photo shoot," Mia said when he couldn't get the words out right. "With me. I do a lot of portraits these days."

"Why would I want to do that?"

I hated having my picture taken. Always had. I looked bigger on film than I did in person, and I always saw flaws that probably weren't even there. It was just part of being me, this aversion to having my photo taken. I dreaded school picture day every year and did my best to blend into the background of the class photos, allowing my students to shine up front.

"Because maybe it'll help you see yourself the way I see you," Blake said. And darn it if he didn't sound completely sincere and adorable when he said it. "I just thought… If you don't want to do it, you don't have to."

But he was wrong about that. Maybe no one would force me to have my picture taken, but it would eat away at me for a very long time if I didn't at least hear her out.

"What kind of photo shoot?" I asked warily.

"The kind that'll help you feel confident in your own skin," Mia replied, a distinct arch in her brow that made her meaning very clear.

"Oh, no. No, I can't—"

"I'll do it with you if you want," Blake cut in. "You and me. Sexy lingerie. Mood lighting…"

"But you look amazing. And you have no problem letting people see you with your clothes off. That's different."

He scrunched his forehead in thought. "How do you know I don't care if people see me?"

"I've heard about naked yoga in the locker room."

Mia appeared to be having difficulty keeping a straight face.

"Oh. Yeah," Blake said, and he had a grin that nearly knocked my feet out from under me. "I guess that's kind of a giveaway. Who told you, though?"

"Dani. Apparently all the guys were complaining about you."

"All of them? Colesy was into me…"

"From what I understand, it was all of them. But Dani has been known to exaggerate on occasion."

"I offered to let Anne film me for *Eye of the Storm*, but she said it's a family-friendly program and she'd have to blur me out. It'd be a lot to blur…"

He winked.

I blushed.

Mia's eyes were traveling between the two of us through this entire exchange, and she had the biggest smile brightening her eyes. "You two are hilarious together. I really want to do this."

I started to argue once again, but Blake spoke before I could get a word out.

"We're doing it. I want you to do it for me, even if you won't do it for yourself."

"For you?"

"I'll be there, too."

"But we've already established that you don't care if people see you."

"No one has to see you but me. And Mia, I guess, since she's the one shooting the pictures."

Mia nodded. "And I have a makeup artist who'll help, but she's awesome and discreet. She can do your hair, help me with styling you… She handles my lights."

"No one else will ever see these pictures? Because I could lose my job over something like this." Not to mention the way my family would react if they ever found out. That *couldn't* happen.

"They'll just be for us. For you and me," Blake insisted.

"I don't know…"

He turned a puppy-dog expression on me, and I melted.

With a heavy sigh, I closed my eyes and said, "What do I have to do?"

Chapter Sixteen

Bea

Blake stayed at the hospital with Mitch, the Quincey kids, and his grandmother while Mia and Angie, her assistant, took me shopping.

Lingerie shopping, to be precise.

I'd never bothered setting foot in a lingerie store before. I mean, not a *true* lingerie store. Since my weight loss, I'd been buying my bras and underwear in stores that specialized in comfort and support, not in sex appeal, because that was what I intended to use them for. And before that, I'd only ever shopped in the stores like Lane Bryant and Catherine's, ones that focused on making clothes for larger women that didn't look like enormous sacks.

Regardless of all that, I wasn't sure I *possessed* any sex appeal. If, by some strange twist of fate, I did have a smidgeon of the stuff, I certainly didn't know how to make use of it.

Still, ever since going under the knife and losing weight, I'd been more focused on hiding my flaws and keeping everything tucked away that ought to be tucked away than I had been on flaunting anything. The thought of finding things to show off my various *assets*, if they could even be called that, was almost enough to have me breaking out in hives.

This entire store already had my skin crawling with trepidation, and we'd barely been inside it for two minutes.

"Bra size?" Angie asked, thumbing through a rack of silky things that had been put on clearance. "And what dress size do you wear?"

"Twelve or large, probably, and I think I'm in a 38D."

"You think?"

"It changed so much so fast… But I'm pretty sure that's where it ended up."

"We'll get someone to measure you," Mia said decisively. She caught the eye of a store employee who had a tape measure draped around her neck and waved her over.

Meanwhile, Angie was grabbing things off the rack seemingly at random other than checking the label for the size, loading her arms full.

"Can I help you ladies?" the clerk asked a moment later as she bustled to join us.

Mia angled her head in my direction. "She needs to be fitted for a bra. And we need you to open a dressing room for her. She's going to be trying on all sorts of things."

"Of course," the clerk said, reaching for the enormous pile in Angie's arms. Then she hurried off to comply.

"Now that I think of it, you and I should go with her," Mia said to me, her eyes following the clerk. "You can start trying on the things we bring you while Angie keeps searching the racks."

"And I need your help for that?" I squeaked. Yes, she'd be photographing me in some of these things soon enough, but the entire situation was growing more complicated and uncomfortable by the moment, which would have seemed impossible only an hour ago.

"I need to see what it all looks like on you."

I hadn't ever had a problem with Dani seeing me while I was trying on her clothes, but this felt a lot different. And not simply due to my not really knowing Mia Quincey.

Dani's clothes had been specifically designed to hide all of my problem areas.

These things, though? I took a negligee off the rack and held it up in wonder over what, exactly, the purpose of it might be, since there wasn't enough fabric on it to cover my left boob. There'd be no way to hide while wearing anything sold in this store. "Yeah, maybe if I find something that's got enough covered…" I muttered.

She quirked up a grin at my reaction. "I'll stay out of the room, but you have to come out and let me see things unless they're completely indecent, like you're literally falling out of them or something."

"But if I don't like it…"

"You might not be the best judge of what looks good on you. Typically, we're our own harshest critics."

"Hmph," I muttered, but I headed back to the

fitting rooms with Mia on my tail.

......

Four hours later, the three of us were back at the hotel, and Angie had me seated in the desk chair so she could do my makeup while Mia fiddled with a bunch of portable lights she was setting up.

"Close your eyes," Angie ordered, reaching for a palette of shadows and another brush out of the bag she'd virtually emptied over the handful of empty spaces in the room.

I tugged on the edges of the robe, drawing it closer around me, as I complied.

"And stop trying to hide," Angie murmured.

"If only I *could* hide. That would be brilliant right about now."

"This is going to be an amazing experience for you," Mia insisted over her shoulder. "You just have to give it a chance."

I scowled at her.

"Give *me* a chance, then," she begged.

I huffed out a sigh. "This might be a lot of things, but I'm not sure I'm willing to call it *amazing*. Not yet, at least." And until I'd seen the final results, I doubted I'd ever be able to do so. Most likely not even then.

A knock sounded at the door, and I pulled on the edges of my robe even it was already covering me and I had the chosen lingerie on underneath, so it wasn't as if I was naked.

Angie scowled at me with a *tsk*ing sound as Mia went to answer it.

"You ready for me?"

I couldn't see him, but I'd know Blake's voice anywhere. While his presence might have comforted me in certain other circumstances, in my present predicament, it only made my pulse go through the roof.

"Come on in," Mia said. "What're you going to wear?"

"You tell me. Jeans? How dressed do you want me to be? I could do boxer-briefs…"

"Depends on the boxer-briefs," she replied. "Are they filthy?"

He didn't answer, but I could imagine him giving her an annoyed look in response.

"You wearing them now?" she demanded.

"Yeah."

"Are they clean?"

"Are you serious?"

"I have a husband and two kids, one of them a boy. Yes, I'm serious," she shot back.

"They're clean."

"And you haven't worn them for so long that they're all stretched out?"

"For fuck's sake."

"Like I already said, I have two males in my house. Don't give me that. I know what guys are like."

"They're fine," he insisted.

"Go into the bathroom and strip, then, and let me see if they'll work."

"I could strip all the way…" Teasing laughter filled his tone, and I had to smother a laugh of my own.

"Don't even think about it. Keep the underwear on or you'll be answering to my husband."

He grumbled something about how he wasn't afraid of Q, or at least that was what it seemed like he was saying, but then the bathroom door closed and the sounds of him bumping around in there filled the small hotel room.

"You've stopped breathing," Angie murmured in a tone low enough the other two wouldn't overhear.

I took a deep breath to force my lungs into compliance as she brushed some more powder onto my eyelids.

Blake came back out to join us.

"Hmm," Mia said. "What do you two think?"

My eyes fluttered open. I blinked repeatedly against the glare of the bright lights Angie was using to do my makeup, but then I was finally able to see.

He was gorgeous.

Which, of course, I already knew. But I'd never seen him quite like this before. I'd *felt* him, but that wasn't even remotely the same.

He was all muscle, with a narrow strip of dark hair trailing down from the center of his chest and disappearing under the royal-blue waistband of his underwear.

My throat went dry at the sight of him. He was like a male model, only he was standing right in front of me; he wasn't just a flat image in the pages of a magazine.

He was real flesh and blood.

His body was perfection, and mine was stretched-out flab and lumps in odd places.

"I can't do this," I croaked, but the words were mainly air and no substance.

They all ignored me, assuming they had heard me at all, which they might not have considering how loudly my heart was pounding.

"I like the blue as contrast against the coral," Angie said, reaching for one of our purchases from earlier. "We should put Bea in this one to start with. And it'll all pop against the white of the sheets."

"Yeah, but that bedspread has to go," Mia said emphatically, wrinkling her nose in distaste at the brown-and-orange fabric.

The next thing I knew, Blake had stalked over and stripped off the top layer of bedding, tossing the comforter to the floor. Then he took a seat on the end of the bed and stared at me with so much heat that I thought I might melt.

"Close your eyes for me again," Angie demanded, and I willingly complied. With my eyes closed, I could pretend for a moment that none of this was happening and it was all a dream.

She dabbed a bit more on my eyelids, swiped a soft-bristled brush across my cheeks, and used a small brush to glide gloss over my lips. "All right. I think we're good. What do you think?"

"I think she's perfect," Blake said, and a tingle zipped up my spine.

"Look up at me," Mia ordered, and I opened my eyes again, trying not to blink under the scrutiny of three pairs of eyes staring down at me.

Blake's eyes, in particular, seemed to be calling to me.

"Go a bit darker on the lips, but keep it nude. And tousle up her hair some more. But otherwise, I think we're all set."

"If I kiss her, am I going to mess her up?" Blake asked.

"Kiss me?" I spluttered, but they ignored me.

"We can fix her makeup again if we need to," Mia said. "That's one of the reasons I have an assistant at the shoots—so we can fix hair and makeup as many times as necessary." Then she arched a brow in my direction. "And yes, he's going to kiss you. And touch you. And you're going to be beautiful the whole time."

I swallowed the lump in my throat and reached for a bottle of water to soothe my nerves.

"Put a little powder on him and let's get going," Mia said, and any hope I might have had of escaping was gone.

Blake

Grandma pressed the button on her bed to raise herself up somewhat when we headed back to the hospital later that evening. "When do I get to see them?" she demanded with no preamble.

Bea tensed beside me—I could feel it in her hand. I squeezed to reassure her as Mia and Angie followed us into Grandma's hospital room. Q and his kids were waiting for us there, with the kids busy playing games in the corner.

"As long as it's okay with Blake and Bea, I'm willing to show you the raw footage on my camera now." Mia said.

"Can I see them first?" Bea asked.

They hadn't shown her anything on the camera yet. *You can't see them until I edit them,* Mia had told her, despite Bea's objections. Not that she hadn't asked multiple times—almost constantly, actually, for the first hour or two of the shoot.

But eventually, she'd lost some of her inhibitions and become more comfortable with what we were doing. Her laughs had become more natural. Her smiles had felt less forced. Her kisses had gone softer, more sensual. Her touches had become bolder. And slowly—terribly slowly—she'd stopped tensing up every time I'd touched her.

Every time Mia had captured a particularly perfect moment, I'd known it right away—because her eyes lit up like fire. That was Mia's tell, her sign that all her creative juices were flowing. There'd been a lot of those moments, too. Once Bea had finally let go and started having fun, it'd happened almost nonstop.

But then I'd forgotten all about watching Mia's reactions and focused instead on Bea. In those moments when she'd lost her inhibitions, I'd never seen anything more beautiful. I only hoped that this shoot was enough to convince her of the same.

"I already told you," Mia said patiently. "You can't see them until I've edited them. But Blake's grandmother is a bit of a special circumstance, don't you think?"

Bea scowled, but she relented, and Mia headed over to sit next to Grandma's bed and show her the day's work.

"Thank you," I whispered into Bea's ear.

"For letting your grandmother see them when I haven't?"

"For everything. All of this."

"I don't know why you're thanking me. You're the one who arranged it all."

"And you're the one who agreed to it," I pointed out.

She bit down on her lower lip, which made me want to do the same thing, but then she nodded.

"I hope it helps you the way I think it will," I said.

"It already has," she admitted, but she wouldn't look up and meet my eyes.

"Yeah?"

"I couldn't have done any of that if you hadn't…"

"Pushed you into it?" I offered.

"Something like that."

"Are you upset that I pushed?"

"I think I needed a good push. Your grandmother gave me one, too."

Now, that was a surprise. "What kind of push did she give you?"

Bea tried to shrug it off, waving her hand around the room as if to indicate all the people around us. But the kids were playing their games, Q was in deep conversation with Angie, and Mia and Grandma had their heads close together, going through the images on Mia's camera. They weren't paying any attention to us at all.

"What kind of push?" I insisted.

"Just… I don't know. She wants me to be sure I want you in my life. That I want to be in your life."

This time, it was my turn to lose my ability to speak for a bit. But finally, I said, "And do you? Want to be in my life and want me in yours?"

"I couldn't have gone through with any of this if I didn't."

That was answer enough for me. And suddenly, I felt a lot lighter. My life was still a mess, sure, and I couldn't bear the thought of having to say good-bye to my grandmother soon—probably forever—but maybe in this one area of my life, things were starting to look up.

And thank fuck for that, because I needed something good to hold on to. Might as well have that *something good* be Bea. Especially if she'd allow me to hold on to her like I had during the photo shoot.

......

L̲ater, Mia started gathering up her husband, kids, and camera equipment, but she took a moment to pull me aside while Bea was busy talking to Grandma. "I'll send the proofs over for you both to take a look at in a few days. Once you know which ones you want, just let me know and I'll edit them and send you the final copies. If you want any prints done, I have some recommendations in Portland, or I can have them printed locally and then ship them to you."

"Thanks, Mia," I said. "I just hope it'll be worth it."

"It was absolutely worth it. Maybe she won't see herself the way you see her right away, but she won't be able to deny it for too much longer once she sees the actual pictures."

"We hope."

"Have a little faith in her, hmm? She's been through a lot. It takes time to see the differences in ourselves. It's a lot easier to see them in someone else."

Q came over and slapped me on the back in an awkward former-teammate sort of non-hug. "When are you heading back to Portland?"

"Not sure. Probably soon."

"Say hi to the boys for me."

"You guys are playing San Jose next week, right?" I asked.

"Yep."

"How about you and *your* boys do us a solid and kick their asses to Timbuktu?" We'd been battling it out with San Jose to see who could land at the top of the Pacific all season long. Every time we won, they did, too. We couldn't get any separation from them in the standings.

"That's the plan, but for us, not for you."

"Mm hmm. Just do it."

A few minutes later, the Quinceys were all gone, and suddenly it was quiet in Grandma's room again, other than the beeping and whirring of the machines and the general bustle of the hospital taking place out in the halls.

I took up the seat next to Grandma's bed that Mia had vacated.

"You two need to go back to the hotel and get some rest," Grandma barked.

I snorted. "I think you might be the one who needs rest. You've had kids here for hours. Probably drove you up the wall."

"Okay, then you two need to go back to the hotel and get some nookie. Then you can rest after."

"Nookie?" Bea spluttered.

"Isn't that what you kids are calling it these days? There's that song."

"Limp Bizkit hasn't been a thing for a decade or more," I said, glancing over to Bea.

She looked like she couldn't decide between utter embarrassment and ridiculous laughter. Which meant Grandma was having the desired effect on her. That was what my grandmother always went for, but it rarely worked with me. I didn't embarrass easily.

"That's still what you're calling it, though, right?" Grandma insisted, catching Bea's eye.

"I don't..." She couldn't finish her thought. Her embarrassment was beyond adorable.

"You won't hear any arguments from me," I said, but Bea wouldn't meet my eyes. Or maybe it was that she couldn't make herself, which was kind of cute. "Sorry," I added, looking her way. "But you know Grandma doesn't mince words."

"It's not— I'm just—"

"She's just frustrated because she wants to see the pictures and your photographer friend wouldn't show them to her. And now we're making jokes about sex, and she's a teacher, which means she's more dignified than all of that. But they look good, honey." Grandma gave Bea a reassuring pat on the back of the hand. "And you'll need to get over the need to be dignified if you're going to spend much time with either of us."

"It's not that," Bea insisted.

"Mm hmm," Grandma replied. "Well, either way, you look good."

"Good enough to eat," I said, and my stomach growled.

After rolling her eyes at me, Grandma said, "Sounds like you need to feed him or he might try to eat you."

"That's not the worst idea you've ever had," I said.

"What? Getting some food in you? Or eating her?"

I shrugged, raising a brow in challenge in Bea's direction. "Either? Both?"

And just like that, Bea was on her feet, with her coat and backpack in her arms, and on her way out the door. I happily and readily followed her…with Grandma cackling in our wake.

......

"I had a good time today," I said later, when Bea and I were curled up together on the bed. We were both still fully clothed, other than our shoes, but she was at least allowing me to spoon her.

The soft coils of her thick, curly hair tickled my nose as I nuzzled her neck. I'd discovered just how much I enjoyed the sensation earlier, when Mia had asked us to lie in this position for a few shots. My dick liked it, too, so I kept having to think boring thoughts to keep from getting too far ahead of myself.

"You might be surprised to hear it," Bea murmured after a moment, her voice thick and husky and so sexy I couldn't stand it, "but so did I."

"So it wasn't all torture?"

She laughed and turned her head, looking back at me over her shoulder. "Not *all* torture. But there was still plenty of it."

"You looked hot in all of it. But that green thing?" Cautiously, I slid a hand down the length of her side, settling it on her hip.

She didn't jerk or pull away, thank fuck. "What about the green one?"

"It's going to fuel my dreams for months. And once we get the pictures, it'll probably do that for the rest of my life."

"Don't tease me, Blake."

"I'm not teasing you. That's total jerk-off material."

"Classy," she said, but at least she was laughing.

"You know I say whatever pops into my head." And seeing her in that lingerie earlier was going to remain in my head forever. "I've been into you for a long time, but today just cemented it. I need you." I inched closer, and my hard-on nestled against her ass. She was so soft and inviting everywhere. I couldn't get enough. But then I had to fight back a groan, because all I could think about was slipping between her thighs and settling more fully into her warmth and softness. "But even more than that, I want you. I want to be with you."

"I want to be with you, too," she whispered, as if it was one of the worst things she could ever confess.

It might be pressing my luck, but I had to try. "I bought condoms today, while you three were out shopping."

She went unusually still against me, almost rigid.

Damn. Too much, too soon. "We don't have to—"

"I want to," she interrupted. "But this has been a lot for me in one day."

"Too much for one day? Do you need me to wait a bit longer?"

Shaking her head, she rolled toward me, but she buried her face in the space between my chin and my shoulder so I couldn't see her expression. "I don't want to wait anymore. I just…"

"You just what?" I prodded when she fell silent.

"Can we have the lights out?"

My heart dropped into my stomach. "Even after today?"

"Even after today. I might get there eventually. I hope I can. I'm trying to."

"But not yet," I finished for her.

"Not yet. I want to be with you," she rushed to say. "But—"

"But you're not ready to let me see you naked."

She nodded so softly I barely felt the movement.

Patience, I reminded myself. Rushing her wouldn't do either of us any good. Besides, I'd already pushed her enough for today.

"But as long as we keep the lights off?" I asked.

In answer, she reached over to the light switch next to the bed and flipped it off with a single outstretched finger.

And then she kissed me.

Chapter Seventeen

Bea

The quiet sound he let out fell somewhere between a growl and a sigh, and he opened his lips, allowing me entry.

I pressed up onto an elbow for a better angle.

As I tentatively slid my tongue against his, he pressed a hand to the back of my head, tangling his fingers in my unruly curls and somehow steadying me at the same time. But he didn't draw me closer; he only provided enough pressure to prevent me from falling away from him, not enough to set the pace.

Apparently, making the next move was up to me—and I wasn't sure how to react to the realization. Should it make me feel strong or possibly anxious about getting something wrong, doing something that would prove my inexperience? Not that either of us could have any doubt about my lack of skill in this area—it was as evident as the nose on my face. And anyway, just now, I felt both strong and anxious in equal measure.

I took my time, exploring his tongue and lips and teeth with my own until I was breathless and panting and had to pull away to gain a moment of clarity.

"I want to touch you," Blake rasped into the dark.

My tongue went thick, but I replied, "So touch me, then," with a heck of a lot more bravado than I could properly account for.

He slid his hand from my hair to my shoulder, the tips of his fingers trailing along the back of my arm with a featherlight caress and leaving gooseflesh in their wake. When his progress finally came to a stop, he settled his palm on my hip for a moment before gently kneading my bottom.

I had to fight the urge to stop him because the pathetic, drooping skin of my butt wasn't very sexy, but his touch made me feel warm and tingly and nice.

Besides, he would *have* to touch me if we were going to go through with this. And I had every intention of going through with it. Maybe this would be the only time I'd ever be with him or any man, because he'd likely be repulsed beyond any chance of recovery once we went through with it, but I wanted at least this one time to happen. It was enough that I'd probably be sad, lonely, and single for the rest of my life after this.

But I wanted to rid myself of my virginity first, at the very least.

"You're so soft everywhere," he murmured with a hint of amazement before fusing his lips to my neck and stealing my ability to wonder whether he meant that in a good way or a bad way.

I splayed my hands over his abdomen to steady

myself. His skin was supple and smooth, but everything beneath the surface was hard—he was nothing but strong cords of muscle everywhere I could reach.

Just how dissimilar could two bodies be?

Apparently very.

I might not be fat any longer, but I was all lumps and bumps (each existing in places they didn't belong), stretched-out skin, and every inch of my body was covered with the sorts of ugly marks that supermodels never bore. Or maybe they'd been thoroughly airbrushed to hide their flaws? If so, I could hope that Mia Quincey would do a bit of airbrushing in Photoshop to make my photos look better than I did in reality.

But thinking about all of that wouldn't help me in the present. I had to get back into the moment, keep my mind away from the things that would haunt my waking hours as much as my sleeping hours. Besides, I was beyond fascinated by discovering the differences between Blake and me.

I tugged up the bottom of his shirt, baring his skin to my touch. His abdominal muscles jumped slightly when I slid first my fingers and then my palm toward his chest. I almost stopped because of that virtually insignificant movement, thinking I'd done something wrong, but he kissed me again before I could, urging me on.

"Is this all right?" I asked, smoothing my hand over his skin when he let me up for air.

"You can do anything you want to me, Bea."

"Anything?" I trailed my fingertips down his chest and abs again, moving them toward the waist of his jeans.

His almost-black eyes locked to mine, he said, "Anything."

That whole breathing thing that humans were supposed to do all the time? Yeah, right. I doubted I'd ever breathe normally again after hearing the heat in that single word.

Undoing his button and fly turned out to be more difficult than it should have been because my hand was shaking and I needed my other arm to support my weight. Blake helped me by lifting his hips and shucking the jeans, then tossing them somewhere on the floor.

My fingers hovered over the elastic waist of his briefs, but I couldn't seem to lower the fabric. My bravado was already fading, giving way to anxiety.

"Touch me," he pleaded.

I swallowed the lump filling my throat. "How?"

"Any way you want."

"I don't know what I want," I lied.

"Well, I do."

"What do you want?"

He chuckled. "No, I mean I know what *you* want."

"Tell me, then," I said, breathless. *Or better yet, show me.*

He removed his briefs, too, flinging them away into the darkness. Circling my wrist with his powerful fingers, he guided my hand toward his pulsing heat. I slid my palm over his length, reveling in the soft hiss of air from his lips that intensified when I gave him a gentle squeeze.

"Rub me," Blake said, rough and needy. "That's what you want. You want to touch me. You want to feel every inch of me. You want to make me hard and hot so I'm aching to be inside you."

Only somewhat surprisingly, he was right. I did want all of that, but I was also nervous to follow through with what I wanted because I was sure it would lead to all my fears coming true.

Still, my fingers tightened around him, and I stroked.

It was tentative at first.

No, *I* was tentative, not some random *it*.

But there was a sort of power I felt with Blake on his back beneath me, his pleasure literally in my hands—and I'd never experienced anything quite like the headiness of this sensation before in any other area of my life.

"Like this?" I asked.

He nodded, but then one of his hands came down over the top of mine, adding more pressure, and he closed his eyes with a deep groan. "That's so fucking good."

And maybe it was good for him, but it was *amazing* for me. There'd been plenty of times I'd thought about doing something like this, but the act of experiencing fell into an entirely different realm than I could arrive at through mere imagination.

His free hand came around my waist, and he drew me closer to kiss me again. He tangled his tongue with mine; I could get drunk off the taste of him and the heated sounds he made. When he broke away, he kissed a trail down the column of my neck, stopping to suckle at the soft hollow below my voice box.

My hand stilled.

"I want to touch you," he said, his voice reverberating against my skin. "I want to make you come. I need to be inside you, Bea."

I shivered from the neediness in his tone and the

anxiety racing through me and making my blood go hot and cold all at once. "Then touch me," I replied.

Faster than I could blink, he was out from under me and had us flipped around so he was hovering over the top of me. With his lips fused to mine, his practiced hands went to work tugging the waist of my shirt free from my jeans and undoing buttons and zippers. It was as if he'd done this many times before.

Well, who was I kidding? No one but myself. Blake was a young, sexy, professional hockey player. Women likely threw themselves at him all the time—women younger and hotter than me. He probably did this a lot more often than I even thought about it. But allowing my thoughts to stray to ideas like those wouldn't help me get through this at all, so I shoved them aside.

He tugged my shirt over my head. I shivered in the moment before he covered me again, warming me with the heat of his own body while he worked my jeans down my hips.

Then his mouth was on mine, and his hands were everywhere at once.

Finally, blessedly, my brain shut down and all I could do was *feel*.

Blake suckled on the sensitive skin where my neck and collarbone met, and I shuddered. He slipped his hand inside my bra and cupped my breast with his palm, and I moaned against his lips. He pressed a knee between my thighs, grinding the top of his thigh against the spot that was throbbing with heat and need, and I stopped breathing.

If only I could stop thinking, too, because now my brain was racing at a pace of a thousand miles a minute.

"Do you want this?" he asked, his voice like gravel as his lips hovered over my skin.

My body zinged when he slid his fingers beneath the elastic edge of my panties, and I nodded desperately.

"Tell me," he insisted. "Tell me what you want."

I squirmed to get more of his touch, and I felt him smile against the overheated skin of my neck.

"This?" Blake asked, lightly swirling the tip of a finger around my clitoris.

I shuddered and drew up my knees, opening myself to him. "More."

One long, thick finger slipped easily inside my opening while he continued to rub my clit with the pad of his thumb. "Like this?"

I nodded, biting down on my lower lip.

"Can you take another finger?" He kissed my shoulder blade, his tongue darting out to lick my overheated skin. "You're so wet, Bea, but I don't want to risk hurting you—at least not any more than I have to. I want to take this nice and slow."

"I—" My breath caught in my throat when I felt a second finger joining the first. But even though the way he stretched my body was slightly uncomfortable at first, the discomfort quickly gave way to a pleasantly full sensation. I nodded, closing my eyes with a moan.

His mouth seared my neck again before making a wet path along my collarbone, veering toward my breast. "Take off your bra for me," he said.

I didn't even think about ignoring him. Slipping my hands behind my back, I unhooked the clasp. My breasts tumbled free almost immediately, but he caught one in his palm before lowering his mouth to suckle my tit. I felt the suction all the way through my body; it seemed to draw everything in me tighter, making me hot.

"Fuck, you're so wet," he murmured, moving his

lips to my other breast while his fingers continued working their magic between my legs.

"Blake," I pleaded.

"Hmm?" He lifted his head briefly, and I imagined he was trying to meet my eyes.

"Hurry."

A rich laugh rumbled through him, reverberating all around me. "I'm just trying to be sure you're ready for this."

"I'm ready," I insisted. Or as ready as it was possible for me to be. Thirty years ought to be long enough, right?

He swirled his tongue over my breast again, but then his weight shifted away from me on the bed. I rolled toward him, partially due to the effects of gravity but also due to my need for his heat.

The sounds of him opening a foil wrapper competed with my heavy breathing, and then he was rolling toward me again. He lifted himself above me, his legs settling between my thighs, bracing his weight with his arms on either side of me.

I reached up and splayed my hand over his chest. His heartbeat thundered against my palm, almost as erratically as mine.

"Kiss me," he said, deep and husky.

"Hmm?"

"Kiss me."

As soon as my lips met his, his hips rocked forward and he thrust into me. My cry of surprise was swallowed up by his mouth. But it was only surprise and not pain, so I quickly got over my shock—and myself—and reveled in the moment.

"I'm not hurting you?" Blake asked.

"No. It's—" Beautiful. Perfect. Heaven. None of

those words quite covered it, not even when they were all combined into one. Because, having spent my entire life as the Designated Ugly Fat Friend, I'd resigned myself to the fact that I'd never experience anything like this. "It's good," I finally forced out.

Blake held himself up with one arm and used his other hand to explore my body. His touch was almost reverent and definitely possessive. Or maybe that was all in my mind, just what I wanted to believe for this brief foray I was taking into someone else's life.

"Can you take more?" he asked, squeezing one of my breasts in the most delicious way.

"More?"

I'd barely gotten the question out when he went deeper, harder. His hip bone ground against my clitoris, and an unfamiliar sound ripped from my throat.

"Too much?" he asked, all concern.

I shook my head, wrapping both of my arms around his shoulder and holding on for all I was worth.

I wanted to capture every moment of this. It was something I could hold on to once he'd moved on and I was back to existing as an old, fat, single teacher, one whom no one like Blake would ever look at twice.

But Blake stopped, buried deep inside me, and he tipped my chin so I'd have to look at him. "You're not with me. You're in some other world."

"I don't— I'm not—" Words failed me.

He rolled over, dragging me with him, not stopping until I was straddling him with his arm around my waist to steady me.

I had to brace myself with my hands on his shoulders so I wouldn't topple over and fall onto him. In this position, my breasts flopped and drooped pathetically. Thank God the lights were out so he couldn't see them.

"What are you doing? What's wrong?" I demanded.

"Nothing's wrong for me. But something's wrong for you."

"I don't understand."

"You were lost in your head. I want you to be here with me."

"I'm here."

"I want you to set the pace, Bea."

Set the pace? "But I…"

"Ride me." He reached for my hands and dragged them lower onto his chest, flattening my palms on his body. "Brace yourself like this, and you decide what feels good."

"You feel good," I argued feebly.

"Fucking right, I do. As long as I'm inside you, I feel better than I've ever felt before."

"That's not—"

"Use me, Bea," he cut in. "Figure out what you like."

"I like you," I mumbled.

"Good, because I like you, too. More than like you. Like doesn't even begin to cover it. So use me. My body is at your disposal. You can do anything you want to me."

He'd told me that, or at least something very similar, not too terribly long ago. But I still didn't know what I wanted.

"Come on," he said, and he ran his hands over my hips, the tips of his fingers pressing in just enough to avoid tickling but not enough to push me into anything. "Move around a bit and see what feels good."

I locked my eyes onto his, and, steadying myself

with my hands on his pecs, I rolled my hips in a circular motion.

"Fuck, that's good," he said.

I concurred, but I couldn't spare the energy to say as much. I was too busy doing it again, moving in a wider arc this time.

"Tell me what you want me to do," Blake said.

"Meaning?" It was almost too difficult to form the single-word question since my brain was otherwise occupied in taking in all the sensations I'd never experienced before.

"Do you want me to play with your tits? Rub your clit? Just keep my hands on your hips to help steady you?"

"I don't kn— Touch my breasts," I finally said.

Almost immediately, he brought his hands up to cup me like a bra, gently kneading every time I rolled my hips toward him.

I leaned forward, changing the angle, which put pressure on my clitoris every time I ground against him. That slight shift drew a new moan from my lips.

"Make yourself come," Blake said. "Use me to make yourself come."

"I don't want to use you. Not like that."

"I want to be used." And as if to prove he meant it, he slipped one of his hands down to my hip again and pressed down, adding more friction to my most sensitive place.

A moan slipped out involuntarily.

"That's it," he said when I started rolling my hips over him again. "Take what you need."

I rolled my hips, rising and falling until I was running out of steam and couldn't keep it up any longer. Then I dropped forward over Blake's body, my chest pressed to his, my face buried against his neck, and let the friction of our movements take over.

He fisted a hand in my hair, holding me close to him, his other hand caressing my back, my butt, my thighs, roaming all over me while the climax built inside me.

And then it exploded. Or maybe I did.

"Fuck, that feels good," Blake murmured in my ear.

Every muscle in my body went loose and limp as he drove into me from below a few times, using my body the same way I'd used his, until he reached his own completion.

I lay on top of him for a long time, trying to steady my pulse and remember how to breathe. He kept stroking his hands over my back, my bottom, my thighs, his body heat keeping me captive in a warm cocoon.

But then he stilled.

Was he asleep? I couldn't tell, but it seemed possible, especially with the way his breathing had gone slow and deep, his chest rising and falling beneath me.

I should probably try to disengage my limbs from his. Could I manage it without waking him? Doubtful. Still, I ought to try because we couldn't stay like this. *I* couldn't stay like this. Allowing him to touch me while we had sex was one thing; but now that we weren't moving anymore, and my skin was just sagging all over him…ugh. No. I couldn't stay like this at all.

I tried to inch my way off his prone form.

"Where are you going?" he murmured in a thick, sated, sleepy tone.

"I just… I should—"

"Stay here." Blake's arms tightened around my waist, tugging me closer.

"But I should really—"

"I need you," he cut in.

That was enough to get me to stop in my efforts to disengage my body from his. I'd been prepared for a lot of things, but not that. "You what?"

"I need you. I need you to stay, Bea. Hell, I just need you."

The thing that scared me, though, was that I was starting to need him, too.

Chapter Eighteen

Blake

After a few more days at the hospital with Bea by my side, taking our relationship further every night we spent together in the hotel while keeping the lights off to appease Bea, Grandma insisted that we had to leave her.

"You've both got jobs to do. You've got lives to live. Can't do that while sitting on your asses and watching me die."

I'd tried to argue with them, but to no avail. Eventually, Bea and Grandma had ganged up on me. They'd even gotten Brett—the male nurse Grandma kept harassing—in on it. It seemed Bea had to return home for her niece's quinceañera.

Before I was ready, Bea and I had given Grandma our hugs, and we were on a late-night flight back to Portland together. Bea spent most of the flight working on her laptop, doing some lesson plans or grading or something, so I took out my phone and played Sudoku until my battery was almost dead, wishing I had some of those coloring books—the special ones I'd ordered—to fill the rest of the time. Granted, I supposed I could color some mandalas, but whatever.

It was after midnight in Portland by the time we landed, which meant it was the middle of the night for Grandma. Hoping it wouldn't wake her, I shot off a quick text message to let her know we'd gotten back safely, checked my other messages—including one from Mia with a link to the unedited photos from our shoot—and then I gathered our bags off the carousel.

I'd left my car at the airport, but Bea had taken an Uber to get there so she wouldn't have to pay for parking over an undetermined period. I hauled our bags to my car and loaded them into the trunk before helping her in the passenger side.

Exhaustion might as well be my middle name right now. Too bad I'd never mastered the art of sleeping on a plane—I just couldn't relax up there—maybe it was the altitude or something. Whatever it was, I hadn't gotten a wink of sleep, even though Bea hadn't been any sort of company for me, since she'd worked the entire flight.

In the time I'd been with Grandma, my body had started to adjust to East Coast time and to not getting the workouts I was used to. Jetlag was going to kick my ass; practice and games would kick it even harder.

"Guess you need to get home to Neville and Luna, hmm?" I said, unable to stifle a yawn as I started the ignition.

She nodded, but there was a question in her arched eyebrow.

"What?" I asked, unable to stifle my grin.

"Just surprised you remembered their names."

"I remember shit when I make a point to remember it. When it's something to do with you," I said, barely stopping myself from saying *when I care*. "So I'm taking you home, then?" I asked as I backed out of my parking spot and navigated my way out of the PDX lot.

"My neighbor checked on them after she got home from work today. They'll be all right on their own for one more night."

"Yeah?" My pulse kicked into high gear. I shot a glance in her direction. She was blushing, which was barely visible on her skin, especially with the darkness surrounding us, but it was sexy as fuck. That blush had to be as hot as anything to do with her had ever been.

We'd explored each other every night since that first one. No lights, but still.

I couldn't get enough of her. And it wasn't purely physical. For a long time, I'd thought I would never love anyone but Grandma—not *really* love them. But I couldn't have been more wrong. I was absolutely in love with Bea Castillo, only I didn't know how to convince her of it. More than that, I wasn't sure she'd ever be able to love me. Putting up with me was one thing—loving me was a lot to ask of anyone.

"I just don't think you should be alone tonight," she said, interrupting my thoughts. "I mean, we can go back to my place if you'd rather…"

"Mine's good." Mine was better than good, actually, because I had condoms there, and I was ninety-nine percent sure we could make use of them, given the change in our relationship over the last few days we were in New York. Plus, there wasn't a doubt in my mind that Bea wouldn't have any handy.

Her inexperience was both endearing and sexy as all hell.

I glanced in her direction when I pulled up to a stoplight. She bit her lower lip and nodded, once again proving how innocent she was. My house it was, then.

"We can look at the pictures together when we get there," I said.

"The pictures? She sent them already?" Somehow, Bea's voice had gone up an octave or so. She dug out her phone and powered it on. "I don't have anything."

"She sent them to me."

"Let me see."

"We'll look together," I insisted. "Once we get back to my condo."

Bea pouted, but the light turned green so I couldn't exactly whip out my phone and pull them up for her just now, anyway. I chuckled at her indignation.

When we went inside twenty minutes later, I took a quick look through the massive pile of mail that had accumulated while I'd been gone. Bills, junk, more bills, lots more junk, and a couple of packages at the bottom… I took the junk straight to the trash can in my kitchen and grabbed a couple of bottles of water from the fridge.

"Can we look at them now?" she called out from the living room.

I set my packages and bills on the counter for a moment. I could go through them later. "Impatient much?" I teased, but I knew exactly how anxious she was to see them. Hell, I was pretty anxious to see them, myself, because I had high hopes this would be exactly the impetus she needed to help her see herself the way I saw her. Granted, there was every possibility it could have the opposite effect, but I was choosing not to allow my thoughts to go there.

"Hmph," she said.

"I'm coming," I said, my arms laden with water and some snacks for us both, as well as the mail I intended to open. "We'll look at them together."

Her phone rang just as I joined her again on the couch. She glanced at the screen, and then her expression dropped.

"What's wrong?" I demanded, opening both of our water bottles and setting hers on the coffee table in front of her.

"I'm sorry. Have to take this. It's my mother," Bea grumbled.

"At this hour?"

"She knew when our flight was due." But when she swiped her thumb across the screen and placed the phone at her ear, her tone immediately turned syrupy-sweet. "Hi, Mama." For a long time, she just listened, her face dropping by degrees until it was nothing but a mask of annoyance—an expression I was all too familiar with, as she'd often sent that same look in my direction. And when she finally spoke, it was all in Spanish, so I didn't understand a lick of it. But there was no hiding the agitation in her tone.

Five minutes later, she hung up and looked like she wanted to toss her phone through my wall.

"What was that all about?" I asked cautiously, tearing into the first bill and starting to sort them into piles.

"I missed the dress fitting Mama had arranged for."

"And that's bad because…?"

"Because Mama says it's bad," she bit off, pressing her eyes closed. "I'm sorry," she said when she opened them again. "I shouldn't be taking this out on you."

"It's okay."

"No, it's not. It's not okay at all. Mama just—"

"You don't get along with her?" I scanned another bill, but this one was just an invoice—the payment was set up to pay out of my bank account automatically—so I set it in a separate pile.

"I wouldn't say that, exactly. She just wants to run my life for me. My family—they're not like your grandmother."

"No one's like Grandma," I readily agreed.

"No." Bea's sigh was palpable. "So any chance you're busy on the eighteenth? Do you have a game, or better yet, a road trip?"

"Why do you want me gone?" I asked, unsure whether I should laugh or be concerned.

"Because if you're gone, then I have an excellent excuse for why you can't come with me to Paola's quinceañera."

"What's a quinceañera again? I still don't get it."

"It's like a Sweet Sixteen party, only she's fifteen. It's kind of like her Welcome to Womanhood party or something."

"And you don't want me there?" I tried not to sound hurt, but it definitely stung. Bea had been by my side through everything with Grandma, so I'd hoped we were moving into meet-the-family territory on her side of our relationship equation, too.

"I just don't want you to have to face my family yet."

"Or maybe you don't want them to have to deal with me," I bit off. Was she embarrassed to be with me? Sure seemed that way.

"No!" she insisted. "That's not it. It's just—my family—they're a tough pill to swallow, even for me.

And for you, they might be overwhelming."

"I'm going to have to meet them eventually."

Her brows shot up. "Are you?"

"Aren't I?" I bit off. "Or maybe I'm just reading too much into the last week or so."

"What do you—"

"I just thought that after you flew all the way across the country to be with me, maybe that meant you were ready to be my girlfriend. I thought that since you finally let me touch you, you were ready to be with me."

"I am ready—"

"To be *with* me," I cut in. "Not just sex. That's not what this is about."

"Then what is it about?" she demanded.

"It's about you not wanting to bring me around your family. It's about you being embarrassed about me for some reason."

"No! I'm not embarrassed about you. That's not— I just—"

"I get it," I said. "I'm not the kind of guy you want to bring home to meet the folks."

"More like I'm not sure how you'll respond to them."

"Well, try me. Seems like a good way of finding out. At least to me."

"But what if…"

"What if what?" I prodded.

Bea sighed. "You don't understand. They're not like your grandmother."

"No one's like Grandma."

"But she's the only family you're used to."

"Are you trying to tell me they embarrass you? It's not me, but it's them?"

"Maybe a bit of both?" she squeaked, almost

apologetically. "They'll be glad I'm finally bringing a man around, I suppose."

"But not a man like me?"

"You're not what they'd expect for me."

"Not what they'd ex—"

"You're not Hispanic," she interrupted before I could get the question out, raising a brow pointedly. "Which doesn't matter to me, and it shouldn't matter to them, but it does. And you're younger than me, which again shouldn't be a problem, but it will be. And to be honest, I think they're convinced that I'm never going to get married or have kids, so I can be the one to take care of my parents in their old age or something. I'm the perpetually single one."

"So maybe it's time you show them who you really are. Or who you want to be."

"I've tried. I mean, they didn't like it at all when I had weight-loss surgery."

"Why the hell would they be upset about you making a choice about your own body, something for your health?" I ground out. All of a sudden, I was starting to hate her family, and I'd never even met them. This wouldn't bode well for whenever I did get to know them.

And if I was going to this quinceañera thing, that would apparently be very soon.

She turned apologetic eyes on me. "It's something they talk about before you can have the surgery. I had to see a counselor about it. People treat you differently afterward."

"Meaning?"

"Meaning my family lost control over me in some ways, because when I was fat they knew they could force me into certain things because I didn't have any other options, so now they're trying to regain that control in other ways."

"Well, maybe you just need to convince them they can't control you at all," I said.

"It's not that easy. Not in a family like mine."

All the more reason I supposed I needed to meet them.

"So when's this keen señora thing again?"

"The eighteenth," Bea said, almost hopefully.

I dug out my phone and glanced at the calendar. The eighteenth was coming up soon. "Looks like I'm all yours the whole day." And I tapped in a reminder, just to be sure I didn't forget and plan on anything else that day. There wasn't a chance in hell I'd be letting her go to that thing alone. Not if her family was half as bad as she made it sound.

She groaned.

I winked.

"Aren't you going to open that package?" she asked in a clear bid to change the subject.

I shrugged. "They're probably just some adult coloring books I ordered. They can wait."

"You ordered more?"

"Different kinds of them. It would've been nice to have them while we were gone, actually. Would've given me something to do while Grandma slept and you were working. Something other than playing games on my phone."

"You had some stuff with you."

"But these are better."

"Better?" She arched a brow but didn't press me. "Too bad they took so long arriving."

"Tell me about it," I said, grinning. "Now…how about we take a look at these proofs Mia sent me?"

"Can't I look by myself first?"

"Nope. We took them together, so we're going to see them together." Because I didn't know how much longer I could go without her letting me see her.

Bea

"Take out your laptop," Blake said. "I've got it open on my phone but we'll be able to see them better on your monitor. They'll be bigger."

"I don't know if bigger necessarily means better," I muttered, unzipping the laptop sleeve and slipping the machine out.

"Sure it does. Just ask any Texan. Rachel Campbell will tell you. She's always telling me and anyone who'll listen how everything's bigger and better in Texas."

"Rachel is the tiniest woman I've ever come across."

"Cadence Babcock is probably smaller."

I furrowed my brow, thinking of the tiny blonde figure skater married to the younger of the two Babcock brothers on the team and comparing her to the redheaded pixie. "Not by much."

"Okay, so maybe the people aren't all bigger and better, but everything else is."

I snorted. "I think they're talking about the size of their state."

"Whatever." He rattled off his Wi-Fi password so I could log on, and then he forwarded Mia's email to me so I could open the image gallery for us to see.

It seemed to take forever for the first image to load. Or maybe I was just impatient because I was sure these photos would prove my point, and Blake would realize his mistake, and this would all come crashing to an end.

But as soon as the first photo popped up on my screen, my breath caught in my throat. That couldn't be me. Or if it was, Mia had to have Photoshopped the heck out of every tiny detail in the picture.

Because that woman in the picture was kind of hot.

The whole thing looked sexy as all get-out, especially the heat in Blake's eyes in every single shot.

In a handful of them, I appeared shy—not a surprise. The whole experience had been uncomfortable for me because it had dragged me kicking and screaming out of my comfort zone. But as we scrolled through the gallery, my confidence during the shoot had visibly grown. By a third of the way through, I was laughing and leaning in toward Blake. By the midpoint, a definite sense of lust was visible in my eyes.

The thing that came as a true shock to my system, though, was the pure desire staring back at me in Blake's expression—in all of them. Unless it was a trick of the camera, he was completely into me and what we'd been doing.

My tongue lodged itself in my throat, and I couldn't swallow.

"You like them?" he asked, his voice thick and deep.

I nodded. "I think I do." To my complete and utter shock.

But now I really had to wonder just how much editing Mia had already done, even though she'd said she wouldn't be doing much until after we'd picked out the ones we wanted. Did I actually look like that?

"Good. Because they're hot as hell. *You're* hot as hell." Blake leaned in and captured my lips in a determined kiss that made me forget my insecurities, at least for a bit. "So which ones should we have her finalize for us?" he asked, giving me another quick peck.

We spent the next twenty minutes poring over every image Mia had sent us. With each photo, Blake inched closer to me. Not that I minded in the slightest. His heat was intoxicating; his scent was addictive.

Finally, we finished going through the shots and sent Mia a message to let her know they were ready for her to finalize.

With his arm draped around my shoulders, hugging me to his side, Blake buried his nose in my hair. He took a deep whiff, then sighed. "After this, you think maybe you'll be ready to let me see you soon?"

"Maybe?"

"So we can try it?"

"Dim lighting, at first?"

"I can compromise like that. I'm good at compromise. Grandma made sure of it."

But could I follow through? I wanted to, but I just wasn't sure what would happen once my clothes came off but the lights stayed on. Even just thinking about it had my pulse galloping at lightning speed.

"You going to stay with me tonight?" he murmured.

I nodded, tentativeness warring with desire.

He pressed a quick kiss to my temple and got up. "Give me ten minutes to get ready for you."

"Get ready?" I stifled a nervous chuckle. Shouldn't I be the one who might need a bit of time to prepare? I tried to remember when I'd last shaved my legs. Was it two days ago or three? I was probably stubbly.

"I just want to change the sheets. I'm not sure when I did it last…"

"Oh." That was a bit of thoughtfulness I hadn't

expected from him. I nodded him on his way. But then I realized I should do something so I wasn't sitting here getting more and more anxious by the moment, but I wasn't sure what. Settling in for a bit of work didn't seem like the brightest idea, so I shut down my laptop and set it aside.

The padded mailer was still sitting on the coffee table in front of me, though—the coloring books Blake had ordered. Surely that had to be what it was. I could open his package for him, get rid of the trash, and maybe have a look through the images just to get a better sense of what had struck his fancy now that he'd been doing these crafty things for a while. It might come in handy for me later—in case I wanted to get him a gift at some point down the line.

Random bumping sounds filtered into the living room from the direction of his bedroom. It shouldn't take him too much longer to finish changing his sheets.

I tore open the mailer and took out the coloring books. The first one made me laugh out loud. It was called *Swearing Words for Dirty Mouths and Dirtier Hands*. That fit him to a T. I flipped through a few pages to get a sense for what was in the book—the images were frilly, flowery letters with cute animals surrounding them like bunnies, kittens, and puppies, and they spelled out words like *cumbucket*, *dipshit*, *twatwaffle*, *douchecanoe*, and *thundercunt*.

After almost snorting in laughter and turning another page, I closed that first book and set it aside, making a mental note to remind him *not* to bring anything like that to my classroom. I could already imagine the angry emails and phone calls I'd be getting from parents if their children went home saying things like *fucktrumpet*.

I switched that book to the back of the stack and brought the next one forward, and my tongue suddenly felt really thick.

Dirty Girls Doing Dirty Work was the title, and it had an image of an almost nude pinup type girl, wearing nothing but a tiny apron that barely covered her overly enhanced assets. Her impossibly long and curvy legs were spread shoulder-width apart, and she had a feather duster in one hand.

I opened the cover and found more of the same. The next one had an almost-nude sanitation worker riding on the back of a trash truck, her ridiculously large and buoyant breasts practically spilling out of her tiny uniform.

Every page I flipped to was more of the same.

I wanted to vomit.

Because this was what Blake was *really* attracted to. Not me. Maybe he could pretend he was into me, but I could never be what he was truly attracted to. He wanted a Barbie doll in human form, and that was something I wouldn't want to be even if I had any control over it.

I'd only been fooling myself to think he could want *me*—no matter how hard he had tried to convince me otherwise. The photo shoot we'd done? That was probably nothing more than his attempt to get me as close to what he'd find in the pages of this book as he possibly could.

If that was his goal, it'd been an utter and complete failure. Maybe I looked better in reality than I could have believed about myself, but I would never look like this. Not even if I could afford plastic surgery to tighten things up a bit, and that wasn't ever going to happen.

I dropped the coloring books on his coffee table and started gathering up my things, debating how long it would take to get an Uber to come and pick me up at this hour. That would be easier than trying to take my suitcases with me on the Max. And now that I'd thought through my options, I took out my phone and opened the Uber app so I could start the process of arranging a ride.

"What are you doing?" Blake asked, his impossibly perfect body filling the doorway and making me want to be with him again even as I wanted to punch him in the nose. He must have stripped down to his briefs while he was changing his sheets. Perfect, glorious muscle filled my eyes, making me want to lick him to see if he tasted as good as he looked.

Bad line of thinking. This wouldn't help.

Well, good. If he was in his underwear, he wouldn't come chasing after me when I left.

"I'm going home," I bit off, but my voice wobbled. I silently cursed myself for allowing him to see just how upset I was. He didn't need to have that kind of power over me.

"But I thought we—"

"But nothing, Blake." I slammed my laptop back into the outer pocket of my suitcase—probably harder than I should have—and zipped all the pockets.

The hurt in his eyes nearly killed my resolve.

Nearly. But not quite.

"What did I do wrong this time?" he demanded.

"Nothing. This is all me."

"If you're not ready—"

"I'm not," I cut in. "That's it. And the truth is, I'll probably never be ready."

"I don't understand."

"I shouldn't say probably. I'll never be ready. Okay? This can't happen. I need to get home to Neville and Luna."

"But—"

My Uber app dinged. I glanced down at the screen of my phone. A driver had accepted the fare and was pulling in, ready to pick me up. "I've got to go," I said.

Then I grabbed the handle of my suitcase, tossed the strap of my purse over my shoulder, and headed out his front door.

Only once my hand was on the door to the Uber driver's car did I allow the first tear to fall.

Chapter Nineteen

Blake

What the fuck had just happened? It took about ten or fifteen panicked seconds for my brain to kick in. I scanned the room in a desperate attempt to figure out what I could have possibly done wrong this time, what I was missing. Nothing came close to cluing me in until my eyes landed on the adult coloring books I'd ordered sitting on the coffee table—the one with pinup girls at the very top of the stack—with the ripped-open mailer haphazardly discarded next to them.

Just like that, everything clicked.

Not bothering to put on clothes or even shoes or a coat, I took off after Bea. Even though she could power-walk like nobody's business, my legs were still longer than hers, my stride far more powerful. I caught up to her just as she was loading her bags into the trunk of her waiting getaway car.

"Bea!" I shouted and reached for her hand to stop her.

She whirled around on me, her cheeks wet with tears, her arm raised as if to slap me, her fingers curling like she wanted to punch me in the nose.

Maybe I deserved it.

Actually, I was almost positive deserved it. I usually did. That was the way most things in my life always went, wasn't it?

Only, now that I thought about it, I wasn't sure I did this time. She'd misinterpreted something, a huge mix-up, but that wasn't my fault. I'd still let her hit me, though, if it meant getting her to come back into my condo so we could talk through the misunderstanding, because I hadn't explained things in advance.

"Let go of me," she bit off, jerking her arm with more force than I'd realized she could produce. She was a hell of a lot stronger than she looked, which turned me on in a twisted sort of way.

I stifled the lust coursing through my veins. "No, I won't let go of you. Not yet. I'm not letting you leave like this. We need to talk."

Willing to take whatever she could dish out, I stood my ground, refusing to release the hand I'd grabbed because I couldn't let her leave. Not like this, at least. I was already losing Grandma, and there wasn't a single motherfucking thing I could do to prevent that; I couldn't lose Bea, too, especially not over something we could talk through like adults.

She didn't strike me, but it seemed like a near miss. "Let me go," she ground out, her voice laced with a devastating combination of anger and pain.

"You agreed to explain shit to me. Now's a good

time to do that."

"I have *nothing* to say to you."

"Well, I have things I need to say to you, and you're going to listen."

"You okay, lady?" the scrawny, pimpled Uber driver asked. He had his cell phone in his hand, and it was already halfway to his ear. "Need me to call for help?"

"I'm fine," she bit off and turned back to me. "What the *hell* could you possibly say that I would want to hear? And just why do you think I'll be willing to listen?"

The fact that she'd used a curse word, however mild, only further proved how upset she was. I'd never heard her say so much as *darn it* before. I wasn't even positive words like that were in her vocabulary prior to spending time around me. Probably weren't, because of her students. She'd never curse in front of them, which was just one more thing I adored about her.

And that was what she had to understand. I loved her. I loved her more than I could bear, and she loved me, too.

Didn't she?

"You're going to listen because you love me," I said, and she froze, glaring at me.

I hoped like hell I was right.

No one had ever loved me before other than Grandma, though, so I could only cross my fingers that I wasn't reading too much into the ways Bea had been responding to me lately.

"You love me," I continued, "and I love you, and we need to find a way to make this work."

"You don't love me."

I noticed she didn't deny that *she* loved *me*, latching on to her admission by omission as a lifeline. "Bullshit.

I do. And so do you. And it isn't just physical, either." It *had* to be more than physical. She would never have allowed the physical side of our relationship to get as far as it had if she didn't love me, or so I had to believe.

"It's definitely not physical on your side."

"And whose fault is that? Who won't allow me to see her?"

"Whatever, Blake. You just think you can control me, the same as my family's always done. But you don't love me; you just want to use me. You want me to fill certain needs you've got, but that's all it would be— using me. And then you'll meet your other needs by going behind my back to do it. You can probably have any woman you want while you're on the road with the team."

"And why the fuck would I want someone else?"

"You want someone who looks like those women in that book you ordered."

"You mean those drawings? The ones that aren't even remotely realistic? I've never met a woman in real life who looks like those pictures. I want a fucking real woman."

"Yeah, a real woman with a perfect body," she bit off with a sob.

"I don't want a fucking Barbie doll. And there's no such thing as a perfect body."

"Obviously not where I'm concerned."

Fuck, this wasn't going well. Getting through her haze of self-hatred was proving to be far more difficult than I'd ever imagined. Should've realized it would be next to impossible, though, because getting anything through *my* thick skull was next to impossible. Why should it be any easier with her?

"I want you," I insisted.

"A perfect Barbie doll or two in every city you play in," she continued as if she hadn't heard me, "just like in that coloring book. And stupid, fat Bea will be back at home waiting for whatever crumbs you feel like throwing her way."

"It's just a coloring book. I don't want you to look like those pictures. I knew what I was getting when I signed up for this."

"Yeah, and what's that? Some old fat chick who isn't good enough for you, so you can use her for whatever you want."

"*You're* the one who doesn't think you're good enough for me—not me. You might as well have just said as much yourself. I think you're perfect. Or at least you're perfect for me, which is all that matters."

"You just want me to take the place of your Grandma," Bea spluttered, tears bubbling over as she blatantly ignored every argument I made.

"What?" I demanded.

"You want someone who can take care of you. That's all I am to you. I'm just a replacement for your grandmother once she's gone."

Talk about kicking me when I was already down. "Don't go there. Don't bring her into this."

"Why not? It's the truth. Even *she* could see you needed someone else to keep you in line. That was the only reason she encouraged me to go along with any of this."

"I'm not using you!" I almost shouted. "I want to be with you."

"Yeah, right. Whatever you say, Blake." She tried to shrug me off again, but I tightened my grip.

"Blake?" the driver said, making us both jump since we'd essentially forgotten he was there. "You're Blake

Kozlow, right? The Storm player? I thought you looked familiar."

"We're kind of busy here," I bit off.

"You don't have to be rude to him," Bea said.

Fuck a duck, she was right, and the last thing I needed was for this guy to spread shit all over social media. I'd already done enough of that on my own for one lifetime.

Maybe Jim Sutter had been willing to overlook my foul-up once before, but I couldn't delude myself into believing I had carte blanche with him.

"Sorry," I said, glaring in his direction, and he shook his head, holding his hands up in surrender even though he wasn't the one who'd done anything wrong. I could only hope he wouldn't immediately pull up Facebook or Twitter and start posting a bunch of shit about me having a fight with my girlfriend out in the street.

Girlfriend. The word felt right. We hadn't made anything official, but hell if I didn't want it to be as official as I could make it. That lit a new fire under my ass.

"I'm still not buying it," Bea said. "Your interest in me has never made any sense. Not if I use my brain."

"Maybe your brain is what's fucking with you, then. Wouldn't be the first time."

"I think we both know that's the truth."

"Exactly. We do. So what's the problem?"

"I don't think it's all *only* in my head. There're too many signs pointing toward me being right about this."

"What fucking signs? A goddamned coloring book?"

"Yes."

"Seriously?" I almost shouted. "That one tiny thing

is enough to send you into a tailspin after the last couple of weeks?"

"And the photo shoot. You were trying to make me into something I'm not."

"I was trying to help you *see* that you're not what you think you are!" I countered, my frustration starting to boil over. "Everyone else can see it. It's just you. You and your fucking twisted brain screwing with you."

"It isn't just me." And this time, she really did start crying, damn it all. "Everyone who looks at us will see it. They'll wonder why someone like you would bother being with someone like me."

"Who the hell is this 'everyone' you keep bringing up?"

"Everyone! The whole world. Dani—"

"Let's leave Dani out of this. That chick hates me."

"Maybe she's right to hate you. Maybe I should, too."

"But you don't," I insisted. "You don't hate me. You fucking love me."

"You sure you don't need me to call the cops?" the driver interrupted. "I'm thinking I should maybe call them."

"Do you want him to call the police?" I asked Bea, forcing myself to remain as calm as possible. Bea was already agitated enough for the both of us, and that damned driver wasn't much better. "Do you want to have me arrested?" That'd go over *really* well with the team.

Yeah, the team had agreed to give me a second chance, but getting arrested for fighting with my girlfriend out in the middle of the street while wearing nothing but my fucking briefs?

Timbuktu, here I come. I'd never play another game in the NHL.

"No," she finally muttered, her scowl directed at her feet.

I breathed a sigh of relief. "Then can we go back inside and talk about this like adults? It's cold out here."

"Not my fault you didn't put on any clothes before chasing after me. Doesn't seem very adult-like."

My eye roll was so big it should've given me a crick in my neck. "Yeah, I know. I'm stupid and immature."

"I didn't say—"

"If I'd done that," I interrupted, "you would've been gone by the time I got out here. Running away instead of confronting me? Also not very grown up. I'm not the only one being immature."

Her expression soured and turned sulky, so I knew I'd scored on that point.

"Come on," I said, deciding it was time to take advantage of her too-brief moment of acquiescence. I dropped my grip on her arm and threaded my fingers through hers. I wanted to coax her to come with me, not force her.

She allowed it, so I tugged her bag out of the guy's trunk again with my free hand.

"I'm not so sure about this," the driver said. "I don't like it."

"I'm fine," Bea insisted.

She wasn't fine, but I didn't want to argue the point out here. As it was, we'd be lucky if none of my neighbors were filming us and streaming it live on the internet. Besides, the sooner I could get her inside so we could talk, the sooner I could help her get *fine* again. Or better than fine if I was lucky.

I really hoped I could get lucky—in more than one way.

"I'd give you a tip for sticking around and waiting for her through all of this," I said, glancing over my shoulder at the guy, "but I don't have any cash on me."

"I wouldn't want it even if you did. Not keen on touching money that's been rubbing up against some other guy's junk or something."

A few dozen stupid comebacks tickled my tongue, begging me to let them fly, but I kept them in check. Maybe I was finally learning to keep my lips zipped when necessary. I could hope, at least.

Instead, I headed for my door, tugging both Bea and her bag in my wake.

"I'll tip you through the app," Bea called out over her shoulder, but he was already back in his car and driving away, fastening his seat belt as he went. Probably wanted to get the hell away from the crazy, almost-naked dude chasing after a chick and arguing in the street despite the freezing temperatures.

I made a mental note to call Jim Sutter once this was all sorted out—just in case the driver or one of my neighbors was posting about the fiasco online. But that would have to wait until Bea and I were okay again.

I'd left the front door open on my way out, but I closed it behind us when we reentered.

Bea looked ready to bolt again just because of that, so I intentionally left the door unlocked. Didn't want her to think I was forcing her to stay.

"I know why you're upset," I said.

"You don't—"

"It's those coloring books."

She scowled.

"I thought we'd agreed we would talk about things

instead of jumping to conclusions."

"Didn't seem like there was anything we needed to talk about."

"No? Just proves that you've jumped straight to the worst possible conclusion."

She crossed her arms in a self-protective gesture. "Well, what else am I supposed to think? It's obvious what kind of woman you go for."

"Yeah, I'd think so, but it seems not. Women who can kick my ass when I need it—that's what I want. And apparently I need my ass kicked often."

"More like women who look like supermodels," she scoffed.

"Do you see any supermodels in here?" I demanded.

She pointed at the fucking coloring book with a *duh* expression obscuring her face.

"The only supermodel I see in here is you. The only supermodel I *want* is you."

"Yeah, sure. Supermodel." She must have been taking eye-rolling lessons from Dani Williams, because she'd never rolled them quite so impressively before.

"Do you need to look at the pictures from the shoot again?"

She glared, but I could tell her façade was starting to crumble.

"What the hell do I have to do to convince you that I want you? *You*, Bea. Only you."

"I don't—"

But before she could finish her thought, I cut her off by kissing her like I'd never kissed her before—like I was desperate.

Because I was.

I was desperate for her to believe me.

Desperate for her touch.

Desperate to be inside her again, and I didn't think there was any better way of convincing her than by showing her exactly what I wanted and craved and *needed*.

Desperate to convince her I loved her.

At first, she pushed against my chest, trying to fend me off, but she didn't put much effort behind it. When I slid my tongue along the seam of her lips, she opened with a frustrated groan of longing, and then her fingers were digging into my shoulders with the same kind of frenetic lust that was coursing through my body.

Only for me, it wasn't just lust. And I didn't think it was for her, either.

"Condoms," I murmured against her lips. I took hold of her hand and tugged her to her feet. "Need a condom. In my bedroom."

Both of us ripping at her clothes as we went, I nudged her backward through the hall toward my bedroom, but we bumped into the wall and ended up staying there. As soon as I got her shirt up and over her head, I dug my fingers into the softness around her waist and kissed a wet trail from her chin down to the soft swell above her bra.

"Not like this," she said, the words coming out sounding both frantic and heated at once. "Turn off the lights. There's too much light."

In a condo like this, there would always be too much light. I had huge, open windows spanning the entire outside wall, so during the day it was as bright as the outside world and at night the lights of the city brightened every room.

Or maybe I should say that there would be too much light for her until she finally gave up and realized that she was beautiful.

And apparently, it was up to me to convince her.

And besides that… "I need to see you, Bea." I slipped a finger inside one cup of her bra and tugged it down enough that I could lower my head and flick her hard nipple with my tongue. "I need to touch you. I need to be with you. I need you."

Her entire body shuddered, which gave my semi all the encouragement it needed to grow up and join the big boys' club.

I ground my hips against her softness as I raised my head again, claiming her lips for a searing kiss before tasting every fucking inch of her flushed face, her sleek neck, her perfect shoulders.

Instead of pushing me away, she flung her arms around my shoulders, one hand pressed to the back of my head and guiding me where she wanted me.

Fuck yes. My dick stood up at full attention.

"How do you do this to me?" she demanded, breathless and bossy at the same time, which only made me harder.

"Same way you drive me crazy."

My lips found hers again, and she barely needed any prodding to open up and let me in. And then we were both pawing at what remained of her clothes, discarding them as quickly as we could. I lifted her off her feet, leaning into her and pressing her back against the wall, one knee between her thighs to help her balance. Her shoes hit the wall and clattered to the floor as I fumbled with her button and fly.

She shimmied her hips around. I backed away enough that she could free the jeans from her hips, and then they tangled around her ankles.

We both laughed like loons.

Fuck, but I loved laughing with her. I missed that. We'd laughed so much on that first date, all those months ago, with Dani and Harry.

Her laughter turned me on more than anything I thought possible.

I held her steady so she could kick her jeans free, my palms settling on the soft flesh of her outer thighs. But the laughter fizzled away when I lowered my lips to the silky spot just above her bra. Her breathing turned sharp, erratic.

I pointed my tongue and licked a trail across her collarbone, and she shuddered, her legs squirming against me like she couldn't decide what to do with them.

All I wanted to do was wrap those thighs around my waist and drive into her until I couldn't think anymore. Until *she* couldn't think anymore—actually, that seemed like it ought to be the ultimate goal. Until all she could do was call out my name while her pussy quivered around me, if she could even remember my name with all that happening.

To that end, I hitched my hands beneath her thighs and carried her into my bedroom.

"What are you doing?" Bea demanded, sounding frantic as she squirmed in my grip.

"What do you think I'm doing?"

"Put me down. I'm too heavy. You'll hurt your back or something."

But despite her squirming, I managed to flip on the light switch in my bedroom.

"No lights," she pleaded, trying to cover herself.

"Yes."

"Blake…" She tried to fling an arm over her breasts, but I tugged her hand away so they'd fall however they would. "They just jiggle so much. It's embarrassing."

"The jiggly bits are my favorite bits."

She arched a disbelieving brow. I kissed her just there.

"You don't really understand men, you know that?" I said, ripping back the blankets so I could sit down and haul Bea onto my lap.

She straddled my thighs, her wide, dark eyes full of heat, holding her weight off me. "How do you mean?"

"The parts you want to hide are the parts we're into the most."

She let out a *hmph* of disbelief and sent her hair flying. "You shouldn't have done that. Carrying me like that." But she didn't try to pull away or climb off me.

I shrugged. "Too late to undo it."

She almost smiled. "You're awful."

"I know." I pecked her on the tip of her nose. "And you're hot."

"Don't—"

"You're hot," I repeated, pressing a finger to her lips to shush her before she could tell me more lies about how unhot she was.

She pursed them and kissed the very tip, which made me think about those lips kissing the tip of another part of my anatomy. But frankly, I'd rather have that part of my anatomy kissed by a different pair of her lips.

"I'll never look like those comics," she said.

"Good. I don't want you to."

"I don't look like I should be with you."

"What the fuck is that supposed to mean?" I demanded.

"You're famous." Her dark eyes locked on mine. "People have expectations."

"People can go fuck themselves, then. They don't get to decide who I take home with me." But then another thought struck me. "Are you worried what they'll say about you online or something? On Twitter?"

"Not exactly…"

"Which means you are," I inferred. Damn it. She might have a point about the fans saying shit, but I didn't want her worrying about anything like that.

"I don't care what anyone says about me. I don't pay attention to that stuff. But you've got a history…"

Yeah, I did. And not a good one. That very history was what had led to us getting to know one another, though, so it wasn't all bad. "Leave it to me to handle that. I'll get the team's PR crew to help me if it comes to that."

"Just don't do anything stupid," Bea said.

"I'll do my best. On one condition."

She arched a brow.

"You stop arguing with me and let me show you just how fucking gorgeous you are."

Bea tried to give me a stern look, but then she dissolved in laughter.

I swallowed her laughter with a kiss…and flipped us around until I was on top of her. Her dark curls splayed out across the mattress, and a surprised look widened her eyes, but her body softened beneath me.

Because I tickled her ribs, and she laughed. She laughed so hard that she snorted, which made me laugh, too.

But then we were kissing again, and stripping off the rest of our clothes. I kissed and caressed her all over, worshipping every inch of her skin and making sure she knew how much she turned me on.

Even after I made her come and she curled up in my arms, she was still laughing.

I hoped I could always make her laugh.

Chapter Twenty

Blake

"How's your grandma?" Babs asked as soon as I walked into the locker room the next morning. One thing about our captain—he could always be counted on to remember the little details about the rest of us.

Granted, Grandma wasn't exactly a small detail in my life. And I supposed I had been gone for a couple of weeks, so the boys were bound to notice my absence, even if it was only because the room was a lot quieter without me or something. Still, I doubted many of the other guys would know or care why I'd been gone for so long. They probably just appreciated the fact that I hadn't been doing naked yoga in front of them for a while.

Shrugging, I solemnly shook my head. I couldn't put words to any of it. Not yet. My throat swelled closed just thinking about how she was when I'd left her. My tongue got so thick I couldn't swallow. The fact that I probably wouldn't ever see her in person again—or at least not until I returned to bury her—just about did me in every time I allowed my mind to go there.

If I was lucky, the doctors might be able to give me enough warning that I could tell her I loved her one final time. But I knew better than to count on it, living all the way across the country and potentially being on the road with the team whenever the time came.

I wasn't counting on being lucky. Luck had never been on my side before.

Babs slapped me on the back in commiseration, which was about as much emotion as I was willing to accept from anyone just now, and we both headed out to the ice for practice.

And it was one hell of a doozy. This morning's practice kicked my ass, and it wasn't just because I hadn't been getting in any kind of decent workouts while I'd been on the other coast, either. Sitting by Grandma's bed and having wet dreams with Bea sleeping so close to me was about all the physical activity I'd managed to get in while I was gone, and that clearly wasn't enough. My first game back was going to be brutal.

Not only that, but Bergy seemed determined to kick all our asses from here into next week.

Turned out that the boys had gone on a week-long losing streak just before my return. I should've been paying more attention to the scores, but frankly, hockey and my teammates had been the last things on my mind. In my absence, they'd dropped four straight games—all but one of them against divisional opponents, no less, and only one resulted in any points in the standings due to reaching overtime—and now we'd fallen from first place to fourth in the Pacific Division.

We were only holding on to a playoff spot by the skin of our teeth.

Yeah, there were still several months to go before the playoffs started, but gaining ground in this league was hard, even though losing ground could be surprisingly easy. My team had just proven the latter.

The skid couldn't continue. It had to end, and it had to end now.

By the time we finally hit the showers after practice, almost every guy on the team was huffing for oxygen and dripping buckets of sweat. At least it wasn't just me—although my exhaustion went well beyond that of the others, due to my lack of activity.

My linemates, at least, seemed happy to have me back in the thick of things.

"Coop is good," Luddy said, jumping under the shower spray in the stall next to me. "And he's getting better. But he's not you."

"Thought that might be a good thing," I shot back. "Change of pace. Keep things interesting."

"So did I." He grinned.

"Don't tell me you missed me."

"Only on the ice, man. Only on the ice."

When I came out of the showers, Burnzie popped my ass with a wet, rolled-up towel.

"The fuck was that for?" I demanded, rounding on him, ready to lash out. My nerves were already frayed, and Burnzie poking the bear didn't help matters any.

"Brie wants to know how the photo shoot went."

"Photo shoot?" Babs asked, looking up from putting on his shoes, and about half a dozen of our other teammates leaned in to find out what was going on.

"Fine," I hedged.

"Is Bea okay with Brie seeing them?"

"Bea?" Harry said, slowing down on his way past us to his own stall. He finished drying off his insanely red hair and tossed his towel in a waiting laundry cart.

Well, hell. This wasn't supposed to be happening just yet. I wasn't sure if she'd be willing for the entire team to know we were an item. But we were an item—weren't we? Pretty sure we were. So they'd all find out eventually, including Dani Williams.

Might as well happen now, I supposed.

"Dani's Bea?" he continued. "The same one from—"

"Yes, the same Bea," I cut in.

"What kind of photo shoot?" Hammer asked on his way to the trainers' room.

"The kind that you'll never get to see evidence of," I shot back, and half the guys snorted in laughter.

"But Brie can, right?" Burnzie asked. "She's been bugging me about it ever since you first hit her up for ideas. 'When's he going to be back? When do I get to meet his girlfriend? When is he going to show us the pictures? We need to make plans for the WAGs shoot if we're going to do it.' I don't even know what this fucking WAGs shoot she's talking about is, but she won't stop pestering me about these pictures."

And I probably wasn't the right guy to fill him in on any of that, either.

"I need to double-check with Bea to be sure she's okay with it, but probably."

Grayson Kowalski piped up with, "Who the fuck is this Bea chick, anyway?" as he headed for the showers.

Gray was new to the team this season—a late signing. He'd only joined the team about ten games into the season, to fill a hole we still hadn't filled. Lower-line winger.

I wasn't sure he'd be lasting long with us. Didn't seem to gel with the rest of the guys. He might even be a worse fit than me, which was saying something.

There'd been a part of me hoping that they'd bring Luke Weber in, instead. The kid had practiced with us before training camp had started. No one else had signed him. Maybe he wasn't quite as skilled as Gray, but his attitude was a hell of a lot better. Sometimes, attitude was more important.

I didn't want to think about that too much, though, because my own attitude was easily as obnoxious as Gray's. Maybe even more so. But my teammates were willing to put up with me because I produced on the ice.

The only thing Gray had been producing so far was a bunch of time spent in the penalty box. I tended to spend more than my fair share of time in the sin bin, too, but at least I added a goal or assist more games than not. Plus, the coaches relied on me in the face-off circle more than anyone but Riley Jezek.

"Someone you'll never get to meet if you keep acting like a fucking douchecanoe," I finally replied.

"I'm not the douchecanoe who abandoned his teammates for a couple of weeks," Gray shot back. "Right in the middle of the fucking season, with the playoffs on the line."

The urge to rip the guy a new asshole nearly overwhelmed me, but Bergy walked into the room just then. I couldn't afford to do anything else that might land me in his doghouse. I bit my tongue and threw on my clothes, wanting to get the fuck away from Gray before I did something else I'd regret.

"Kowalski," Bergy grumbled in a menacing tone. He stood near the entry to the showers, arms crossed, with a glare permanently etched into his features.

Shocked that he wasn't griping at me, I ducked my head and tried to pretend I wasn't interested.

"Coach?" Gray replied.

"You have a problem with your teammate taking care of his family?"

Gray tried to answer, but Bergy cut him off before he could get a word out.

"I'll be sure to remember that when your wife goes into labor. She can handle delivering twins without your help, right?"

Gray mumbled something that no one could make out, and then he headed for his own stall and left me alone.

I caught Bergy's eye and gave him a nod of thanks.

He glared for a moment, then gave a brisk jerk of his head and left the room.

I took that to mean I was supposed to follow him, so I dragged on the rest of my clothes and headed for the hall.

"You doing okay?" he asked gruffly, without preamble, when I caught up to him.

"Not really."

He nodded curtly. "Sophie sent something with me to give you."

"Sophie?" What the hell could his stepdaughter have sent me? Whatever it was, he didn't seem happy about giving it to me. But then again, he was never happy about anything to do with me, so his mood wasn't a good indicator.

"In here," he muttered, heading for his office.

I followed him inside, and I took a seat in the chair he pointed at. He sat in his usual chair on the opposite side of his desk, bending over to dig something out of the Storm duffel bag he always carried with him to the practice facility.

When he finally came up again, he tossed me a stack of heavy art paper, bound on one side with yarn threaded through a series of holes. On the top was a watercolor painting that I could only assume was meant to be a portrait of me, as I could make out a Storm jersey and the number fourteen on the sleeve. But I was surrounded by kids with smiling faces. One of them at the front—who had a smile just like Sophie's—was hugging me around the waist. The words painted over the top read "Just Like Me."

My tongue felt thick. I couldn't swallow.

I opened the cover and scanned every page in the book. Every piece of artwork had clearly been created by a different kid. The styles were obviously different, not to mention the skill levels. But it was obvious that I was a feature in every one of them.

And several of them had me holding hands with a gray-haired woman, who I had to assume was Grandma. A few others had a different woman next to me—one with dark, curly hair. Must be Bea. My favorite picture had to be the one that had an ugly imitation of my grinning face, with almost all of my teeth missing.

"I don't understand," I said. But that wasn't entirely true. I just couldn't wrap my brain around the fact that these kids, who ought to hate me for the things that I'd said a while back, had made something for me.

Bergy scowled. "Sophie and some of her middle

school classmates went to Bea's school while you two were gone. It was a field trip—something where the older students could help the younger students. They worked together to make this book for you. I told them I'd deliver it when you got back. They're expecting you back in the classroom soon, but not right away. They know you have a job to do on the ice."

I nodded, too choked up to say anything. But I'd have to eventually come up with something to say to Sophie, at least.

That little girl had the biggest heart of anyone I'd ever met.

I nodded my thanks and Bergy sent me on my way.

Before leaving the practice facility for my pregame nap, I took out my cell phone and shot off a message to Bea, letting her know about the book and asking if it would be all right to share the images from our shoot with Brie Burns.

Bea was at school right now, so I didn't expect an answer until quite a bit later. Color me shocked when I got an immediate response.

> Bea: *It's fine for Brie to see them. But ONLY Brie. I haven't even shown Dani yet. Not sure I will, actually.*

> Me: *Done. But why aren't you willing to show Dani?*

> Bea: *She's not your biggest fan.*

> Me: *But she is yours. Wouldn't she want to be part of this?*

Bea: *Maybe. I'll think about it.*

Me: *As long as it's just me you don't want her to see and it's not about you hiding…*

Bea: *My kids told me about the book today. They'll be excited that you got it. When's the next time you can come read to them?*

Me: *Maybe the week after your niece's quinceañera?*

Bea: *We'll sit down with a calendar and figure it out soon.*

Before I could second-guess myself, I shot off a quick text message to Brie with the link to the image gallery and a note that it was for her eyes only, and she was not to share these images with anyone, including her husband.

Then I headed home for my pregame nap. Lord knew I could use the rest.

Bea

One good thing to come from spending as much time on the East Coast with Blake as I had was that I'd demolished any possibility of going through with the dress fitting my mother had been insisting on for Paola's quinceañera. The seamstress Mama had arranged for would never be able to finish a dress in time, which meant I could wear whatever I wanted—

within reason, of course.

Of course, "within reason" for me meant something entirely different than it did for my mother. But that was what had led to the fashion show I was putting on for Dani Williams before the Storm's home game against the Ducks.

"You're *not* wearing brown," she muttered, giving the first dress I'd held up the stink eye before dipping her spoon in the Halo Top ice cream I'd brought her as a bribe. She savored the bite like she was experiencing nirvana. It was Red Velvet, which I knew was her favorite. Obviously, I've never been above bribery and tricks.

"Brown looks good on my skin," I countered, eyeing the dress I'd held up for her. It was perfectly acceptable—it even had a few shimmery bronze and gold details, so it wasn't completely plain and boring. This was the sort of dress that would allow me to blend into the crowd of other older women at the quinceañera, and blending in sounded ideal.

"Everything looks good on your skin," Dani argued. "You've got amazing skin. You can get away with anything with your coloring." She stabbed her spoon into the carton again. "What color is your niece wearing?"

"It's kind of a deep burgundy."

"Then you should pick something in the same color family." She narrowed her eyes, scanning the rack of dresses I'd brought with me. Her eyes lit up, and she pointed her spoon toward the end of the rack. "What's that red thing look like?"

"It's...nothing." I shouldn't have even brought *that red thing*, as she'd described it, with me today. It was a slinky, silky dress that Mia and Angie had pushed me to try on while we were lingerie shopping. I'd been so stunned by how I'd looked in it that I'd bought it, never mind the fact that I had no earthly idea where or when I might wear it.

As a teacher, I didn't have too many opportunities to dress up. Certainly not in something slinky.

"Nothing, hmm?" Dani muttered. "I think that means you need to show me."

Grudgingly, I took the hanger off the rack and held it up for Dani to see.

"Put it on, smart-ass."

"The only smart-ass I see in here is you."

"And proud of it. Now strip and let me see you in it."

There wasn't much point in arguing anymore. This was the whole reason I was here, after all. But first… "No one in your family's going to walk in on me like this, are they?"

"They're all at the game. The guys are playing. Dad's coaching. Mom and Katie are in the box. Luke is working. It's just you and me, *chica*."

Taking her at her word, I stripped down to my bra and undies. Then I drew the slinky material over my head. "I'd have to get into some shapewear first to keep all my bulges in check, but you can get the general idea."

The fabric shifted into place after a few slight tugs, and Dani's eyes lit up. "Omigod. Bea Castillo, you've been holding out on me."

"I told you. I can't wear something like this around my fam—"

"This is *exactly* what you need to wear around your family. Let them see what a hottie you are. Who needs an LBD when you've got an LRD like that one?" She set her carton of Halo Top aside and waved me over to the bed. "Can I make a few alterations?" she asked, tugging at the hem and reaching for a stuffed red tomato-shaped cushion full of pins.

My wary-o-meter started going haywire. Mainly because the look in Dani's eye couldn't possibly mean anything good for me.

"What kind of alterations?"

"The kind where I take it up about an inch or three at the bottom." She folded the fabric and put the pin in place so that it fell a few inches above my knee instead of a couple of inches below.

"That's more like six inches!" I complained.

She kept placing her pins, though, somehow managing to avoid poking them through my skin. "Hardly."

"That's half a foot. You're insane."

"What else is new? I've been on bed rest forever and a day, and this baby isn't going to come out for a while yet. Anyone would be insane in my shoes. But go look in the mirror with it like that."

When I didn't immediately comply, she shoved me away from the bed, reaching for her ice cream again in the same motion.

I stood in front of the mirror and grudgingly admitted to myself that she had a point.

"So?" she demanded. "Can I fix it up for you?"

"Fine," I grumbled, tugging the fabric over my head and tossing it her way. My girl Dani might have all the tact of a bulldozer on steroids, but she was usually right when it came to what I should wear.

"Bring me my sewing kit," she demanded, grinning as widely as I'd seen in months. "It's on the desk in my work room down the hall. I can hand stitch this and have it done for you in no time."

"I know where your sewing kit is," I muttered. But first, I finished putting all my clothes on again. Didn't want to take any chances of someone walking in on me when my flab was hanging everywhere, and I wasn't entirely convinced that no one in her family would be stopping in. Yes, the guys had a game tonight, but with Dani's pregnancy complications, everyone had been checking in on her far more often than usual.

No one stopped in, though, and an hour later, by the beginning of the first intermission, she'd finished her alterations—including adjusting the neckline, which I hadn't been expecting.

"Just enhancing your assets," she said with a smirk.

"Mm hmm."

The game was still a scoreless tie, and Blake had only ended up in the penalty box once, for a minor tripping call when he'd gotten caught out of position and was too gassed to catch up to his guy. All in all, it seemed like he was having a reasonably good game for his first one back after such a long absence.

I put the dress on for a final fitting. "This is a lot sexier than I'm comfortable wearing at my niece's quinceañera," I complained, examining my reflection in the mirror.

"Which is exactly why you need to wear it. You've got to show them who you are now."

I'd be doing enough of that just by showing up with Blake Kozlow on my arm. "My family won't know what to do with the idea that I have a date. Dressing like this is going to be well beyond anything they can handle."

"I still can't believe you're dating Koz."

I chuckled to myself and climbed onto the bed next

to her, dipping my own spoon into her carton of Halo Top. "Can you try to be nice to him for me? Or at least nicer?"

"Only until he fucks up and hurts you. As soon as that happens, though—" She drew a finger across her neck and made a slashing sound.

"What if he doesn't hurt me?" Because so far, the only one who'd been hurting both of us was me, although I wasn't sure Dani would ever believe it. She was too loyal to me by half, and too dead-set against him.

"As long as he doesn't hurt you, I'll be civil to him. Or at least I won't bite his head off. Too much. But that's about as good as he'll ever get from me."

"That's about as good as anyone gets from you," I pointed out.

She stuck out her tongue at me.

I winked.

The game returned, and they zoomed in on Blake sitting in the penalty box, looking as surly and disgruntled as ever.

"Oh, no," I murmured.

"Get used to seeing him there if you're serious about being with him. The guy spends more time in the box than out of it."

"That's right, folks," the TV commentator said. "Blake Kozlow is once again in the sin bin, but believe it or not, this time it actually isn't his fault."

Dani snorted in disbelief.

"The Storm took a bench minor just as time expired at the end of the first," he continued, "so Kozlow is doing the time."

I breathed a sigh of relief that he wasn't being penalized due to something he'd done himself.

The Storm's penalty killers put up a heck of a fight, and they came away unscathed.

But the best thing was what happened as soon as time on Blake's penalty expired. The seconds ticked down. He stood ready at the door. As soon as the time keeper opened it, he shot out onto the ice, and the puck soared straight to his stick.

He picked it up mid-stride and flew into the offensive zone with a few of his teammates on his tail and the other team's defenders frantic to catch up.

But no one would.

He faked a shot, got the goaltender to bite, and then sent the puck heading for the opposite corner of the net. It went in, the goal light lit, and the arena went wild.

"I might forgive him if he keeps that up," Dani mumbled.

"Mm hmm."

"They need to get out of their slump. Bad."

"You know, he's a good guy underneath it all. Once you get to know him."

"But that would require me getting to know him." She dug into her now-empty carton of Halo Top, then scowled at me. "You're going to make me get to know him, aren't you?"

"I can't make you do anything."

"Yeah, but you're dating him."

"I am," I agreed.

"Damn you. I don't want to like Blake Kozlow."

"I adore you, too," I said. And to prove it, I dug a piece of dark chocolate out of the super-secret stash in my purse and tossed it her way. I kept some in there just for occasions like this.

"Just give me lots of warning before you marry him.

I need time to prepare myself."

"Prepare yourself?" I spluttered, but what I was really thinking was *marry him?* Who said anything about me marrying him?

"So I don't show up in all black and declare an official state of mourning."

"Mourning for what?"

"Your sanity. Duh."

I laughed so hard my stomach hurt, and still I couldn't stop.

Chapter Twenty-One

Bea

"You look so fucking hot in that, I'll be thinking about how to get you out of it the whole time we're here," Blake murmured in my ear, just before he eyed me hungrily. "How long do we have to stay?"

We were in the Uber car on our way between the hotel and the civic center my brother had rented for the big day. And this was precisely why I shouldn't have let Dani talk me into wearing this dress to Paola's quinceañera. Mama would have a cow, seeing me like this. I'd never hear the end of it.

"Probably only a couple of hours," I said, tamping down the heat that was building within me again. If I could wangle it, we might escape even sooner—although my reasons for wanting to escape were far different than Blake's. "It would've been longer, but Mama couldn't arrange for the mass to be on the same day, so they had Paola's mass yesterday."

"Mass is part of it? Like a Catholic mass?"

"Traditionally. And my family is nothing if not traditional."

"Huh. So do you go to church and stuff?"

"Not as often as I should. Don't really have time for it these days."

"We could make time," Blake said. "I haven't been to mass since I lived with Grandma."

"I never would've pegged your grandmother for a regular church-goer."

He grinned and winked at me. "She likes to be unpredictable."

We'd flown down to San Bernardino this morning and checked into a hotel—a nicer one than I'd have chosen on my own, but Blake had insisted.

But after we'd checked in, Blake had continually pawed at me while we'd been getting ready to go. It was a miracle I'd managed to get my dress on and that my makeup and hair looked halfway decent, because he'd acted like a man on a mission to muss me up and leave me hot, sweaty, and aching for more.

This was going to be a quick trip. We were spending one night in the hotel tonight after the party, and our flight back to Portland left before lunch tomorrow. Frankly, I was glad we had the excuse of work (for me) and team obligations (for Blake) to keep the visit short and sweet.

So to speak.

I wasn't convinced it would be overly sweet. Paola would be, of course, and it was her big day. She was the reason I was here. And my grandmother might not understand my dietary needs, but she loved me no matter what.

Everyone else, though? Debatable. I was hoping we

could get away without a massive confrontation, since today was supposed to be about Paola and not me, but I wouldn't hold my breath. I knew my family too well to risk death by familial asphyxiation.

"Do you wish you lived closer to them?" Blake asked, slipping his hand into mine in a practiced, comfortable manner. I could get used to that—him touching me like there was nothing else that would make sense for him to do.

I didn't have a coat or jacket that would really go well with this dress, and it was a lot warmer here than it was back home—but it was a bit chilly for me, still. I kept hoping that one of these days, my internal thermostat would settle somewhere in the middle of where it had been before the weight loss and where it was now, but no luck as of yet.

"Not even remotely," I replied. "I like having enough distance between us that they can't randomly show up at my front door."

"But they're your family."

"I think I told you before—they're not like your grandma."

"No one is."

"True. But they're *really* not like her. I needed some space after I got out of college. Some room to breathe." I inadvertently shivered from the chill. This dress might make me look hot, but it was too flimsy to help keep me comfortable.

"Hmm," was his reply. But he firmed up his grip on my hand, lending me some of his warmth.

I greedily inched closer to his side to soak up more of it. One of the many things I'd started to appreciate about having Blake in my life was that he was like my own personal heated blanket that required no electricity to operate. Especially when he held me snug to his side in bed at night. His body was always putting off the most delicious heat, which made me want to curl into him as often as possible.

Lucky for me, Blake seemed only too eager to allow it. The more he could touch me, the happier he was.

Before I was ready, we were walking inside the civic center my brother and sister-in-law had rented for the party, and we were slipping through a gaggle of overly excited teenaged girls in frilly dresses and pimpled boys who looked like they'd rather be anywhere else.

I tightened my grip on Blake's hand for reassurance before skirting around the clot of teenagers. I dropped my gift for my niece on the appropriate table and headed straight to the kitchens, where I knew Abuelita and my parents would be, and possibly my brother and sister-in-law, too.

Sure enough, Mama looked up with a huge, welcoming smile the second we walked through the open entryway. She had an apron covering her dress to keep it clean. Her happy expression faded away as fast as it had come.

"Beatriz!" she chided. "What are you wearing? Go change before Maria sees you."

Maria was my sister-in-law.

I said a silent prayer for patience. "If you want me to come back in my pj's, I can change. Otherwise, this is what you get." I arched a brow in challenge, but she just stood there, spluttering indignantly.

Then I headed to the stove so I could kiss Abuelita's cheek, with Blake trailing behind me. He hadn't let go of my hand, and I got the sense it was more to keep me calm than it was for his own sake. I had to lean down to kiss her, and I wasn't an overly tall woman—

my grandmother was tiny and growing smaller with age. The footstool she always kept in her kitchen had been brought here for her use so she could reach the counters and stove.

She reached up and patted my cheek absentmindedly with one hand and then went back to putting the finishing touches on the *trés léchês*.

Papa came barreling in through the other door, but he stopped cold when he saw Blake standing next to me. Or, more likely, he stopped cold when he saw Blake's hand on mine, our fingers threaded together.

"Who is this?" he boomed into the cavernous, echoing space. His voice was as big as he was—there wasn't any doubt as to where my issues with my weight had come from. Everyone on his side of the family weighed upwards of three hundred pounds, and he might very well be the largest of them all.

Well, everyone but me, at least. Not anymore.

I steeled my spine to answer, but Blake spoke up before I could.

He reached out his right hand to shake my father's. "I'm Bea's boyfriend."

"Boyfriend," Mama spluttered. "But…but…you're not—" She couldn't seem to bring herself to say what she was thinking.

Hispanic? Old enough? Someone they knew?

I honestly wasn't sure which statement she was aiming for, but it didn't matter.

"No, he's not," I said emphatically. Then I turned to Blake as calmly as I could, silently begging him with my eyes for patience, before facing my parents again. Granted, he seemed to be taking everything in stride; I was the one who was a jumbled mess of nerves.

"Papa, Mama," I said. "This is Blake Kozlow. Blake,

my parents, Jose and Isabella Castillo, and my grandmother, Guadalupe Vasquez." Abuelita waved a hand over her shoulder without bothering to turn from her cooking. She'd never been one to say much, especially not when my father was in one of his moods, which was often.

"Pleased to meet you all," Blake said, still holding out his hand.

But my father didn't reciprocate, Papa's face turning a dangerous shade of red that almost matched my dress. Mama immediately launched into a tirade about how inconsiderate I was, bringing a *gringo* to my niece's big day just to upset everyone—all in Spanish, of course, so Blake couldn't understand a lick of it.

I couldn't decide whether I was glad about that or not. He probably deserved to know what she thought of him.

Of *us*.

But it might be better for me to fill him in later, when we were alone.

Paola chose that moment to race into the kitchens and wrap me up in a hug. "I worried you weren't going to be here when you didn't make it to mass yesterday!"

"I wouldn't want to let you down," I said, patting her on the back. Too bad she and Abuelita were the only reasons I had to come. I hooked my arm with hers and led her away from everyone else, catching Blake's eye and nudging my head in that direction so he'd know he should come with us. Leaving him in my parents' clutches seemed like a disaster waiting to happen.

When he reached us, Paola's eyes went wide. She cupped a hand over my ear and whispered, "He's hot."

I burst out laughing. "I know."

"And he's famous."

"I know that, too."

"Are you two…you know?" She shrugged.

"Dating?" Blake supplied.

Paola nodded.

He winked at her. "Yeah. You could say that."

"You're seriously dating Blake Kozlow?" she spluttered. "And you didn't tell me until *now*?"

"Sorry?" I supplied.

She batted at my arm playfully. "You should be. You're holding out on me, Aunt Beatriz."

"Well, now you know."

Her eyes turned wicked, and she glanced over at Blake. "So are you friends with Austin Cooper, then?"

"Coop?" he said, scratching his head in confusion.

I recalled one of my students asking Riley Jezek about Austin Cooper last year, when Riley and his wife had been coming to read to them. "He's too old for you, so don't even bother," I quickly interjected.

"But he's—"

"Not looking to end up in jail for corrupting a minor," I cut in. "You're fifteen, but that doesn't make you an adult. And I don't know how old he is, but he's too old for you. Got it?"

"You don't have to be mean about it," my niece said sulkily, but then she grinned so I'd know she was just giving me a hard time.

I glanced up at the clock on the wall. "It's almost time. Are you ready?" I asked her, tucking a curl of her hair back into place and inspecting her corsage.

Just like that, all her nerves and excitement were back. She nodded eagerly.

"We'll leave you to it, then." I hooked my arm through Blake's. "See you in there?"

"You'd better," Paola replied.

"Wouldn't miss it for the world."

Blake and I headed out into the ballroom, which had been decked out better than my senior prom. Flowers and candles lined every table, and the ceiling was covered with a balloon canopy, which made the lighting atmospheric.

I waved and smiled at a few familiar faces, and Blake found seats for the pair of us.

"I have no idea what's going on," Blake murmured in my ear.

"It's okay. Just sit back and enjoy it. Or try to, at least." To be honest, I didn't understand many of the traditions associated with the quinceañera, and I'd been through one, myself. "Here she comes," I whispered as my niece was being escorted into the ballroom by four young men—her *chambelanes.*

Once they were all present, the music started, and she danced with the boys.

Everyone applauded them profusely, and my niece curtseyed when they were done.

Then my brother got up to present her with *la última muñeca*—her last doll.

"This symbolizes her journey from childhood to womanhood," I whispered in Blake's ear.

"At fifteen?"

"Yeah. Tradition." I shrugged.

Then one of the boys who'd been among her chambelanes brought her a bouquet of flowers, and she blushed profusely. I made a mental note to ask her if she had a crush on him, or maybe they were already dating and no one had told me she had a boyfriend. It was possible. After all, I was dating someone and hadn't bothered to tell any of them until I'd arrived with Blake at my side—well, I'd kind of told Mama, but not really. She knew I was dating someone, but she didn't know any details.

Finally, it was time for the *piñatas*. Fifteen of them. "She's got to break a *piñata* for every year of her life," I explained to Blake as she took the baton and started swinging.

It took her a while. A *long* while. My niece was a delicate little thing and didn't have much upper-body strength.

"I wish I could go help her," Blake whispered in my ear.

"She'd probably love that. But no, you can't. She's got to do it on her own."

Suddenly, I realized that Blake and I weren't the only ones in the ballroom whispering amongst ourselves. All around us, tables of guests were bending their heads together and having heated conversations while my niece swung her baton—and several of them were pointing in our direction.

This…couldn't be good.

At all.

My spine stiffened as my brain whirled at a rapid pace, trying to determine what they were whispering about.

Was it my dress? Or the fact that I was here with a man that they felt wasn't good enough for me at the same time as they felt I wasn't good enough for him?

I itched to escape, to run out of that room, dragging Blake with me, and never look back. But I wouldn't do that to Paola. My niece hadn't done anything to deserve it. So, despite my unease, I forced myself to stay put as the whispers grew louder, the fingers pointing in our direction more numerous.

Paola swung again and connected, effectively bursting her fourth *piñata*. Hundreds of pieces of candy spilled to the floor, and she moved on to the next one in line.

"Why are they all talking about us?" Blake murmured in my ear.

That was when I knew that it wasn't all in my head, and it was really happening. Blake wasn't terribly perceptive about these things. If he was picking up on it, then it was far worse than I'd initially imagined.

I shook my head, shrugging.

"Do you want to leave?" he whispered. "You look miserable."

I wanted to leave, but I couldn't. "Let's stick it out awhile longer," I insisted. "At least until the cake."

"You're not going to eat any of it, though."

"No, but you can." I angled myself away from him, determined not to draw any more attention our way, and watched Paola swing at her next *piñata*.

A faint buzzing sounded from the general vicinity of Blake's pocket. He took out his cell phone. And then, "Fuck," he muttered beneath his breath, but it still carried through the ballroom. Dozens of eyes turned in our direction. I wanted to sink beneath the table and disappear. I wanted to be invisible again, like I had been when I'd weighed more than three hundred pounds. But wearing a dress like this, and with a man like Blake at my side, there was no chance of invisibility.

I steeled my spine and tried to ignore the whispers and stares.

"I have to go make a phone call," Blake whispered in my ear.

"What? Now?" My voice was sharper than I'd

intended. More heads turned to stare in our direction.

"I'm sorry. I'm really, really sorry." And in truth, he sounded absolutely devastated. "Sorrier than I can ever say."

"Is it your grandma?" I asked, but he was already halfway to the exit. I couldn't get up and follow him without creating a huge scene and drawing Paola's attention in the bargain.

So I stayed put, watching her swing at her seventh *piñata*, and worried.

But the whispers and pointing only increased in Blake's absence, and my feet itched to book it out the door behind him—more due to my own discomfort than worrying about him, though.

When Paola started on her eighth *piñata*, my brother sat in Blake's empty seat, his expression a combination of fury and concern.

"What?" I demanded in a heated whisper.

Instead of speaking, he wordlessly passed me his cell phone, with the screen open to one of the photos from the shoot I'd done with Blake and Mia—me wearing a sexy negligee, the strap falling off my bare shoulder, Blake in nothing but his briefs, his tongue darting out to lick my bare skin.

"What? I don't—" My throat swelled closed, and no more words would come out.

"It's all over social media—Twitter, Facebook, Instagram. Blowing up as we speak. He's been tagged in them, and they're trying to figure out your name."

"But I don't understand. Those were supposed to be private." My eyes burned with unshed tears—both because of the betrayal and the fact that if the school board got wind of this, I'd lose my job faster than I could blink.

"Probably why he just booked it out of here," Miguel groused. "If I get my hands on him…"

I didn't want my brother to get his hands on Blake, though.

That was all for me.

Or at least it would be, as soon as I could pull myself together again.

"Tell Paola I'm sorry," I said with as much composure as I could muster. Then, with a modicum of dignity and a pinch of get-the-heck-out-of-Dodge, I slipped out the side exit of the ballroom and burst into tears.

Blake

"You're the only person I sent them to," I shouted into the phone.

I'd never yelled at a teammate's wife before, but neither had I ever felt so much panic before. This could ruin everything I'd built with Bea, everything I'd been working toward.

"You never sent them to me," Brie Burns insisted again. She'd already sworn the same thing twice, but I didn't believe her. How could I? No one else had access to them, so it had to have been Brie. "Keith said you were going to," she said, "but I never got them. I never got anything from you. No text. No email. No phone call. Nothing."

"Bullshit. I texted you the link as soon as he brought it up and Bea gave me the go-ahead."

"Well, maybe you should check your phone, then. Did you send them to the right number?"

In my fury and panic, that thought hadn't crossed my mind. I put Brie on speakerphone so I could scroll through my messages. Shit. Nothing there. But then I remembered I'd forwarded her an email. I pulled up the email client on my phone and found it in my sent messages. "It was an email, not a text message." I rattled off the email address I'd used.

"My email address is Brie dot Burns at mail dot com, Blake," she said calmly. "There's a dot between my first and last names."

Fuck. While I still had her on speaker, I checked the address I'd sent it to, again. "So who the hell has that email address without the dot?"

"No idea, but I'd guess they're your leak. Just call Jim and let him know so he can get the PR team on it ASAP. It'll be okay. They managed to dig Harry out of whatever mess he found himself in last year, so they'll dig you out of this one, too."

"I'm not worried about *me*. I don't care if people see me like that. I'm worried about Bea. She didn't want anyone else to see them. No one. And now the whole world is seeing them, and it's all my fault. Or at least she's going to assume it is."

"Oh," Brie said. "Ouch. Yeah, that's a bit touchier."

"She's going to kill me. She's going to *murder* me."

"I'm sure she'll understand it was an honest mistake," Brie insisted, but she didn't sound overly convincing.

"Maybe *she* will, but will her school district? She could get fired over this." Holy fuck. The thought of Bea losing her job because of something stupid I'd done burned in my gut. She loved her job. She adored those kids. And she was fucking good at it, too.

I probably just got Bea fired.

"But can they prove it's her?" Brie suggested hopefully.

"You tell me," I said. "The pictures are everywhere. What do you think?"

"I haven't met her," she pointed out.

Well, there was that. "Do they really need to prove it?"

"To fire her? I'd hope they need to prove it."

"Hoping doesn't do much good in the real world," I said. Grandma's health was enough proof of that. "Besides, aren't school districts more concerned about the kids? They can always find another teacher." Just like a hockey team could always find another player to fill a hole. Maybe someone with a different skill set, but there was always someone else coming along to take someone else's place.

Brie started to say something else, but Bea raced out of the building just then, so I cut my teammate's wife off mid-sentence. "Got to go."

"Keith and I'll get Jim and the PR team on it," she said just before I hung up.

I shoved my phone into my pocket and power-walked over to where Bea had flung herself down onto the curb, her arms wrapped tight around her knees, her head buried against them. Her shoulders were shaking, and I couldn't fool myself into thinking it was due to laughter.

"Bea?" I said cautiously.

Her head shot up at the sound of my voice. She glared at me with red, wet eyes.

"I'm so sorry. I didn't—"

"Why?" she cut in before I could get another word out. "Why would you do something like this? I was right all along, wasn't I? You were just using me for—

"

"I wasn't using you," I insisted. "I would never use you."

"Oh, sure, Blake. Whatever you say."

"I'm not using you," I repeated. "I love you. It's killing me that I did something to hurt you."

"Just stop, already."

I sat down next to her and tried to put an arm around her shoulders, but she tore away from my grasp, leaping to her feet. She was halfway across the parking lot before she stopped, dropping to her knees on the pavement.

"I sent the link to the wrong email address," I called out, slowly inching my way toward her.

"You really think—"

"I thought I was sending them to Brie Burns, just like you said I could. But apparently I got a digit wrong."

"You *seriously* expect me to believe—"

"It was an honest mistake, Bea," I cut in again. I hated to keep interrupting her, but it seemed to be the only way I could get a word in edgewise. "I know you don't want to believe it, but it was. Look, I can show you." I held my phone out like a peace offering.

"Why do you always think I'll give in to you?" she shot back.

"Why do you always assume the worst of me?" I countered.

"Because everyone always gives me the worst."

"Not everyone." I took a chance and crossed the parking lot to join her, dropping to my ass beside her. "I didn't mean to hurt you. It's killing me that I hurt you. You've got enough people in your life who're doing that already."

"Don't bring my family into this."

"I didn't. *You* did," I pointed out. "But are you seriously going to try to argue that they're better for you than I am?"

"You can't—"

"You've told me yourself that they want to keep you how you've always been. They've got you in a box and expect you to stay there, and they don't like it when you do anything outside of the norm. I'm the one trying to help you bust out of that box."

"Yeah, by getting me fired."

"Have you been fired already?" I asked, my stomach sinking all the way to my toes.

"Already got a call from my principal. I've been suspended pending a formal disciplinary hearing."

Fuck fuck fuckity fuck. "I'm so sorry. I didn't mean for any of this to happen."

"Maybe it's a good thing that it happened," she said. "Now, I mean. Before it was too late. Before things got too serious between us."

"Things are already too serious between us."

"We can end it now without causing too much pain," she continued, as if she'd never heard me. "It'll be better this way."

End it? This was worse than I'd imagined.

"Better for who?"

"For everyone."

"Bullshit."

"I think you should leave now," she said. "You should go back to the hotel. I'll stay with my parents tonight—"

"Bea," I cut in, tipping her chin so she'd have to look up at me. The pools of tears in her eyes nearly broke me. But then again, I was already broken.

"Please," I croaked.

She blinked hard a couple of times, somehow keeping her tears from spilling over. "You should leave, Blake. I've got to go back in there and do damage control with my family."

Chapter Twenty-Two

Blake

Bea stayed true to her word, spending the night with her parents instead of coming back to the hotel with me. She sent her grumpy brother to pick up her things. I could only assume it was so she wouldn't have to deal with me.

He made it clear he wasn't a big fan of mine. I had difficulty not letting him know what I thought of the way he and the rest of his family always treated her, but that probably wouldn't help things any, so I somehow kept it in check.

I wanted to say, *See, Bea? Sometimes I can control myself!* But that wouldn't help anything. And besides, she was giving me the cold shoulder, so I couldn't say anything to her at all.

She arranged for the airline to switch her seat on our flight back to Portland so she wouldn't have to sit next to me on the way home.

She wouldn't respond to my texts, no matter how profusely I apologized.

I felt like enough of an ass already, but the way she was completely shutting me out of her life was enough to do me in.

Grandma called me the day we got back to Portland, before I could make it in to the PR meeting Jim had informed me I was required to attend.

"Just keep your head on," she said. "You made a mistake. Everyone makes mistakes. Don't say anything stupid."

"I always say stupid things."

"Not always. Not if you slow down and think. They'll help you figure this out, Blake."

"It doesn't even matter what the team does to me at this point," I told her. I'd never sounded more morose before, not even to my own ears. "I'm just worried about Bea. Her family won't take it well, but it's worse than that."

"Worse how?"

"She could lose her job over this."

"Well, if she does, she's better off without them."

"She's better off without a job? A job she loves?"

"Teachers don't get enough appreciation anyway. She could do a lot better for herself doing something else."

"But she loves those kids, Grandma."

"So...what are you going to do about it?" she demanded.

"What *can* I do about it?"

"If you want her back, you'll think of something. If you want to make things right, you'll figure it out. You're a smart man, Blake. Always have been. You've got a brain between your ears. Time to use it."

"Not really helpful," I said, and she just cackled the way she always did when the answer was staring me right in the face but I couldn't see it.

......

"From the team's standpoint, there's not a problem here," Jim said the next morning, folding in the earpieces of his bifocals and setting them on his desk. "We know our players have lives outside of hockey. Those photos are clearly not pornography. There's nothing indecent or inappropriate about the photos."

"But we still have a problem on our hands?" I asked, because I wasn't quite following his train of thought.

"We still have a problem," Bergy said, crossing his arms in an intimidating posture. He and the other coaches were present, too, as well as about a dozen other bigwigs from the Storm's front offices.

"Our problem," Mr. Sutter said, "is that Ms. Castillo is a teacher, and her students are young and also very impressionable—more so than many of their peers—and we don't know how the school board will handle this."

A breath of relief whooshed out of my lungs. "You're telling me that the team is going to help Bea with this, right? That's what you're saying?"

"It's made national news, both here and in Canada," he said calmly. "If she'd done that photo shoot with almost any other man, it wouldn't have been newsworthy, and it never would have become an issue for her. The only reason anyone cared about posting those photos online was because *you* were in them, too. The perpetrator didn't know who Ms. Castillo is, or at least it's highly doubtful. We have to treat this with the belief that they only made the images public because *you're* a public figure. So we, as an organization, feel that we have an obligation to Ms. Castillo to help fight her case with the school board."

"You're being serious? You're not fucking with me—I mean screwing around with me?"

"I'm being serious. Any chance you can find out when her hearing is scheduled?" Mr. Sutter asked.

"She's cut me off. I don't—"

"I can find out," Webs interrupted. "Dani will know."

"Good," Mr. Sutter said. "As soon as we know that, we can get our legal team involved and begin the process of moving forward."

Holy hell.

I didn't know what I'd done to deserve this kind of loyalty from Mr. Sutter and the Storm organization, but I was beyond glad I'd done it. Bea might have a teacher's union that could help her, but getting the power of the Portland Storm's legal team on her side was beyond anything I could have hoped for.

Maybe, if we were able to help her out of this mess, she'd eventually forgive me.

Maybe I'd be able to convince her I loved her, even if I sometimes fucked up.

Maybe she'd eventually give me another chance. And maybe I wouldn't destroy it as soon as I got it.

Maybe, just maybe, she'd believe that loving me was worth it.

That *I* was worth it.

Hell, maybe I wasn't, but she sure as fuck was.

Bea

When I walked into my disciplinary hearing with the school board, I nearly fell over in shock. I'd been expecting the board, my principal, and maybe one or two other people from my school to be present. I was *not* prepared to find more than half a dozen men I didn't recognize in the slightest—most of them tall, muscular men in expensive suits—alongside a woman in a dark gray power suit.

One of the unfamiliar men, a graying gentleman with bifocals and a firm handshake, came over to me with a smile. "Jim Sutter," he said. "General Manager of the Portland Storm. Blake filled us in on what was happening, so we thought we'd bring our legal team out to lend you a hand. This is Mattias Bergstrom," he added, indicating a very intimidating gentleman next to him with sleek, dark hair with a silver streak on one side and a build that would rival Blake's and any of his teammates'. "He's the Storm's head coach. The rest of these gentlemen and Ms. Farnworth work in our PR department, and Mr. Dalton, over there" —he indicated a blond-haired man in a dark gray suit—"is our lawyer. We'll be assisting you today if that's all right."

"Blake sent you?" I spluttered.

"Not exactly, but since it was his mistake that led to your suspension and this hearing, we believe it's right for us to get involved."

"With your lawyers?" I repeated, still trying to wrap my brain around it. I'd been preparing to argue my case on my own, and if necessary, I thought I'd ask the teacher's union to provide me with legal counsel. That was one of the benefits of having a union, after all. I wasn't sure their legal help would be of quite this caliber, though.

Jonathan Grissom, the president of the school board, scowled and waved a hand toward an empty chair. "If we could get started," he said impatiently. If I had to guess, I'd say he hadn't been expecting half a dozen bigwigs to show up in my defense any more than I had been.

I took the empty chair he'd indicated, and Mr. Sutter sat next to me, looking perfectly calm and in control of the situation.

"Very well," Mr. Grissom said. "Are we all ready to proceed?"

"I'd say so," Mr. Sutter replied congenially. He took off his bifocals and folded the earpieces in, setting them on the board table in front of him. "Our lawyers have put together a list of comparable incidents around the country, as well as the actions taken in each case."

Mr. Grissom looked as taken aback as I felt, but he quickly pulled his features under control. "This isn't just any old *incident*, Mr. Sutter, as I'm sure Ms. Castillo will be all too happy to explain to you. Her students are especially impressionable, more so than the majority of the student body. She teaches our special education population—a group of students far more sensitive to outside influence than the average student of the same age."

"We're quite familiar with the sensitivities of special education students," Coach Bergstrom put in. "My stepdaughter happens to be one of them, although Sophie is a bit older than Ms. Castillo's students."

"Yes, we're familiar with Sophie," Mr. Grissom said. "In fact, I believe she and some of her classmates joined Ms. Castillo's class while she was in New York recently, isn't that so? They worked on an art project for Mr. Kozlow while he and Ms. Castillo were supposedly visiting his ailing grandmother. But in reality, she was taking risqué photos with her boyfriend."

"We were with his grandmother the majority of the time we were in New York," I said. "Other than when we were sleeping. Anyone at the hospital can verify that. The reason for my taking the time off was exactly what I said it would be when I put in the request."

"And I don't believe the way Ms. Castillo spent her hard-earned time off is in any way relevant to this discussion," one of the other men on my team said.

Mr. Grissom scowled. "Since her behavior has affected our students—"

"How?" another lawyer interrupted. "How has her behavior affected your students? The leak of the photos only took place two days ago. The Storm's legal team got the article taken down within an hour of it being posted to the internet. The likelihood that any of those students saw them—"

"Whether they actually saw them or not is irrelevant to the discussion," Mr. Grissom interrupted.

"I'd think it would be entirely relevant," Mr. Sutter said.

"They *could* have seen them, Mr. Sutter," the school board president said. "We can't have a teacher in compromising positions like that—"

"Compromising positions?" Ms. Farnworth interrupted. "They were intimate photographs, sure, but there was nothing remotely illicit about them."

"They had their clothes off," Mr. Grissom argued.

"On the contrary, there is no nudity involved," Ms. Farnworth said. "Have you seen them? Because I have copies here for everyone present." She picked up a stack of manila folders, then stood and distributed one folder to each person present. "If you'll take a look, please, gentlemen. So sorry to invade your privacy like this, Ms. Castillo," she said as she handed a folder to me, "but I believe it's necessary for everyone to have a full understanding of the scope of the situation."

My cheeks heated, but I nodded my agreement. The images had already been all over the internet. They were currently featured on no fewer than a dozen of the biggest sports blogs and news sites in the world. There was no hiding from them, whether I wanted to or not.

"Now, Mr. Grissom, would you kindly tell me which image contains the nudity you mentioned?" Ms. Farnworth said pleasantly, a brow raised in expectation. "I'd love for you to show me what I'm missing."

Blake

"You know I still want to murder you, right?" Dani said from over the top of the pint of Halo Top ice cream I'd brought her. "Bringing me ice cream is only enough bribe to convince me to wait until I'm done eating it to deal with you."

"I deserve it," I said, cautiously taking a seat at the foot of her bed.

"You do."

"I fucked up."

"You have a pulse and you're breathing, so yes, I'd have to say I agree."

"I'll never be able to make up for this. She'll never forgive me."

"Not if she's smart."

"I don't deserve her forgiveness."

"You aren't expecting me to argue with you on any of this shit, right?"

"You could try to cheer me up *some*."

"Doubtful."

"Gee, thanks."

"What the hell were you expecting?" Dani bit off.

"I love her, all right? I know I fucked up, but I love her. And she loves me, too. We need each other."

She scowled, resting the carton on her growing belly. "Help me sit up straighter, hmm?"

"I don't know. If I come close enough to touch you, you might find a way to shove that spoon up my nose or something."

"Better your nose than your ass."

"Am I supposed to find that reassuring?" I shot back.

"If you don't, I'll get my husband to bring me a gun so I can shoot you."

"We don't own a gun," Harry called from somewhere nearby.

"We should do something about that," Dani called back.

"Nope. I don't trust your mood swings."

"If you're close enough to hear her," I shouted, "why don't you come and help her sit up so I don't have to? She's *your* wife."

"And you're the one who fucked up with her best friend," he called back. "You two are having a private conversation. I'm only listening in to be sure I don't need to call the cops to protect you from my wife's wrath."

"Maybe you should protect me in here, then."

"Hush," Dani said, digging her spoon in for another large bite. "And for the record, you would've scored more points if you'd brought me the Chocolate Chip Cookie Dough flavor."

"I'll make a mental note for next time."

"Assuming there is a next time."

"There's going to be a next time," I insisted. "There has to be." I refused to believe that Bea would cut me off from her life forever. I had to convince her to give me another shot. "So how'd the hearing go?"

Dani shrugged. "Thanks to the team's lawyers, better than she expected."

"She's reinstated?"

"Not yet. Apparently the process is going to take a couple of weeks, maybe longer, no matter which way things go. But the lawyers were able to point out the numerous flaws with the school district's case."

"But she will be able to keep her job?" I pressed.

"Too soon to know for sure, but it looks a lot better than it did before. The suspension is bad enough, though. It's killing her."

It was killing me, too.

Dani stabbed her spoon into the carton and drew out another bite. "She's miserable, you know."

This wasn't helping my morale any. "I hate that she's having to deal with all of this because of me."

"I mean without you. She's miserable without you."

A frisson of hope came to life inside my chest. "I'm miserable without her, too."

"Don't ask me why she's into you. I couldn't tell you. I've never understood it."

"I couldn't tell you, either. All I know is I love her, and I fucked up worse than I ever realized it was possible for a person to fuck up, and it doesn't look like I'll ever be able to fix it. She's never going to let me make it right."

"I know why she's into you."

The familiar voice coming from the doorway made my heart stop. I glanced at Dani's face to determine if the voice had only been in my head, but she was staring at the doorway with an expression I couldn't name.

I tried to swallow the lump in my throat, but it wouldn't budge.

No part of me would budge.

I was completely stuck.

"She's into you because you've got a heart as big as the ocean. And because she gets why you screw up. And because you refuse to let her see anything but what you see when you look at her. She's into you because you make her laugh. And because you make her feel sexy, when she's never felt that way before in her life, even if it scares her sometimes. She's into you because you're everything she never knew she was missing until you walked into her life. She's into you because you're willing to move unmovable mountains when you make a mistake in order to make things right again. And because you love your grandma with your whole heart. And now that she's shut you out, she's miserable. Just as miserable as you are."

Bea's words fluttered through my ears and settled around my heart, filling the holes that I'd gouged in it as well as the ones others had left behind.

"That doesn't sound very nice," I forced myself to say. "Being miserable."

"It's not. It's lonely." She came to the side of the bed and sat next to me, her hand settling on top of mine.

Cautiously, I threaded my fingers with hers, staring

down at the place where we were joined.

"I'm lonely," Bea said.

"So am I."

"I don't want to be lonely anymore. I don't want to be scared of what everyone thinks of me anymore. I don't want to be the DUFF anymore."

"The DUFF?"

"You've never been the DUFF other than in your own head," Dani interjected, reminding me we were still sitting on the edge of her bed and she was listening to the entire conversation.

"Designated Ugly Fat Friend," Bea explained.

"You're not—"

"I know I'm not fat anymore," she said, pressing a finger to my lips before I could get a head of steam going.

I kissed that finger. Couldn't stop myself. "And you've never been ugly."

"That's not the point I'm trying to make."

"So what *are* you trying to say?" I demanded.

"That I'm sorry I jumped to the worst possible conclusion again. And I know you didn't intentionally hurt me. And I want us to try to figure this out."

"Your family'll hate me."

"Not all of them," Bea said. "Abuelita just wants me to be happy, even if I won't eat her tamales."

"But your father…"

"Maybe he'll come around. Maybe he won't."

"Are you okay with it if he doesn't?"

"They've never come around to see that I'm not who they want me to be," Bea said. "They can't love me for who I am, so why would they love the man I love?"

A grin took over my lips. "Told you."

She shot up a brow in question. "Told me?"

"That you love me."

"You're so freaking cocky," she said, laughing uncontrollably.

"Is that a bad thing?"

"Not for me, it's not."

"Good," I said. "Because I don't want to figure out how to deal without having you in my life."

Bea picked up our joined hands and pressed a kiss to the back of mine. "I don't want that, either."

"Are you two finished already?" Dani interrupted, and I jumped. I'd forgotten we were sitting on the edge of her bed.

"For now," Bea said, thoroughly unfazed by her friend's disruption of our flirting. "Why?"

"Because you're as sappy as a Hallmark Christmas movie, and my hormones are going haywire, and if you're going to make me cry and shit, you owe me chocolate. Copious amounts of chocolate. Stat."

"You only get to say *stat* in the case of an emergency," Bea said with a grin.

"Chocolate is always an emergency for a pregnant bitch."

My girlfriend looked toward the open doorway and called out, "Note that she's the one calling herself a bitch, not either of us."

"She knows the truth," her husband replied, returning to the bedroom with a small handful of Dani's favorite individually-wrapped dark chocolates. "But chocolate helps."

I dug out my phone and tapped some shit into my notes app.

"What're you doing?" Bea asked.

"Making reminders for myself, since we all know

I'm not good at remembering things."

"What sort of reminders?"

I shrugged. "Chocolate gets emergency status—for when you're pregnant."

Her eyes went as big as saucers.

"I'm not planning on knocking you up anytime soon. Right now, we're doing fine with Neville and Luna. Just—you know—for whenever we're ready."

That shy, sexy grin I loved so much slowly crept over her features, and she squeezed my thigh. Which, of course, made me wish she'd squeeze a different part of my anatomy, a little bit higher.

"Ugh," Dani groaned. "Don't you two *dare* start making sexy, googly eyes at each other. Not while I'm lying here like a beached whale."

"You're a hot beached whale, though," Harry said, smirking. "And you're mine."

I caught Bea's eye. "I think that's our cue to get the hell out of here."

She threaded her fingers through mine, and we made a hasty retreat.

Together.

Epilogue

Bea

"You shouldn't have come," Blake said again, holding my hand so tightly it was a wonder I had any circulation. But he couldn't let go, and I didn't have it in me to complain. His muscles all seemed to be in a permanent state of contraction, as if they'd never relax again.

"I wasn't about to let you do this alone," I said. "What kind of girlfriend would I be if I did that?"

"But this isn't— You didn't sign up for this. To hold my hand and watch me blubber and shit."

"That's exactly what I signed up for." I stretched up onto my toes and kissed his cheek. It was a soft kiss, no heat at all. Just tenderness. The scrape of the facial hair he'd been growing—getting an early start on his playoff beard, he said, even though that didn't sit well with some of his more superstitious teammates—

scratched my lips. "Just like you signed up for dealing with all my body image issues."

"That's different."

"Hardly."

A small stream of people gradually joined us. Some brought flowers. Others merely shook Blake's hand or wrapped him up in a tearful hug. I did my best to thank them all for coming, because Blake couldn't seem to find the words. He wasn't being rude—just grief-stricken.

I recognized Brett, Lil's favorite nurse, as he made his way toward us. He looked different wearing a jacket and tie instead of his traditional blue-green scrubs, but there was no doubt it was him. When he reached us, Brett handed us each a card.

"They're from Lil," he said solemnly. "She asked me to give them to you both when it was time."

I was so taken aback that I had to blink away a fresh wave of tears, so I couldn't imagine how the latest turn of events must be affecting Blake. Mutely, he nodded and accepted his card, then shook Brett's hand.

I wrapped the nurse up in a brief hug. "Thank you for all you did for her."

"She did more for me," he said with complete sincerity, and he moved on down the line, making way for the next mourner to offer Blake their condolences.

The service was small and brief.

A few of her friends and neighbors offered their memories in eulogy. Lil's longtime mailman stopped in with an arrangement of gorgeous white lilies.

Mitch and Mia Quincey brought a casserole and a six-pack of beers for Blake, and Mia pulled me aside when there was a brief lull.

"I've had my lawyer working with the Storm's legal

team. They're trying to find out who initially leaked the photos. They've been doing all sorts of IP searches and whatnot, and they've found the guy. We're suing for copyright infringement. It won't undo what was done, but it's better than nothing. And if we win, I'm sending it all to you."

"You don't have to do that," I argued.

"I want to," she insisted. "It's the principle of the thing. And you're the one who's been fighting to keep your job over it. My business has skyrocketed. You inadvertently made me into a highly sought-after photographer for these sorts of intimate shoots."

"Really? I mean, I don't doubt it, but…"

"Really." She hugged me.

"Well, at least some good came from it, then."

"I hope more good came from it than just for me." She arched a brow. "You doing any better?"

I blushed and scanned the room to be sure no one was looking, because it felt inappropriate at a time like this. "Much," I admitted, heat scorching my cheeks. "Better than I ever imagined." Partially due to what we'd done in that shoot, sure…but mostly due to the way Blake loved me. It was impossible to hate my body when he loved it as much as he did.

And it was even more impossible to hate myself because of his love.

Even Dani was starting to come around to him, although she still threatened him with a rusty spork every now and then out of habit. But she couldn't hate him when I loved him. She'd tried and failed. "Seeing you light up like this makes it impossible, since I know he's the one behind it," she kept telling me.

"I still can't believe all that drama with the school district," Mia said. "It was all over the news here, too."

"But it's all sorted out now."

In the end, I hadn't lost my job. I'd had to sit through a lengthy suspension while it was investigated and decided, but in the end, my students' parents had petitioned the school board for me to be reinstated. They'd argued that the pictures had allowed them an opportunity to help their children learn about having healthy body images. Plus, apparently, their kids had complained vociferously about my replacement, who didn't bring famous hockey players to school to read to them.

"Well, I'm glad," Mia said. She pulled me in for another hug. "And I'll be seeing you again soon."

"You will?"

"Storm WAGs charity calendar," she said. "Brie and I've been making plans. We're going to wait for the weather to warm up a bit. I'll be there when the kids have spring break."

We talked for a few more minutes, but then she gathered up her husband and kids, and they said their good-byes as most of the other mourners were starting to trickle out.

I glanced over at Blake from across the room. His eyes were red from all the tears he'd cried over the last few days, but he had a huge smile on his face as he spoke with an older gentleman. Since he was busy, I started organizing the flowers, finding people to send them home with. We couldn't take them on the plane with us, and there was no reason for them to all go to waste.

Around the time I found a new home for the last of the arrangements, Blake inched up behind me and wrapped his arms around my waist, dragging me back against his chest.

"You doing okay?" I asked.

He shook his head, his chin resting atop my scalp. "Better now."

"How come?"

"Because I'm with you." He kissed the top of my head. "You read your card from Grandma yet?"

"To be honest, I've been putting it off."

"Me, too."

"Think we should slip off somewhere and read them?"

In answer, Blake threaded his fingers through mine and led me to a quiet room off the main hallway. There was a couch near the window, a picturesque, snowy winter scene outside, and we dropped onto it, practically falling on top of one another because the cushions were broken down.

"Oops," I said, and we both laughed.

It felt good to laugh.

After planting a kiss on the end of my nose, he removed his card from his jacket pocket, and I dug mine out of the inside zipper in my purse. With one more look at him for reassurance, I slid my finger under the seal and retrieved my card while he did the same.

> *Dear Bea,*
> *I'm sure you know that you're not perfect. No one is. But you are perfect for my grandson. Life won't always be easy, but you know that. You expect the hard times, which is good. It means you're strong enough to withstand them when they come knocking at your door. But don't forget to enjoy the good times, too.*
> *It's not a bad thing to be soft around the*

*middle sometimes. It'll give him a soft place to
fall—and we both know Blake will fall. You
two can get back up again together.*

*And don't forget to laugh. Laughing together
is one of the best things you can do. You'll have
a longer, happier life if you always remember
to laugh.*

*Thank you for loving my boy. It's time for me
to pass the baton.*

Lil

I had to reach for a tissue and blow my nose loudly. Blake was in much the same condition.

"What'd she say to you?" he asked once he'd pulled himself together.

"Made a crack about being soft around the middle," I said, trying to laugh it off.

"I like you being soft around the middle," Blake said, sniffling again. "Makes it easier to get a grip on you."

"What'd she say to you?" I asked.

"Drew a picture of her tattoo."

"The one where she's flipping off cancer?"

"One and the same. And she said she loved me."

"She did. She loved you better than anyone else ever has." Fresh tears filled my eyes.

"Not better than anyone else," Blake said. "She didn't love me better than you."

"Time to pass the baton," I said, repeating Lil's final words to me.

"You ready for this?"

"Yes. I'm ready."

Roster

Name	Position	Nickname	Number
Cole Paxton	Defense	Colesy	3
Lauri Vanhanen	Defense	Van	4*
Levi Babcock	Defense*	501	5
Chris Hammond	Defense	Hammer	6
Keith Burns	Defense	Burnzie	7
Cody Williams	Defense	Harry	8
Brenden Campbell	Left Wing	Soupy	11
Andrei Sokolov	Center	Socks	13
Blake Kozlow	Center	Koz	14
Austin Cooper	Center	Coop	16
Jamie Babcock	Right Wing	Babs	19
Axel Johansson	Right Wing	Jo-Jo	20
Dylan Poplawski	Right Wing	Pops	21
Leif Sorenson	Defense	Thor	24
Cam Johnson	Left Wing	Jonny	28
Nicklas Ericsson	Goal	Nicky	30
Konrad Jokelainen	Goal	Loki	32
Preston Hutchinson	Left Wing	Hutch	39
Aaron Ludwiczak	Left Wing	Luddy	43
Tony Bridger	Center	Bridge	62
Nate Golston	Left Wing	Ghost	83
Riley Jezek	Center	RJ	91

About the Author

Catherine Gayle is a *USA Today* bestselling author of more than forty contemporary and historical romances. She's a transplanted Texan living in North Carolina with three extremely spoiled felines. In her spare time, she watches way too much hockey and reality TV, plans fun things to do for the Nephew Monster's next visit, and performs experiments in the kitchen which are rarely toxic.

If you enjoyed this book and want to know when more like it will be available, be sure to sign up for Catherine's mailing list. You can find out more on her website, her blog, at Facebook, on Twitter, at Instagram, and at Goodreads. If you want to see some of her cats' antics and possibly the occasional video update from Catherine, visit her YouTube account.

Books by Catherine Gayle

Contemporary:

Breakaway
On the Fly
Taking a Shot
L ight the Lamp
Delay of Game
Double Major
In the Zone
Holiday Hat Trick
Comeback
Dropping Gloves
Bury the Hatchet
Home Ice
Smoke Signals
Mistletoe Misconduct
L osing an Edge
Ghost Dance
Dreaming Up a Dare
Game Breaker
Rites of Passage
Defensive Zone
Power Play
Rain Dance
Neutral Zone
Free Agent

Coming Soon:

Drream Catcher
Journeyman
On the Warpath
Sleigh Bells & Slap Shots

Historical:

Twice a Rake
Saving Grace
Merely a Miss
Wallflower
Pariah
Seven Minutes in Devon
The Devil to Pay
A Dance with the Devil
An Unintended Journey
To Enchant an Icy Earl
Flight of Fancy
Rhyme and Reason
Thick as Thieves
Wanton Wives

Free to newsletter subscribers only:

Ice Breaker
Subscribe at: http://eepurl.com/GXcwr

For a printable booklist, please visit www.catherinegayle.com